Also by Sophia Watson

Her Husband's Children
Strange and Well Bred
The Perfect Treasure

Sophia Watson was born in 1962 and educated at Durham University. She has worked in publishing, as a feature writer for the *Daily Mail* and as a ghost writer. Her non-fiction books are *Winning Women* (1989) and *Marina* (1994), a biography of the Duchess of Kent. Her novels, *Her Husband's Children* (1995), *Strange and Well Bred* (1996) and *The Perfect Treasure* (1998) are all published by Hodder and Stoughton. She has four young daughters and lives on the edge of Exmoor.

Only Pretending

Sophia Watson

FLAME
Hodder & Stoughton

Copyright © 2000 by Sophia Watson

The right of Sophia Watson to be identified as the Author
of the Work has been asserted by her in accordance with the
Copyright, Designs and Patents Act 1988.

First published in Great Britain in 2000 by Hodder and Stoughton
First published in paperback in 2000 by Hodder and Stoughton
A division of Hodder Headline

A Flame Paperback

10 9 8 7 6 5 4 3 2 1

A CIP catalogue record for this title is available
from the British Library.

ISBN 0 340 68890 4

Typeset by Palimpsest Book Production Limited,
Polmont, Stirlingshire.
Printed and bound in Great Britain by
Mackays of Chatham plc, Chatham, Kent

Hodder and Stoughton
A division of Hodder Headline
338 Euston Road
London NW1 3BH

For Jake and Anna, true friends.
With my love

I would like to thank the explorer David Hempleman-Adams, who made time to see me just before setting off for the North Pole, when he really had other things to do

Chapter One

All these years of wasted loving.

Penny let herself into the empty house, switched on the hall light and left the door to slam behind her. She ignored the post on the door-mat. There would be nothing from John: this was a trip to a world without post-boxes. In the sitting room she drew the curtains, turned on the lamps, and lit the fake-coal gas fire in an attempt to make this comfortable shell feel like home. She poured herself a gin and tonic and lit a cigarette. She was home too late to watch the early-evening news, and anyway was not in the mood to give a damn about the rest of the world.

Outside, the streets of London had that pre-Christmas glow she used to love. Tonight, though, she had glowered at the chestnut roaster on the corner of the street, hating his phoney merriment as he stood warming his hands over the brazier. This year, as last year, John would be away for Christmas. This year, once again, she would have to rely on some psychic link for him to feel the love she sent half-way around the world towards him. This year, as so often before, she would buy him presents suited to his London life while all his energies were concentrated on his other life. It was no longer enough for her.

It had seemed a fine thing at first: wonderful and bold and romantic. She had loved the look in her friends' eyes when she told them whom she was to marry: surprise turning into interest, vicarious excitement into envy.

'John Brunel?' they had asked. 'Not *the* John Brunel?'

'Well, yes. I suppose *the* John Brunel,' she had agreed, pretending to a modesty and confusion she did not feel. 'But that's no big deal. He's no different from anyone else, really. He's just the same as the next man.'

She was lying, of course. There was no one like John Brunel. There never would be. Nowadays that was a realisation more comforting than exhilarating.

John had become famous almost in spite of himself. He said he hated his fame, that it interfered with his work, and to do him justice he really did believe that. Yet he had married the creator of his legend. Penny found that difficult to puzzle out during the long winter evenings she spent alone with the cat. He had his own impetus, his own charm, his own star-like brilliance, but it was Penny who had harnessed that brilliance, who had guided his footsteps away from the solitude of his calling towards the television studios in which he had made his name. Hating his fame, he never resented Penny for creating it. Perhaps, she wondered, and not for the first time, he just had not put two and two together and realised what a large part she had played in the invention of John Brunel.

The wedding had taken place at St Mary Abbot's, Kensington, four years ago. John, his face as always unseasonably brown, had seemed ill-at-ease in his top hat and frock coat. The coat had been copied from a photograph taken of his great-great-uncle Isambard Kingdom Brunel, a romantic urge he had regretted when the coat was collected from the tailor. Nevertheless, he looked very handsome, and his wife, fifteen years younger, in an ivory silk sheath dress and her grandmother's rubies, looked overwhelmed at her good luck.

The guests at the Roof Gardens afterwards made a crew more motley than is usual at even the most English of weddings. Penny's relations were gathered in a tight knot, conventional clothes and pearls, not quite sure what to make of the match. John's relations were few and unused to London, but they seemed almost more at ease than the Knightsbridge and Kensington Latimers. John was one of four brothers, all of whom had started life along accepted lines – Wellington, good universities, in one case a spell in the Irish Guards. But now some rogue gene had spun them all far off the path of middle-class order.

Richard had converted to Catholicism and become a missionary priest, travelling mostly in the Far East. He had joined the Communist party while at Cambridge, seen the error of his ways and decided that the only way to combat the Red Terror was through religion. He had not had a great deal of success.

Patrick, the next brother, was the easiest to explain. He had bought himself out of the army, and farmed on Exmoor. Like John, he had married a much younger woman. She had borne him four sons in seven years and now their energies were mostly directed towards saving the local hunt. Then came John, and lastly Izzy, who might have been the most eccentric of all had he not spent most of the sixties and all of his money discovering the joys of acid and transcendental meditation. Now he spent half of his year in Oakford – a small Devon village an hour from Patrick's farm, filled with like-minded leftovers of that love-filled decade – and half in Nepal. In Nepal he painted, in Oakford he wrote poetry.

All three brothers had their own agenda at the wedding. Izzy recited the snatches of his verse he could remember to anybody who would listen, hoping that one of his new sister-in-law's guests would be able to work the miracle for him that she had worked for John. Where Izzy was confident through lack of awareness, Patrick had the confidence bred by public school and the officers' mess. He also had more appreciation of Penny's world: with the hunt in the parlous state it was, he knew he needed good PR and John, watching his brother move smoothly through the not-so-young women professionals, could not help but admire his brother's nerve. To bring the hunting issue to Kensington, to a wedding, and to north London urbanites like these, showed a dedication John could understand.

Scattered among the two disparate groups of relatives were the friends and colleagues. There were bearded, hairy men with clear blue eyes that saw beyond the confines of the elegant reception. Smartly confident public-relations girls squared their shoulders, eyes glinting in search of unattached men. A few minor television celebrities – even when planning her wedding Penny had remembered her work – smoothed down their hair and checked their reflections in mirrors, wanting as always to look their best, to be recognised. A clutch of Fleet Street snappers had been invited (John's wedding was an Event), some hacks drank too much and talked only to each other, there were university friends, seen every six months or so, and other young-marrieds who had taken an interest in Penny as soon as the announcement was in the paper. It was a motley crew of people with little in common.

John had barely noticed the party, swam through it in a daze of bafflement. Penny, always professional, had seen to every guest's intellectual and physical comfort, all the while thinking of her new life, her new husband, the overwhelming, passionate love she felt almost despite herself.

The most peculiar aspect of her new life was how little it differed from the old. The house she and John shared in north Notting Hill was larger and more comfortable than her spinster flat in Parson's Green, but otherwise nothing much had changed. John, although so much older than she, had few possessions, so the house was equipped with Penny's old furniture, and Penny had bought anything else they needed. A stranger walking through the house might not even have realised that, nominally at least, a man lived here. Only in the small study converted from the half-landing was there any sign of his personality.

'Marriage,' Penny said aloud to her reflection in the mirror over the mantelpiece. 'I used to think it was the end of the story. The grown-ups were right, though. It's only the beginning of the next one.'

Four years. Four years since the marriage. Four years in which she had watched the public side of John's career while knowing as little as ever about the realities of his life. Four years during which she had flirted her way through other men's careers, deadly earnest behind her smiles, and always, always faithful to her hero. He was still her hero, her husband. She still loved the romance in his life, which had now become her life. For it was romantic, was it not?, these long separations, the ecstatic reunions, the letters (when they could be sent) the brief, intense few weeks after John's return when he would commit himself entirely to her before he turned back to the next job, the gruelling weeks of preparation.

When he was not abroad, John spent weeks at a time with Patrick on Exmoor. He said it was as remote a place as could be found in England, with people as open-minded as anywhere on earth. There he could set himself the increasingly hard tasks that kept him fit, and know that no passer-by would look twice at him as he pulled a laden sled across the heather for hours at a time. Penny, when feeling less charitable than normal, wondered whether the inhabitants of the moor were open-minded or just incurious to the degree of backwardness. Her comment had aroused one of John's rare but blinding rages. Next time he went to his brother's house she went too, raved about the glories of Exmoor, kept her mouth shut about stag-hunting and limping sheep, and succeeded in rehabilitating herself with her husband.

She finished her drink and crossed the room from the hearth to pour herself another. 'I'm turning into a soak,' she muttered to herself. 'Perhaps I should watch myself.'

On impulse she picked up the telephone and dialled a friend's number. 'Sarah? It's Penny. Are you doing anything this evening? Oh, well, it doesn't matter. No, of course not. No, I just wondered.'

She hung up and returned to her drink. She was in a no man's land. Neither single, nor really married. Neither part of the man-hunting, wine-bar-haunting group of girls on the make, nor part of the safe dinner-party, small-children world of young-marrieds. She sighed and pulled her briefcase towards her. A publishing house had hired her to organise an author tour. Mario Melzi was a film-maker who had caused an uproar with his tales of urban violence and drug-taking and had now written a novel. Much to the publisher's horror, he had delivered a tale of rural peasant life in Italy that seemed directly descended from Laurie Lee and Miss Read with the occasional lurch towards Don Camillo. Penny had not yet met Melzi, but she had three videos to sit through and a manuscript to read before the end of the week. It would have been silly to make a social plan.

She was still on her second gin and tonic but her third cigarette when the front-door bell rang. She pushed the pause button on the video with a sense of relief. Melzi's film was strong stuff for an early Monday evening, not the sort of thing she relished watching alone. (What would John make of it? Would he have enjoyed sitting there beside her? Would he respond more easily than she to these soulless, grunting creations for whom Melzi claimed compassion?)

More than one head was outlined behind the frosted glass. For a moment Penny felt an upsurge of panic. Oh, God, have I forgotten something? It was always possible. With John away she lived in a selfish world, concentrating on work all day with no one but herself to think about once she returned to the safety of Cambridge Gardens. Perhaps they should have children ...

She was smiling as she opened the door.

'Penny, we wondered if you wanted to join us? What are you grinning at?' Sarah, Helen and Beth stood on the step, faces friendly and affable. She wondered whose idea it had been to take pity on her.

'I was indulging in a rather theoretical spot of family planning,' she said, pleased to see them after the initial flare-up of self-sufficient pride. 'Come on in, have a drink. I need one, I've been watching that Melzi film – *Blood City*? My stomach feels most peculiar.' They followed her in, and she saw their glances go to the half-empty glass and half-full ashtray. 'OK, caught, I need another,' she said, joking, and felt rather than saw them carefully not looking at each other.

The moment of awkwardness passed. They laughed, and Penny poured them drinks. She was much richer than the others – an example of the classic eighties Dinky syndrome – and was well known among her friends for the generosity of her drinks. Only a few had begun to mutter that the reason the tray was always so well stocked was more to do with her own tastes than with hospitality. John was practically teetotal.

'So why did you come round?' Penny asked, video forgotten, as she tucked her feet under herself on the sofa.

'Well, it was stupid of me – I should have thought of it when you rang,' answered Sarah. 'We'd arranged to go out together this evening anyway. I should have just said come along then.'

'But you thought you'd better check whether the others minded first?' asked Penny lightly. The gin was finally reaching her head, freeing her of the inhibitions created by good manners. Sarah looked uncomfortable and the others exchanged glances. No wonder no one ever asked her out if she was going to ruin it with chippiness.

'I'm meant to be watching this film.' Penny gestured lazily at the television set. A frozen picture showed a man with a tie around his upper arm, face grimacing with the effort of pulling one end between his teeth as he searched for an elusive vein. 'But, to be honest, I think I've lost it for this evening. I'd love to come with you, thanks.'

She went to the loo while the others finished their drinks, and as she washed her hands she looked her reflection seriously in the eye. So tonight, Penny,' she said, 'you are with the singles. You will be humorous and light-hearted, and make them glad they asked you to come too. In fact, by the end of the evening they'll be wondering why they don't always ask you along for their girlie nights out. You, too, will enjoy yourself. You will laugh a lot, make them laugh. You're good at that. In fact, Penny, you will squish every silly chippy thought, remember how lucky you are, and be the Life and Soul of the Party.'

Penny had always talked to herself. She did not think she did so more than anyone else, nor did she consider that the habit had become more exaggerated over the last year or so. In fact, she thought, when she did think about it at all, talking to herself was quite useful, a way of bouncing ideas back and forth. She did not always agree with herself — that would be boring. It would also be pointless. She talked to herself because sometimes she needed to hear another person's opinion of her, and she could never do that in the privacy of her own head.

'So, where are we going?' she asked, as she rejoined her friends. 'Italian or French?'

They walked down the street in pairs: Penny and Beth, Sarah and Helen. Four women, like so many others in London, in any big city. Penny, suddenly feeling slightly drunk, did not speak much, just thought about the picture they presented as they made their way down Cambridge Gardens towards Ladbroke Grove. Beth, in her platform boots, skinny-knit jersey, short flared skirt, could only be a city-dweller. She never wore anything more than eighteen months old, made up her face with exquisite care, more for the most recent fashions than for its shape, was a junior writer on *Harper's* and had visions of greatness. Sarah, a university friend of Penny's and the most earnest among them, dressed expensively but unimaginatively. You could almost see 'Buy a few classics and they'll never date' stamped on everything she wore. Her velvet hairband and pearl stud earrings told everything about her background and her future expectations. She managed a branch of a large estate agent in Chelsea. And then Helen: staggeringly beautiful, her face had the simple lines of a Raphael angel and her hair the lustrous waves of a pre-Raphaelite nymph. Had she not been so beautiful she would have been thought too tall, but as it was she was a woman at whom men and women alike found it hard not to stare in frank admiration. She should have been a model, everybody said so, but she worked as an aromatherapist and spent her days massaging far less beautiful women into a state of false assurance of their charms.

None of the other three was married; none of them had a lover.

They walked across the Grove to the Brasserie des Puces. It was the nearest place and, although cold, the evening was clear and dry.

'So, is John home for Christmas?' Helen asked, as they took their seats and ordered their drinks.

'Of course not,' Penny said. 'He won't be back until March, I don't think. Then he'll be here for a while.'

'That'll be the time to get your baby going,' said Beth enviously.

'Oh, I don't know about that,' said Penny. 'I didn't really mean it, you know. I was just thinking that I thought too much about myself and that if I had a baby it would give me someone else to think about.'

'But you wouldn't be able to work,' said Sarah.

'Not for a while. Hey, girls, I was only thinking about it. I wasn't actually making plans. Anyway, I'll probably have forgotten how babies are planted by the time John comes back.'

They giggled. This was what Penny was good for, and she responded to the laugh her feeble joke had raised. 'Perhaps I should find myself a lover,' she went on. 'Maybe a toy-boy to ring the changes.'

'Come on, Penny. Get yourself a lover of your own age and he'd be a toy-boy,' said Beth.

Penny felt herself blush, the painful flush that always started on her chest and wound its way upwards. She laughed, though: her sense of fairness told her that she could not be the only one allowed to make bad-taste jokes at other people's expense. But somehow she preferred making fun of herself, opening ways for her friends to mock her, than to let them find their own causes of mockery. She bit back the quick answer, the one that would hurt, the one that would remind them all that, absent though he might be, at least she had a man. Instead, she laughed, her eyes bright. '*Touché*,' she said. 'Anyway, it's all fantasy. I have a photograph of my hero to go home to and for now that'll have to be good enough.'

'So let's fantasise,' said Helen. 'Our heroes. Who would yours be, Beth?'

And so, over the lamb ragoût and Beaujolais they imagined their ideal men. Mr Darcy, Mr Rochester, Mel Gibson, Yul Brynner (from Beth), Kojak (from Penny). They giggled and bickered and slurped at the house wine, and Penny laughed the loudest, made the most outrageous suggestions, feeling the diners at other tables looking at them, envying them their youth (comparative), high spirits (exaggerated) and good looks (above average).

Later they walked back to the Grove, where they took their separate ways home. Penny felt lonely as, stumbling slightly, she made her way down Cambridge Gardens. 'I'm glad they asked me,' she told herself, side-stepping to avoid a dog's mess on the pavement. 'We had a good time. I did show off a bit, didn't I? But it's what they expect. I made them laugh. I might as well make them laugh.' She thought of another group of women who had eaten in the restaurant that night. There had been five of them, heads lowered, talking earnestly, only one bottle of wine but three of mineral water between them. They had all chain-smoked but never laughed. 'They must have wished they were us,' she went on. 'And how grim it would have been to be them. And we could have been, if we hadn't laughed. I love Sarah, she's a good friend, but she's not exactly *fun*, is she?'

A man walked past her, looking at her curiously. 'Are you all right, love?' he asked.

She smiled, but the kind voice had almost brought tears to her eyes. 'Oh, yes, I'm fine,' she said. 'I often talk to myself, I live alone, you see.'

He laughed, but his eyes were still concerned. 'You're a bit young for that, love – I mean, talking to yourself.'

'Oh, no.' Her smile was bright, well rehearsed after the evening. 'It's good practice. For when my husband comes home.'

'Well, if you're sure.' He looked at her more closely, uneasy now.

The look went to her heart. 'I live just down the road,' she said. 'Thank you for asking. And I'm not a mad old woman. Not yet.'

'Well, don't practise too hard at it,' he said, and she watched him walk away from her, whistling to himself, his stride rolling and rhythmical. She wondered where he was going, if he was happy, if he had a girl somewhere, waiting for him to walk through the night to her. She thought of John, beard frozen against his skin, sleeping the half-sleep of the man never off his guard. She thought of the strange man's kind voice and her own loud laughter and poor jokes, and felt the tears slide down her cold cheeks.

'Oh, shit,' she muttered, and, suddenly sober, walked the last few steps to her front door. She wondered if the man would look back at her, notice which door she had opened, come calling one evening with a bottle of wine ... 'Oh, shit,' she repeated, fumbling with the key.

Inside the house she looked at the mess of glasses and ashtrays in the sitting room, saw her open briefcase, the jotted notes, the videotapes. 'I should have stayed at home. I should have worked. But we had a good evening. I made them laugh. I showed them how well I manage.'

'Helen? Are you busy?'

'No, I've a client at half eleven.'

'So what did you think?' Beth spent a great deal of time on the telephone, mostly from work. Occasionally she felt a twinge of guilt, but journalists always stressed the importance of contacts, and she could always say she was trying to persuade Helen into modelling.

'About what?'

'Penny.'

'Penny? She was on cracking form.'

'Crack? Do you think that was it?'

Helen laughed. 'Hey, I'm meant to be the goofy one. *No one* takes crack any more. And you working for the style-setters – you should know that.'

Beth laughed too, glancing around her office at all the youngish women so competitively dressed in the height of fashion. 'Yeah, well, you know. So what was with her?'

'With Penny? Nothing. She made us laugh. She always does. So what's the deal?'

'Come on, Helen. You saw her. We turned up, she was already on the bottle, she'd smoked God knows how many cigarettes, she was watching that weird movie . . .'

'Beth, you're imagining things. That movie was for work.'

'So she said. And what about the gin? Don't tell me she's working on the Gordon's PR account, too.'

'OK, maybe she'd had a drink before we got there. But why shouldn't she? She's a grown-up. She'd die of thirst if she waited for John every time she wanted a drink – or one of us, come to that. How often do we ring her, or drop by and ask her out? You and I went to the cinema last week – we could have asked her, we didn't.'

'No reason why we should.'

'None at all. All I'm saying is that she probably spends

more evenings on her own than any of the rest of us, for all she's married. And she works really hard ... None of us had even considered spending the evening in to work. We never do. At least I don't.'

There was a pause. Beth's boss was striding around the office and Beth fiddled with some papers, telephone cocked under her chin, in an effort to look busy. The silence forced her into thinking about Helen's words. 'The trouble with you,' she said crossly, when she thought she could speak, 'is that you're too damned reasonable. You're right, of course. Everything you say makes sense. But everything I say does too. She does drink too much, she was too frantic. We're meant to be her friends, not her audience.'

'Well, then, be a friend to her and she may not feel she needs an audience. Think about it, Beth. She's got us, her girlfriends. But it's not the same. I wonder if she ever sees a man who isn't someone else's husband or her own brother? She might be lonely.'

Chapter Two

Penny shut her briefcase with a smart click. She had had enough for one day. She had spent the morning fighting a faint hangover and the afternoon dealing with the hysterical, wounded wife of an MP who thought hiring the services of a PR company might keep the tabloids away from her front doorstep and bring her husband back to her bed. Enough was enough. There were the joys of Melzi to look forward to, and a cool glass of Semillon. She put her head around the door of the senior partner's office. ''Bye, then, Herbie.'

'What? Oh, yes, 'bye.'

'I'm sorry to rush off, but I need to catch up on Melzi before the meeting with the publishers, and I'm meant to be going out tonight.' The last was a bit of a lie. In fact, it was a total lie, but who knew?, someone might come knocking on the door. She thought briefly of the man who had walked her almost to her doorstep the night before. He had been good-looking, kind, you never knew . . .

'Yes, yes, fine. See you in the morning.' Herbie looked up and smiled. He liked Penny, but their relationship had never crossed from professional to personal. Something in her eyes made him hesitate to go back to his paperwork. 'Penny, Christine and I have been meaning to ask you – would you like to come to dinner with us, um, the week after next? I think it was Thursday Christine mentioned.'

'Oh, Herbie, thank you.' Penny was surprised, and it showed.

Herbie was almost hurt, but thought it must be his fault. She must be lonely, he thought. Her husband away so much. I wonder who she's seeing this evening? I wonder if she has a lover?

Penny pretended to think, but knew how blank her evenings were. 'I'd love to, Herbie. Thank you. That's very kind of you – of Christine. I shall look forward to it.'

She made her way home on the lurching tube, looking at the *Telegraph* crossword without really seeing it. Dinner at the Langabeers', well, well. She had not been just polite in saying she would look forward to the evening. She was curious about Herbie's home life, always had been. He was so proper at work, friendly yet formal, falling into none of the traps laid for men working among women. Christine was a shadowy figure, often mentioned, seldom present even at work shindigs. Penny wondered who else would be there. Some new people, she hoped. It was so hard to meet new people socially when you were not on the party circuit.

Herbie eased his black BMW through the flow of the north-bound traffic and cursed softly. Why on earth had he done that? Christine would be livid, but she'd have to see sense. Some impulse of pity had moved him to ask Penny to dinner, something in her brown eyes that asked for attention in direct contradiction to everything else about her. He often thought that she looked more French, or possibly Italian, than English. Continental, anyway. Her hair was cut short and severely about her small head, and she possessed a natural elegance that made all clothes hang well from her slightly broad shoulders. She was an asset to the company, he knew that, and he did not want the company to lose her. Maybe it was time she was paid more – if Christine would allow it.

He pushed a tape into the machine and let Rachmaninov blare around the car. For all she was so competent, there was something vulnerable about Penny. She made him feel almost fatherly. That was it, he shifted in his seat and grinned to himself. Tell Christine he felt paternal towards Penny, that would be all right, and glide over the moments when he wanted to comfort her, to soothe away her troubles. If she had any troubles.

Christine was in the sitting room, makeup slightly askew, hair perfect. The sitting room was at the front of the house, a detached thirties monstrosity in Barnet built by her father. She had been brought up here, loved every brick, every rhododendron in the shrubbery. Herbie had always planned to sell when they inherited, but Christine had insisted on moving from Pimlico, and with so little else in her life that satisfied her he had not dared to insist. Now he knew that every evening, no matter what time he returned from work, Christine would be sitting in the same chair on the same perfectly plumped cushions, with this week's or month's version of the same magazines, waiting with the same wordless patience for her husband to pour her first drink of the day.

At one stage of their marriage he had tried to catch her out, he had longed so much to walk into the house and find her doing something. Anything. Even plumping the bloody cushions. But never once had he succeeded. The dinner was always in a state of incipient readiness, the house clean and tidy, the lemon sliced on the drinks tray, the ice in the bucket, the wife on the sofa, looking a little like the curtains, still pretty but slightly faded.

'Christine.' The same routine. The kiss on the upturned face, the return to the hall where he hung up his coat and put the car keys into the bowl on the small table, then back to the sitting room, to the drinks tray, and the pretence at asking, 'Would you like a drink? Gin?'

Two glasses poured, the satisfying crack of the ice in the tonic before Christine spoke.

'Did you have a good day, Herbie? Meet anyone interesting?' Hand out for the glass, eyes on her husband.

'Yes, my love, a good day, thank you. And you?' Maybe one day she would surprise him with her answer, would say, 'Yes, lovely, thank you. I met a polo player in Harvey Nichol's and went back to his hotel for a licentious afternoon.'

Maybe. But not today. 'Yes, very nice. I had lunch at Sonia's and we played a rubber of bridge. Very enjoyable. I thought I'd like to invite her and Malcolm to dinner soon. I seem to lunch there so much ... What do you think?'

Well, this was a minor surprise. It was rare that Christine came forward with a suggestion of something they should do together. At any time Herbie would have encouraged her, but now relief at the opportunity she had given him made him garrulous. 'An excellent idea. Yes, Malcolm's a nice chap, we hardly ever see them. In fact, I was thinking, Christine, that we should invite Penny Brunel to dinner. She's on her own again, and I can't help feeling that it would be kind ...'

'Kind?' For the first time Christine looked at him with a sharper focus. 'I hope you're kind to her in the office, but I see no reason why you should be any kinder to her than that.'

'She's on her own,' Herbie repeated. 'Her family is all over England.'

'I'm sure she has friends.'

'Yes, and I'd like to think I'm one of them.' Desperation made him bold. He had asked Penny already, after all, and sometimes Christine had to be made to toe the line.

'Don't suggest that I might become one.' Her tone was icy. She held out her glass for another drink.

He took it, dropped ice in, poured a healthy measure of gin. 'Oh, never mind, Christine. It was just an idea. Common civility, good manners, that sort of thing. No, I doubt you'd be friends. You're very different women. But she works hard, I like her, I just thought . . .'

Christine took the drink and sat back against the cushions. 'Manners,' she murmured. 'You're right, of course. Yes, she must be asked. She is not the kind of woman I warm to, although I know that the very things that make me distrust her are those that make her valuable to you. I know she's important to the company.'

Herbie, his back to his wife, pulled a face of distaste. He wanted to ask Penny here because he liked her, not for the sake of office politics. But if that was what was needed to persuade Christine that there was no harm in inviting her, so be it.

Now he had to think of some other people to entertain her. Malcolm was all right, but Sonia . . . He pushed all disloyal thoughts from his head and turned back to his wife with a smile. 'What do you think about the cinema this evening?' he asked.

The doorbell did ring that evening, to a visitor almost as unexpected as Penny's Good Samaritan would have been. It was nine thirty, and Penny had just finished a bowl of Covent

Garden soup (carrot and coriander) and a sandwich (cheese). She had thought Melzi would leave her with no appetite, but she had been wrong. She suspected that he would be a great deal more interesting to work with than the average film luvvie. Maybe he would even be a new friend ... quite a catch, Melzi would be, in her circle. Penny was beginning to tire of the sameness of her group of friends when John was away. He had few friends, but the ones he had were far removed from her middle-class professional world. An Italian-immigrant film director with a brutal view of modern life and the soul of a seventeenth-century poet would certainly have something different to offer.

'I'm selling him, of course,' she said to herself, standing at the counter in the kitchen and gazing at the blue and white Portuguese tiles on the wall, 'but I must be careful not to sell him to myself before I meet him. There's getting to be a danger of that. But there must be someone interesting in this world apart from John. And he's so far away ...' She thought of John, almost alone in the ice. She wondered if he would ever tire of his loneliness. 'At least I'm not lonely,' she said. 'At least I have people around me. People to play with, to talk to, *react* with.'

Her gaze shifted from the tiles to the bottle of red wine open in front of her. 'Oh, why not? I've only had one gin and tonic tonight. Another glass of wine won't hurt.'

And then the doorbell rang.

Penny hesitated, looked at her watch, wondered whether to pretend to be out. But the lights were still on, it wouldn't be very convincing.

She looked through the peephole in her front door. The man on her step stood with his back to the door. He, too, was looking at his watch. Perhaps he was reconsidering his visit. Something about him was familiar. Who was it?

He turned towards the door, hand raised to the bell and

Penny opened the door straight away. 'Tel! What on earth are you doing here?'

He was not quite as tall as John, but there was no mistaking the resemblance. The mouth was slightly more curly, the chin a shade weaker, but the build was the same, the long legs, the head, which was surprisingly finely set above the strong shoulders. Only the eyes were different. Not only the colour — a murky hazel compared to John's blue — but there was always a hesitation in his expression, a lack of confidence. 'You never look as though you'll be welcomed,' Penny half scolded. Sometimes Terence's diffidence touched her, sometimes it irritated her.

'Well, it is rather late,' he said, gesturing hopelessly.

'It is. Are you all right?' She looked at him more closely. 'It's so hard to tell with you, Tel. You always look worried.'

He smiled. 'I'll go on being worried until you let me in. And maybe offer me a glass of that wine.'

'Oh, God, of course, come in. And tell me all about it.'

Penny liked Terence but she felt uneasy with him. His very existence cast a little shadow over her hero.

His first words, as he sat in front of her fake fire with a hastily made cheese and pickle sandwich on a plate on his knees and a glass of red wine in his hand, activated the prickle of discomfort he always gave her. 'So where's Dad now?'

The very way he said the word 'Dad' was all wrong. Penny knew it, but she wondered if Terence was aware of how false it sounded coming from him.

'God knows. I next hear from him in five days' time. Unless, of course ...' There was always the 'unless'. 'In some frozen tundra or whatever they're called, looking for some place that will look the same as the place he's just come from, but will have the advantage of never having been looked at before.'

'You sound bitter. But you make a good cheese sandwich.'

She smiled. 'Oh, Tel, I'm not bitter. But sometimes I wonder—' She stopped herself and poured them both more wine. 'I wish I had more of him.' She intercepted his look, and added hastily, 'Of course I have more of him than you do.'

'Than I ever had.'

'Now who's sounding bitter?'

She did not know how to deal with Terence. Flirting was out of the question – he was her stepson, after all. Only four years younger than she, but still a stepson. However, she had never wiped his nose, or his bottom, or taken him to a James Bond movie or done any of the things that stepmothers were supposed to do. She just did not know how to play him.

He sighed, looked forlorn. 'I'm sorry. I was hoping to catch him.'

Penny laughed. 'You are idiotic. He's not a bus. You can't have come over from Ireland on the off-chance of "catching" him. You know how long he goes away for, and how often.'

'Not so much the call of the wild as the call of the polar wastes.'

'Exactly. What did you really want?'

'To get away from Mum.' He grinned, all boyish charm. It was sometimes hard to forget that he was so close to her in age – he was more like a teenager.

'Something to do with Irish charm, or feckless living, I suppose,' said Penny.

'What, Mum?'

'No, no. Oh, God, Tel, I'm even talking to myself in public now. It really must be getting bad.' She told him about last night's street encounter and they both laughed. The ice was broken.

'So – your mother?' Penny prompted. This time she was to play the wise older woman, the stepmother, the discreet arbitrator between generations. A shame, really. She liked to flirt.

'Oh, the same old story. She's got herself a new boyfriend and there just isn't room in the shack for me and her and anyone else. Anyway, it was time I moved on. For a while, at least. I suppose she'll call me when it all goes wrong, weep on my shoulder, expect me to look after her for a while.'

'Hasn't it been time you moved on for years?' Penny asked gently. 'In ex-junkie-speak there's something called enabling. You let her treat you as she does, you should stop her.'

'I have done, by going away.' His gloom turned to petulance.

'But you'll go back to her, you know you will. And so does she.' Her tone was gentle, forbearing. She rather enjoyed this new role.

'Unlike Dad.'

'Oh, come on, Terence, you know that's not fair. She never wanted him. She never pretended she did.'

'That's what he says.'

Penny sat up straight. She was not games-playing now. Loyalty to John was one of the strongest motivating forces in her life. She could not bear anyone to say, or even hint, that his behaviour was not of the best and his motives were not of the highest. 'Yes, he does say it. And I believe him. So do you. You've told me yourself about his visits to you when you were a child, how painful you both found them. He tried to look after you, you told me that yourself, but your mother wouldn't let him near.'

'So she turned him into some sort of myth, not a father.'

'You're being bitter again. He was nineteen, Terence. He didn't know what he wanted out of life. Give him a chance! He was younger than you are now, and you still don't know where your future lies. Yours is uncomplicated by a baby.'

'My mother's was complicated with a baby.'

'Yes, which she decided to take to Ireland. He didn't even know where you were for the first three years of your life. She just disappeared. His parents were willing to help, they've often told me so.'

'Yes, but it's all hearsay. Has it ever occurred to you that the whole of my life is based on other people's hearsay? Mum says this, Dad says that, his parents say this, the various boyfriends say something else. At least by leaving the coast clear Mum won't be able to say I drove Pip away.'

'Pip?'

'The new one. He writes adventure books for ten-year-old boys, and came to Ireland because of the tax thing. He thinks Mum's wonderful, beautiful, romantic — and it saves him rent living at the shack. He's a fraud. Ireland is the furthest he's ever been from Essex, and his six months there is the longest he's ever been away from the mainland. He thinks Mum's some kind of Marianne Faithfull, bruised by circumstances, a tragic heroine of the modern age. And he keeps asking about Dad. I can't answer him, Penny, not even the most basic questions, because I don't know the answers, because I think he's going to put them in some crappy book and then I'll be caught out about how little I know about my own father.'

'So you thought you'd catch him here, gen up on the info Pip needs, go back and shine in both their eyes?'

Terence jumped up, his empty plate falling to the floor, the wine glass safe by a margin. 'Sometimes you are a complete bitch, Penny.'

She did not move, looked up at him in silence, waited for him to react to his own anger.

It worked. He sat down slowly, picked up the plate and put it carefully on to the coffee table. 'I'm sorry, Penny. I shouldn't have said that, and I'm not really sure it's true.'

She raised her eyebrows at him.

'All right, it's not, I know it's not, I know you're only protecting Dad, although why you should . . .'

'Terence, had you been drinking before you arrived here?'

He looked surprised. 'No. One beer on the train, and I came straight here from the station. I never drink much.'

She believed him. She recognised drinkers easily enough. 'So you just sat on the train, getting angry.'

'I suppose so. Oh, Penny, it's not fair to take it out on you. I've cocked up my own life, I suppose. Yes, I should have left Mum years ago, but you know what she's like. She's so messed up . . . I think she would have been whatever had happened to her, but I don't suppose she gave herself the best chance, running away to Ireland like that, small baby in tow, turning her back on her relations – and mine.'

'You forget, she didn't go entirely alone.' Penny's tone was dry. She did not like this presentation of Terence's mother.

'No, but she was dumped pretty quickly.'

'I suppose you're blamed for that, too.'

Terence took a sip of wine. Suddenly he looked every one of his years. 'Sometimes. I did cry a lot as a baby.'

Penny laughed. 'Oh, come *on*, Tel. What a load of rubbish! Are you a man or a mouse? Your mother can't blame the disintegration of her life on the fact that you cried as a baby. Or if she does, you shouldn't let her.'

They had been through this before, of course. Terence could never decide who was the hero and who was the villain in his parents' story. The facts were that John had made Rowena pregnant in the course of a brief, essentially light-hearted affair when they were both eighteen. Her parents, taking a tidy tea on a well-mown lawn in the Home Counties, had received the news badly, with horror, disgust and outrage. His parents, worried and cross at John's carelessness, had volunteered nevertheless to bring up the baby. Rowena had lost her nerve at the thought of abortion, collected several cheques from her father and John's, and disappeared, seven months' pregnant, leaving no word.

It turned out she had gone with a new lover, a man who deserted her soon after Terence's birth but at least contacted her parents on his return to England to tell them about their grandson but not where he could be found. John, secretly relieved that the responsibility was taken from him, had kept in half-hearted touch with Rowena's parents until their aggression took its toll.

'But he did try to find you. And he did find you. And he did try to see you.' Penny was almost thinking aloud, urging John's case to his son.

'In between going to Cambridge *as planned*, getting his degree *as planned*, taking three months in North America, six months in India, a month in Canada *as planned*. Until he took up with the Pole, everything in his life went as planned except for me.'

Penny could not respond to Terence's quavering self-pity. It was too late, she was tired, she couldn't face it. The only question was whether to argue with her stepson or laugh at him. She chose laughter. ' "Took up with the Pole" indeed. It sounds more like a dodgy girlfriend than a way of life.'

'Yes, well, there were one or two of those too.'

Penny did not dignify that retort with an answer. She stood up and collected the glasses and Terence's plate.

'You sound sixty.'

'And you sound sixteen. Which is exactly what I mean. Come on, snap out of it, we can have some fun together—'

She was interrupted by the ringing of the telephone. Startled, she looked at her watch. Ten fifteen was late for a call, perhaps there was bad news of John. 'Hello, Penny Brunel speaking.' She kept her voice calm but felt the tension leave her in a great flood as she heard Herbie's cool voice.

'Penny, I just wanted to confirm dinner. Oh, I'm sorry, I've just seen the time. I hope you weren't asleep.'

'Of course not, I've just finished work.' Her voice was light, teasing. Relief made her talk to Herbie in a way she never would have in the office.

'You shouldn't do that — you should be out on the town. I'm sure John wouldn't want you pining away without him.' He was jocular, avuncular, embarrassed by her change in tone. Too late, she remembered her lie, that she had said she was going out that evening. Oh, what a fool she was! Why did she bother to speak sometimes? More to hear the sound of her own voice talking to another person than because of any information she wanted to share.

She suddenly thought of Terence. Would he still be with her in ten days' time? Should she ask if she could bring him to the Langabeers' with her? She looked at him out of the corner of her eye. He was slumped in his chair, eyes fixed on the wavering blue gas flames. No, better to leave him to his own devices. Besides, she didn't want him to think she spent every night sitting on her own watching videos and waiting for his father to return.

'So, Thursday week — we'll look forward to seeing you,' Herbie was saying.

She laughed lightly as though he had paid her a compliment, thanked him prettily and hung up.

Terence looked up at her with a scowl. 'Bit late to ring, isn't it?'

'My boss,' she explained, picking up the glasses again and taking them to the kitchen.

Terence pulled himself to his feet and followed her. 'Sounded a bit chatty for a boss.'

'I don't know how you'd know. You've never worked in an office, have you?'

'Was he asking you out?'

She washed the glasses before she answered, and put the plate in the dishwasher. 'Yes, he was,' she said, with an exaggerated grin. 'He was asking me to dinner in north London with his charming if reclusive wife and some old men with whom he probably plays golf on a Saturday afternoon. He's doing his duty by me, as I'm doing my duty by him in accepting. If, on the other hand, he had been a man I met yesterday on the tube who had looked at me with come-to-bed brown eyes and asked me to dinner at Tante Claire, I would have said yes to him too.'

'To dinner or to bed?'

'Is it anything to do with you? I'm off to bed, Terence. I'll give you some sheets. I leave at eight, but don't feel you have to get up. Shall I take you out to dinner tomorrow? Or do you have plans?'

'At Tante Claire?'

'192 more like. Unless you're in the money.' She kissed his cheek. 'Come on, stepson, let's be friends. It'll be nice for me to have a companion for a change.'

Terence followed her up the stairs, took the crisp white sheets and thick white towels from her, walked on up past the closed door of his father's office, into the cold spare bedroom. Penny drew the curtains, turned on the radiator, checked that the bedside light was working, turned again to her silent stepson. 'I'll leave a spare set of keys by the telephone in the kitchen if I don't see you in the morning. Don't bother with the telephone — I'll leave the answering-machine switched on, although of course help yourself if you want to use it. You know where the bathroom is. Sleep well.'

Ignoring his glower, she kissed him again and left the room, shutting the door quietly behind her. She hummed as she walked up the next flight of stairs to her own room. Despite his mood swings, it might well be fun to have Terence staying. And perhaps she had found the role he expected of her: not a flirt (at least, not with him), not a mother figure, which was clearly inappropriate, more of a social butterfly, a glamorous figure enjoying her husband's absence. In the purest of senses, of course . . .

She turned out her bedside light feeling much more cheerful than she had for weeks. What a lot there was for her to look forward to, after all.

Chapter Three

Terence idled out of bed and made his way down to the kitchen. He put the kettle on and stood waiting for it to boil, staring at nothing. This stay was not turning out quite as he had planned. He had not necessarily expected his father to be in London – it had been a vague hope but not the sole purpose of his visit. In fact, if he were honest with himself, he had been as interested in checking out Penny as he had been in talking to his often absent father.

And I'm not really getting anywhere, he realised, as he reached for a mug and rooted in a cupboard for the Nescafé. He was never out of bed before Penny left for work and she seemed to spend most of her evenings with her briefcase in front of her, reading and making notes. Somehow, life in Cambridge Gardens was not as he had imagined. Comfortable, of course – there was always plenty to eat and drink, and Penny did not seem to begrudge him helping himself from either her fridge or her drinks tray. Perhaps he should offer to cook her dinner one night.

He made the Nescafé, and some toast and Marmite, which he spread directly on the counter without using a plate. He would wipe it up later. Now he had things to do.

He picked up the telephone, delved in his jeans pocket for a dirty piece of paper and dialled the number written on it in an illiterate hand. 'Hello? This is Terry. We met yesterday in the Percy. Yeah, hi! I just wondered if you were doing anything at lunchtime. Great, all right, see you there, twelve fifteen. 'Bye, then, Mike.' He hung up with a smile. He always found it easy to make friends. If he found himself slipping into a bit of an Irish brogue as he talked to Mike, it didn't really matter. Mike came from the same part of Drogheda as he did, and Terence often found it easier not to proclaim his public-school education with every syllable. Mike might get him some casual work on the site, and although he was living for free he could still do with some money. The beer and chips every lunch added up . . .

There was an hour before he could meet Mike. Terence looked at the shelf of videos but found nothing that attracted his attention. He gave the bookshelf only the most cursory of glances, but more as a way of killing thirty seconds than with any expectation of finding something to entertain him. He wondered about going out for a paper, but could not be bothered. He could buy one when he went to the pub. He resented it slightly that Penny had three papers delivered and took them all with her to work. He had not yet dared to suggest she leave one behind for him.

Tonight she was going out to dinner with her boss. Yesterday he had hinted that she might take him along, but she had not risen to the suggestion. Couldn't she see he was getting bored with nothing to do all day? Couldn't she at least provide him with some social life? She must have friends.

On an impulse he picked up the telephone again and dialled a number he knew by heart but rarely used. He waited a while, giving his mother time to rouse herself from wherever she was lying and answer the telephone. She hated it, had only put one in the house five years ago when he had taken to leaving suddenly, without warning. 'Of course, you're a big boy now,' she had said, looking up at him through her always slightly too long fringe. 'Of course you must always feel free to come and go as you please. You don't need to think of me.'

'Mother, you've always managed to look after yourself.' He only called her Mother when he was trying to assert himself.

'And you.' Her kohl-rimmed eyes blinked slowly up at him. Rowena did nothing at speed.

'And me,' he admitted. 'So it'll be all the easier for you with only yourself to look after.'

'Oh, no, I'll be forgetting to be doing the cooking without you to cook for,' she said. He hated it when she lapsed into Irish brogue. It was totally fake, and they both knew it. Her voice had the clipped enunciation of Roedean and the Home Counties. In her youth she had adopted an Essex twang, but had deliberately lost it with her move across the Irish Sea. Now her accent depended on her mood, on the picture of herself she wanted to paint. No one knew better than Terence how far Rowena really was from the soda-bread baking, Irish-stew cooking, home-making Irish mother she sometimes aped. The only thing of which he was unsure was how much she knew she differed from that picture.

'You won't be on your own for long,' he had said, turning his back cruelly on her. 'I must go and pack.'

That had been his first escape. Not without a twinge of guilt he had kissed his mother goodbye, caught buses and trains and ferries until he arrived in London. These escapes had now become a feature of his life. A few months at home, allowing his mother to look after him, or himself to look after her (sometimes he wondered which way round it really was), followed by a few more months of growing impatience with her, with himself, with Ireland. Then he would pack his bags and leave, sometimes without warning, sometimes after a painful row. He worked on stud farms or in kennels, painted other people's houses, mended their fences. He would take lodgings with elderly ladies pleased to have a good-looking young man for whom they would cook in return for his helping around the house. That was probably the next stage in his mother's career, after the supply of boyfriends finally dried up. At first she would resent playing the part of grateful widow, but she could do it.

Mummy could do everything.

'Hello?' She always sounded frightened when she answered the telephone.

'Mother? It's Terry.'

'Terence! Darling, where are you? I've been so worried.' It was the Roedean voice. She was all right. Pip must still be with her.

'I'm at John's.' He never used the word Dad to his mother. It did not seem right.

'John? John who?'

'John Brunel. My father. Mother, are you all right?'

There was a short silence. When she spoke next Roedean had softened, but she was not yet fully Irish. 'Your father, of course. And how is he?'

'He's away. I'm staying here, though. Penny's being very kind. She's a good hostess.'

'Houseful, is there?'

Terence was puzzled. 'No, just me.'

'Are you sure your father wouldn't mind?'

'Mind?'

'You're a young man, Terence. Closer to Penelope in age than she is to your father. Good-looking, too. He might not like it.'

34

Terence nearly laughed out loud. 'Don't be silly, Mother. She's my stepmother.'

'Don't be silly yourself, Terence, you know she's not, except technically, any more than John is your father, except technically.'

He sighed. It had been a mistake to ring. He had thought that at this time in the morning she would be capable of speaking sense. 'Anyway, Mum, I thought you'd want to know where I was.'

'Although I suppose she has plenty of boyfriends for John to worry about. You won't make any difference.' Rowena's voice was gentle, musing.

Terence suddenly felt uneasy. 'I don't think so.'

'Not that you've seen. But, then, she wouldn't exactly flaunt them in front of you, would she?'

'Mother! She didn't know I was coming, did she?'

'So she struck lucky when you turned up. Are you sure there are no men around? No signs of them?'

Terence had a mental picture of the pair of brown brogues under the table in the hall. Odd that such a tidy woman had not put the shoes away when her husband had been away for what . . . a month? Two months? He hadn't thought to ask. His unease intensified. 'Only of John,' he said. He didn't like his mother in this mood and was not going to give her any ammunition. What was it to her, anyway? She had left his father all those years ago . . . hadn't she?

'Oh, and of course you'd recognise his possessions, wouldn't you?'

Suddenly Terence had had enough. He did not like the poison his mother was dripping into his ear. But wasn't that partly why he had come here? He shook the suspicion away. 'So how are you, Mother? Pip all right? Or is there another boyfriend on the horizon?' He made his tone jocular, but he hoped she picked up the inference. She, after all, was the one with a history of passing men, not Penny. Penny, as far as he knew, as far as he could see, was virtue itself.

'Sure and I don't know what you mean. Another boyfriend? What do you make me sound like? I told you, Pip is different. He doesn't drink, he doesn't shout, he locks himself away all morning with his whatever-they're-called, you know, computer thing, and then in the afternoon he's all mine. This one's going to last, Terry. This one's for real.'

'As long as I stay away?'

'Oh, my darling, you know that's not true. In fact, only yesterday Pip was asking me when you'd be back.' There was a pause. Terence was not going to fall into that trap. She gave in. 'When will you?'

'I can't say, Mother. I'm getting a job here. I don't know how long I'll be committed.' It was part of their relationship that he should stretch the truth about his work, and that she should believe him.

'Wonderful, Terry. Anything interesting?'

'Mother, would I waste my time on anything else?' He had once heard her telling a friend that she thought Terence had a great career in novel-writing ahead 'when he was grown-up'. He had been twenty-four at the time, and selling novelty ties out of a cheap briefcase to secretaries bored at their desks. He had not been offended by her words, though – had in fact taken an obscure pride in them, as though she gave validity to a life that he knew was being lived ineptly. 'He's a clever boy,' she had gone on. 'Realises it's easier to get experience when you're young, is trying everything now. After all, if he'd been conventional, started some career for the sake of it, what would he have to write about?' He had not yet written the seminal novel about tie-selling (or anything else), but there was always hope, there was always a future.

'I'll tell you about it another time,' he went on. 'I'll ring again soon, let you know if I move away from here. All right, Mum, look after yourself. 'Bye.' He hung up before she could remember her role as mourning mother and begin the pressure to bring him home. She was all right, Pip was there, she had the current love of her life under control. She did not need him yet.

The coffee was cold, he made himself some more. Soon his pulse would quicken and he would begin to feel awake.

But something other than caffeine had stirred his blood this morning. He thought of his mother's words, and although he had not liked their tone, had tried to push them away as she spoke, they had a certain power. It was unlikely that Penny was as alone as she appeared. She was good-looking, stylish, intelligent. She was on her own for months on end. If there had been friends who came round, telephone calls even, it would seem less suspicious. But such total silence? He had not once answered the telephone to a man, had not heard a man's voice leaving a message on the answer-phone. Only on the first night, when her boss (if he was indeed her boss) had called and asked her to dinner ... the dinner she was going to tonight, without him, her house guest, her stepson.

A second cup of coffee was left to cool, untouched. Terence paced the ground floor, his mind alive with possibilities. If she was having an affair, what should he do? Should he try to find out the truth, or leave his eyes closed to it? What did he owe his father, his mother? Himself?

The carriage clock on the mantelpiece in the sitting room chimed the hour and brought him back to earth. Twelve o'clock. Enough of thinking. It was time to meet Mike.

*   *   *

The salmon mousse, wrapped in slices of smoked salmon, was laid out on each plate, accompanied by two lettuce leaves and a green olive. Each plate was symmetrically arranged, symmetrically placed. The napkins were folded into boat shapes (a little joke for Malcolm, who loved sailing even more than he did golf). The pheasant à la Normande was covered in foil, keeping warm in the bottom oven. The vegetables were prepared, waiting only to be put into pans of boiling water. The chocolate mousse was in the fridge, the lemon tart on its lemon-decorated plate, the winter fruit salad in a cut-glass bowl. The cream was in its silver jug, the ice was in the bucket, the red wine opened, the white chilling in the fridge, the flowers arranged. The dining-room table was laid with the best silver plate and crystal. And there, right on cue, was Herbie's key in the lock. Christine put the magazine she had been holding – reading was too strong, looking at too active a concept – on the coffee table. She did not like to be doing anything when Herbie walked in, thought she owed it to him to give him her full attention when he had finished a day at the office.

And here he was.

'Christine.' She raised her face for his kiss, watched him leave the room, listened to him hang up his coat and put the car keys in the bowl, saw him return, with pleasure. Without routine Christine felt lost. Herbie's home-coming each evening was perhaps the happiest moment of her day. She felt safe from the moment she heard his key in the door.

'Would you like a drink? Gin?'

The two glasses were poured, she listened for the ice cracking, beginning to melt as her heart had so long ago in the warmth of Herbie's kindness.

'Did you have a good day, Herbie? Meet anyone interesting?' She held out her hand for the glass, kept her gaze on her husband. Her mother had told her how important it was to listen to men, to give them her full attention, to make life as easy as possible for the breadwinner, the head of the family.

'Yes, it was a good day.' Mostly because he had been looking forward to this evening, but that was not something he felt he should tell his wife. 'We had a new client in. Well, he's not the client, Brooker and Hudson are, the publishers, but they've given us a big budget and I think we should have fun with this one. It's one of Penny's, actually, a young film-maker, I don't know if you've read about him.' His glance flicked to the pile of magazines on the coffee table; Christine caught the contempt and the attempt to hide it. 'Melzi?'

'No, I can't say I have. Does he make nice films?' It was always important to show interest in his work, even if it meant nothing to her.

Herbie grinned. 'Not what you'd call nice, no. I've not seen them myself, but by all accounts they're fairly grim. The book, though, perhaps you'd like that. I'll bring you a copy, I'm sure there'll be a spare one at the office ... All ready for dinner? Anything I can to do to help?'

Christine laughed. She had a pretty laugh, a tinkling, girlish laugh, which she practised sometimes during her long hours alone in the day. 'Herbie, my darling, of course not! You've done your job all day, now it's my turn to do mine. It's called corporate entertaining, isn't it? I'm sure I read about it somewhere.'

'No, darling, it's called having your friends to dinner.' Herbie sucked his lemon slice. It irritated Christine, but she irritated him, and it was better that she thought the grimace was caused by the lemon than by her. He wished he were the kind of man to kick sofas, but he was not, he never would be. He would keep on bringing home the cheques and pouring the gin and living in this luxurious box and running Daddy's firm for Christine until one of them found something that would make their hearts sing.

'Do you ever laugh for no reason?' he asked his wife.

'Laugh? At nothing? I don't think so.' Christine's eyes dragged into focus. 'Well, there wouldn't be anything funny, would there?'

'Do you remember doing it? Ever? In your life?' he persisted. The question had come from nowhere but he had to have an answer.

'I doubt it. It wouldn't be very ... tidy, would it? Are you feeling all right? Do you want me to cancel dinner?' Suddenly Christine was concentrating. He could read her thoughts. It would be embarrassing to cancel Sonia and Malcolm, a shame to have to put off Charlie Ackroyd, a relief not to have to see Penny. The Melmottes were cousins of a sort, so they would not mind. The main course could be frozen for another time, the vegetables were not yet cooked ... tick tick tick, went her mind on the boring practicalities that made up her life.

Herbie pulled himself together. 'No, Christine, of course not. I'm sorry. I was just trying to imagine you before I knew you, when you were, I don't know, fifteen or something. They always seem to laugh a lot, girls of that age. I saw some on the way home, just walking along, pushing each other and giggling wildly ... It made me think.'

Christine was relieved. 'Oh, no, I wasn't one of that type, Herbie, you needn't worry. I don't suppose I was much different from how I am now. A little thinner, maybe.'

'Impossible, my love, you have a marvellous figure.' They could both play this game blindfolded, it oiled the wheels of the civilised pretence of their marriage. He had been mad to think about laughing, he couldn't think what had overcome him. Thank heavens they were back on track. 'Another drink?'

Christine took the second gin and tonic, and then, as he had known she would, looked at her wrist-watch (a dainty sapphire and diamond affair her parents had given her as a wedding present) and said, with a start of surprise, 'Heavens, Herbie! The time! I must go and change.'

'I wish you would,' he answered, helping her up from her chair. She did not read the double meaning, which was just as well. He closed the door behind her and poured himself a second drink. Then, avoiding the chair on which his wife had been sitting, he sank into another perfectly puffed chair. She would tut, and repuff, and he would pretend not to notice and so their life was run. He wondered if Christine was as aware as he was of the games they played, the circles they danced around the truth. Oh, Lord, perhaps this was all some ghastly mid-life crisis.

Penny walked through the Langabeers' front door with a broad smile designed to hide her curiosity as well as her nerves. She was never frightened at work, could meet everyone else's heroes with supreme indifference (she had married one, after all), but would sometimes find herself struck with tongue-tying nerves on social occasions. With her own friends, she knew the part to play, the part expected of her. Faced with strangers she would sometimes clam up until she could gauge the temperature of the people around her, and often by then it was too late to make any sort of impression.

'It's not showing off,' she said to herself in the taxi, struck with panic at the thought of an evening with her gentle boss and his shadowy wife, 'not like it is with the girls. It's just I don't know what's expected of me, and I hate that. Oh, God, why did I accept? He was only being nice. He's probably dreading it as much as I am. Or perhaps there are some potential clients we're meant to be seducing. He should have warned me.' She thought a moment about whom he might ask from the client list. Maybe their new novelist, Philip Veysey – he seemed interesting. But not Herbie's type. Herbie handed Penny all the authors, said talking about writing made him feel as though he were still at school. 'Still, I get to see the Langabeer house, which is a plus.'

She thought of Terence, whom she had left drinking red wine in front of her fire. She wished she had stayed with him, thought that perhaps he was lonely and she should be providing him with some social life. He seemed set to stay for a while, and she was beginning to find his lethargy irritating. Perhaps if he found some friends he would go out more often and leave her her space. Then, with surprising strength, she found herself missing John. He never let her work herself into a rage about other people, would always look at her blankly until he made her laugh at herself. 'They don't matter, Penny,' he would say. 'Don't you see they're only pretending?' She wished he were with her so that he could tell her exactly what his son was pretending, what he wanted to be, or to be thought to be. He was never pompous, John, and would deny that he was interested in people, but he was surprisingly wise about their faults. Wise and understanding, but never judgemental. Sometimes she thought he was a little God-like in his appreciation of the people around him, but the thought scared her. He was just a man, after all, just her husband.

So the smile was in place as the door was opened. It was a smile that would do for Herbie, or for his wife, or for any staff they might have. (Everyone in the office knew that the company had been owned and founded by Christine Langabeer's father. The gossip about her inherited riches was one of the staples of lunchtime conversation among the secretaries.) When Penny saw that it was Herbie on the other side of the mahogany veneer, her shoulders sagged with the release of tension and her smile broadened. 'Herbie, hello. I hope I'm not too early.'

'Spot on, Penny, welcome.'

She followed him down the wide corridor, her antennae alert to every detail of décor and design. Nothing much was given away by the striped wallpaper in the hall, the standard mock-antique hall table, the framed engravings of Italian cities. It could be any house in North London. There was a genteel buzz of voices from behind a door on the left. Herbie paused for a moment, hand on the door knob. 'I'm glad you've come, Penny. I'm only sorry we haven't asked you before. Now, then, we've some nice people here to meet you.'

He made it sound as though she were the most important guest, Penny realised, and the thought gave her courage as he pushed the door open.

'Christine, darling, Penny's here.'

One look from her hostess made Penny realise that she was not as important to Mrs Langabeer as she was to her husband. Another quick look around the room and she saw that there was nothing to be frightened of here. A red-faced man in an expensive blazer and diamond cuff-links. He had once been good-looking but too much gin and wind had done for him. An immaculately coiffed woman in a tailored sugar-pink suit and matching lipstick moved a step nearer to him as Penny walked in. Why did a certain sort of woman always think of her as a threat just because she didn't wear her own husband on her arm like a badge of honour? Penny felt a stab of dislike for this woman, who had not yet even spoken. She knew, though, that the woman was right. She could charm the old buffer without any effort at all. The evening would pass pleasantly enough, but would be unmemorable. Herbie had asked her out of kindness, and she would behave properly to thank him, and pray that the conversation did not turn too dully right-wing.

She took a gin and tonic from Herbie, asked him if she could smoke (she had a feeling that his wife would feel no embarrassment in telling her she could not) and turned her most professional smile on Christine while Herbie left the room to answer the front door again. 'It's so kind of you to have me, Mrs Langabeer. We've often met, of course, but always in such a big crowd that we don't really know each other. You're such an integral part of the company that I was really pleased to have a chance to know you better.' It was so easy, knowing which button to push. Had she complimented Herbie, Christine would have given her the same look that the pink woman had thrown her.

Instead, Christine's smile slipped from social to almost warm. 'I did work there for a while, before we married. Daddy hoped I'd stay on, but somehow I always felt that some things were more important than a career.'

Penny caught her breath. So it was gloves off from the start; how interesting. 'Of course,' she agreed. 'My generation's very lucky in being free to make more choices than yours.' She could fight if necessary: although Christine appeared middle-aged, Penny didn't think she was in fact all that much older than herself.

'Oh, I had the choice. Daddy was very in advance of his time. He made it clear from the start that there would always be a place for me in the boardroom. But I looked at how happy he and Mummy were and wondered if their marriage would have been so contented if she had always been off making decisions.

Of course, I know that in your case your husband is away for so much of the time. I do feel for you. It must be very hard being a wife to him.'

Penny drew deep on her cigarette. The woman was right, of course, but not in the sense that she intended. Penny wondered why this mild-looking woman so disliked her. 'Oh, I do know what you mean. Sometimes I feel he's more a client than a husband,' she said sweetly, although a voice in her head was warning her, You promised to behave, Penny. Take it easy, let it ride ...

The red-faced man let out a huge guffaw. 'Oh, I say, I'm sure you didn't mean that the way it sounded – client, indeed, not husband!'

'Malcolm!' the pink woman said softly, moving even closer to her husband. 'Malcolm, honestly, no golf-club-bar humour here!'

Herbie came back with another couple, a bonds dealer called Richard Melmotte and his younger, prettier (presumably second?) wife Sally. Behind them followed Charlie Ackroyd, the publicity manager of a large fashion house whom Penny had met before in the office. Her heart lifted; at least there was one person here to whom she was of no interest, no threat, nothing but an amusing companion. He winked at her as he walked in, and hugged her warmly. Penny handed her glass to Herbie for a refill (the barbed conversation with Christine had made her drain her glass rather fast) and smiled back at him. She would survive this evening with no wounds.

Penny sat back in the taxi with a sense of relief. She had drunk more than she had intended (it had been a mistake to have a gin and tonic before she left home, even though she had needed courage) but she had not behaved badly. She had listened solemnly as red-faced Malcolm had given his views on African diplomats being allowed immunity from traffic offences – what had he been on about? she wondered. It apparently all boiled down to black men being bad drivers. She had even laughed at his golfing stories. She had thanked Sonia for her kindness, but regretted that she did not play bridge, and was tied to the office by Herbie's draconian demands on his staff (girlish laughs all round, admiring glances from the two older men). She had complimented Christine effusively on her cooking, and regretted her own ineptitude in the kitchen. 'Perhaps that's why John goes away so much.' She had sighed. 'Perhaps even seal blubber or whatever he eats is better than his benighted wife's attempts at cordon bleu.'

'Oh, but, Penny dear, you must move on. Cordon bleu is very *passé*, now,' said Sonia. 'It's all rocket and new Italian cooking. Perhaps you'd have more luck there.'

Sally caught Penny's eye, flicked her glance at the creamy sauce in which the pheasant legs floated disconsolately and raised her eyebrows. Penny felt the giggles kick in (for heaven's sake, she was in her thirties, wasn't it time she lost the impulse to behave like a schoolgirl?).

Altogether Penny found that this time the drink had left her mellow and cheerful, if a little wistful. On the way to the Langabeers' she had missed John with an intensity so strong she had felt her gut twist. On the way back she thought about him more gently. Christine Langabeer was the kind of woman Penny never could be, would never wish to be. But perhaps she was right. Wasn't there something rather noble in a woman who gave herself up so totally to the man she loved? Was there anything finer than such self-abnegation?

Penny had watched Christine as she worked the evening.

Her initial prickly approach had softened, she had listened and smiled, laughed a pretty laugh at Herbie's most feeble jokes. Their home was indeed a home, a testament to Christine's love. Penny loved her job, loved her husband, loved her house (so she told herself, as she sat in the back of the southbound taxi), but she found herself envying the calm security of the Langabeers' marriage. How comforting it must be to know what each day would bring.

She arrived at Cambridge Gardens, paid off the taxi-driver and unlocked her door. She heard REM blaring from her sitting room and was surprised to find herself pleased to know that Terence was still up. 'Tel – did you have a good evening? Fancy a beer?'

Terence did not move from the sofa, but looked up at his stepmother with his most endearing grin. 'Penny, I have to admit to having had a few already. But if you're offering, why not? Thanks.'

Penny came back from the kitchen with two Budweisers. 'So how was your evening?'

'I went out to the pub with some guys I met. Might put a bit of words my way, you never know. Time I started paying my way.'

'What sort of work?' Penny did not want his money, but was interested that the thought of contributing had occurred to Terence.

'Oh, nothing grand, a bit of painting, house-painting, you know. Easy enough money.' He paused, expecting Penny to say no, he should not waste his time on matters so trivial, he must save his energies until he found his great work, his reason for being. But she said nothing. He had forgotten for a moment that she was not his mother. 'I hope you don't mind, I rang my mother this morning. Thought she should know where I am.'

'Of course. How was she?'

Terence looked at Penny closely. She did not seem very interested. 'She asked after you.'

'She did?' Penny found the idea unlikely, but supposed he was just oiling the social wheels of life.

Terence, sensing her lack of interest, was nettled. 'She wondered if you weren't lonely without John,' he said nastily.

'Lonely?' Penny roused herself from her bottle of beer. It was time she went to bed.

'Well, aren't you? You should be.'

She looked at him through her eyelashes. Why should she be lonely? Were his work to be taken at face value? Did he mean she should be missing her husband all-consumingly? She did not like his tone, which sounded drunken, and was too tired to work out the message he was giving her. Suddenly she felt old. 'I'm only thirty-one,' she said.

'So? You're still married. That was your decision. I was at your wedding, remember. You were a lovely, blushing bride. You didn't look as though you'd been forced to the altar by my father.' If anything it had been John who looked bewildered, uneasy, surprised at where he found himself.

Penny forced herself up from the sofa. 'I was talking to myself,' she said, with dignity. 'There was no need for you to interrupt. I'm too tired to play games tonight, Terence. Too tired even to work out what games you want to play. No, thank you for asking, I am not lonely. I have friends and my work and my family. And John's family, if I need them. I had a very enjoyable evening, for instance, with Herbie and his friends. I am not at all lonely. Just really rather tired. I am going to bed. I will probably not see you in the morning. You can finish my beer.'

After she left the room Terence stared at her half-empty bottle.' What was she on about, playing games? Had she been coming on to him? The thought horrified him. He shied away from all the implications of this half formed idea. She was his father's wife, for God's sake. Perhaps he should leave. Not now, it was too late, in the morning.

Or perhaps he should stay. Keep an eye on her. Watch out for her, for his father's sake. The thought appealed to him. His father would be pleased, would thank him for his concern. And she would, too, once she had overcome this crisis. Whatever it was. He wished he could meet this Herbie, whoever *he* was. How could she even look at a man with a name like Herbie when her husband, his father, the internationally acclaimed hero, was lying surrounded by ice not knowing what the next day would bring? One thing Terence always knew was what the next day would bring. More or less. Enough to keep him feeling safe.

He fell asleep on the sofa and woke an hour later, sore and cold. The next day would bring him a stiff neck and a hangover, he realised, as he made his way up the stairs to bed.

Chapter Four

'Helen, it's Penny.'

'Hi! I've been meaning to ring you. I haven't seen you for ages. Are you OK?'

Penny hesitated, then opted for a half-truth. 'I'm all right. Just tired. I can't think why. I went to Herbie's last night, but it wasn't late. I suppose I've just been out too much recently and I can't seem to get myself on an even keel. I've been working quite hard as well – a lot of new clients all starting at the same time, which is always a killer. And two of them are writers, which takes more out of me. I'm always scared I'm going to come up against an ego problem. You know how it is.'

'Yes,' said Helen, who didn't. 'Do you want to come round one evening? Chill out with a glass of wine or two and a video?'

'No. Thanks.' That was the last thing Penny wanted. She did quite enough of that already. 'Actually I wondered if I could book myself in with you.'

'For an evening? Lunch?'

'No, no. For a session.' For the first time Penny laughed. 'And I don't mean beers and pizza and football on the telly, either. I mean some massage.'

'Massage? You? But you never do!'

'You needn't sound so surprised.' Penny laughed again, happy at her friend's pleasure. 'I've always said I'd try it some day, and now seems the time. I can't sleep at the moment, and they say aromatherapy is very relaxing. I'd rather give it a whirl with you — as long as you don't mind if I fall asleep on your table — than hit the sleeping pills. Do you mind?'

'Don't be ridiculous. Have one on the house — or would you rather I came round after work and gave you one at home?'

Penny didn't want Helen to meet Terence. Not now. He might let slip that she spent most evenings at home alone with the cat and him. He barely spoke, was almost as silent as the cat, but was a growing presence in her house. He had no work, let alone any friends. She wondered if he was aware of the emptiness of his life. 'No, I'd rather keep it professional, if you see what I mean. You know, come to your treatment room.'

'If you're sure. I'm here to please. So when do you want to come?'

Penny lay stretched out on one towel, wrapped in another, her eyes half closed as she felt Helen's strong fingers work her way across her shoulders and neck, down her spine. They were silent for a while, Helen concentrating on her job, waiting professionally for the client to speak first, almost forgetting that the body beneath her fingers was that of a friend. Penny, who had made the appointment more as a way of seeing Helen than to profit from her therapy, did not now know what to say and found, despite herself, that she was falling asleep. Perhaps she was tired, after all.

'Did you know that Tel had turned up?' she asked at last. 'Tel?'

'Terence, John's son, my stepson.'

'No, when?'

'It seems like weeks ago now. Actually, I suppose it was. Three, anyway. He just turned up out of the blue and doesn't seem to be going away.'

'Do you mind?'

'Not really. He eats like a horse, but I don't begrudge him that. After all, it's his father's house and it's not as though John doesn't pay the bills.'

Helen had always wondered about the Brunels' finances. Penny must earn a good salary, but she talked as though she were kept by John. It made no sense.

'I suppose the company's nice,' Helen said idly, and felt Penny's muscles contract beneath her hands. She pretended not to notice, took her hands from Penny's back and oiled them afresh with lavender. When she touched Penny again her muscles had relaxed a little, though not completely.

'I don't need company,' Penny said. 'Not all the time, anyway, unless it's John, of course, and I never have his company all the time. Although I know what you mean. I did think Tel would be more of a mucker, but it's a bit like sharing a house when you're a student with someone you haven't chosen but have just fallen in with. We get on quite well when we meet, but we don't meet much. We keep different hours.'

Terence had been out late at night more often. Sometimes, alone in her double bed, Penny woke to hear the front door slam as he came home in the early hours. Once or twice she thought she had heard him talking to someone, but no one was ever there in the morning. She would not demean herself by asking, but she did wonder if he had a girlfriend.

'Does he have a girlfriend?' Helen asked, echoing her thoughts.

'I don't think so. Not that he's ever talked about, anyway.'

'Penny! How could you?'

'What?'

'Well, for heaven's sake, you've been keeping a single man under your roof for three weeks and you've rafts of friends desperate to meet new men. Not everyone has your luck, you know. Some of us are still looking.'

'But Terence is only a baby. I never thought of him like that, as anyone's boyfriend. At least, not anyone I know.'

'Well, give us a chance. He's all-right-looking, isn't he?'

'Yes, he looks like John. Different, of course . . .'

'Of course,' Helen agreed. Penny's friends laughed behind her back at her passion for her husband. They laughed without spite, with a certain degree of envy, but they could not help but laugh. 'How is he different?'

Penny thought before answering. There was certainly something to be said for aromatherapy. She was so relaxed she felt almost hypnotised, slightly out of herself. The feeling was very pleasant, made her want to speak the truth, not just give a reply that fitted the moment. 'Well, with John you always feel he's working towards something, whether it's a polar expedition or a visit to the opera. He always knows where he wants to go and is busy making whatever it is happen.' She thought of making love with John, remembering how even then, even at his most tender, his sense of purpose was apparent. She wondered what it would be like making love to Terence and was startled and shocked at herself, shook her head to push the image away. 'With Terence, it's more as though he's waiting for something to happen to him.'

'What?'

'Oh, I don't know, his life, I suppose. He's been spoilt by his mother, never been taught that you have to make an effort. Something will come up, he seems to think, and it always does.'

'Sounds like my kind of man. So what does he live off?'

'Live off? Oh, you mean money. Well, the Brunels set up a trust for him when he was born, and they're not mean, and I think his other grandparents have always helped out, and I don't suppose it costs much to live in Ireland. I don't know, I've never really thought about it.'

'And he's living off you now.'

'Not me, John,' Penny said quickly.

'Don't distance yourself from your own generosity, Penny,' Helen said, and Penny was surprised. She thought she knew herself pretty well but it had never occurred to her that she was generous. It was rather a comforting thought.

'But Terence seems a little different at the moment. His waiting seems to have become more active.'

'What do you mean?' Helen was working on Penny's legs now, could feel that her ministrations were bearing fruit, sensed her friend's languor overtaking her.

'He's always waiting for something unthought-of to happen. Recently, in the last few days, he seems to be waiting for something in particular.'

'A call from a girl, that sort of thing?'

'No, not at all, I don't think. It's as though he's watching, that kind of waiting. Me, I suppose. Watching me. Waiting for me to do something.'

'Sounds spooky. You're putting me off him.'

Penny thought for a moment. 'D'you know, I don't think I'd noticed it even, at least not consciously, until I started telling you about it? Is there some sort of truth drug in your oil?'

Helen laughed. 'Not officially, although I've often wondered that myself. You'd be amazed at some of the things my clients tell me once they're stuck into a massage.'

Normally that would have put Penny on edge. She liked so much to be in control of her thoughts, her words, of the impression she gave. But she felt obscurely comforted at the thought of her truth-telling.

She paid Helen, shrugged into her coat, said, 'Well, I must come again. And, Helen, why don't you come over one night? I'll get some other people round, we'll have some food, laugh a bit. Maybe Terence is just bored. Let's make an evening of it. Can I make another appointment? It was heaven, although I may have to go home and sleep it off.'

Penny sat in her sitting room, waiting. She had sent Terence out on a feeble excuse. She did not want him to know why. She had schooled herself not to look forward to these brief moments of communication with John. Too often they ended in disappointment. It was almost easier when it was impossible to talk to him. That way there was nothing to hope for, no inevitable disappointment.

She had a gin and tonic to hand, a cigarette lit. She would stub it out as soon as the telephone rang. She needed to concentrate.

Finally – but dead on the appointed time – it rang. The noise made her jump. She put out the cigarette, took a deep breath, suddenly unwilling, then picked up the receiver.

'Hello.' There was a dreadful crackle of static. She waited, heard her own voice echoing back at her, tried again. 'Hello?'

'Penny,' and then it was all right. The sound of his voice made her heart leap as though she were newly in love all over again. There he was.

'John. Is everything all right?' Again the echo, the dreadful crackle. Somehow she managed not to care.

'Yes, it's fine. We're making good progress. Only a day or two behind schedule. We should be all right.'

He never told her the whole story over the telephone, saved that to be revealed in bits and pieces when he returned. He was right, of course, she did not need to know about the nights unknowingly spent on the edge of a crevasse, the face-to-face encounters with alarmed polar bears, until he was safely home. She coped with his dangers by refusing to picture them, by pretending he was on a business trip like so many other husbands.

'And the weather?'

He laughed, as he always did. It was a feeble joke, repeated every time they spoke. Once, in the early days of their marriage, she had commented on a long-married couple discussing the weather. 'We'll never be like that, will we? We'll always have something to talk about, something real,' she had said. 'Promise me we'll never, ever talk about pets or the weather. I'd rather be divorced from you than have to look at the boredom in your heart while you discussed Bozo's ingrown toenails with me.'

'Cold,' he said. 'And Spindleshanks?'

'Keeping me company.' She heard herself sounding wistful, heard the tone again in the echo. She took a deep breath. 'But he's not the only one,' she said brightly.

There was a silence of static after her echo had died away. 'John?'

'So who else is keeping you company?' he asked, and suddenly, for the first time in their marriage, she thought he might be jealous. She might have teased him with the possibility, the thought even crossed her mind, but no, not to John. To John at least she always spoke the whole truth, even in jest. John was her touchstone of truth and sanity. She never had to pretend with him, never would.

She was conscious of the other ears listening in on their conversation, the technicians at base camp, anyone else in the world who happened to tune in to their frequency. God, how she hated these conversations. But she could not tell John that: he wouldn't understand. 'Terence. Your son. He came looking for you. Rowena's got a new boyfriend so he's checked out for a while.'

'How long has he been there?'

'A few weeks. Shows no sign of leaving.'

'Is he working? Don't bother to answer that. Oh, that boy . . .'

'Hey, don't worry about it. He feeds the cat, shares a beer with me late at night. It's fine, honestly. I think he thinks he's keeping an eye on me.'

John laughed — really laughed this time, and Penny's heart rose. Thank God. What was she for if not to cheer him in his loneliness. She remembered Christine Langabeer's views on what constituted a good wife and, if it had not been for those unseen ears on the wire, would have asked John if she were the right one for him. She pushed the impulse aside. They could never really talk to each other when he was away. They just had to make do with inanities.

'Let him think so, but you keep an eye on him, too, won't you? See if you can't talk him into some kind of job — career, even.'

'One with a pension and a proper structure?'

'Something like that. Like his parents,' John agreed, and laughed again.

'I went to supper with the Langabeers,' Penny volunteered. She thought he liked to know about the everydayness of her life. At least he could imagine her without waking in a cold sweat of fear.

'Time's running out', he said, suddenly distracted. 'Penny, are you sure everything's all right with you? You don't need anything?' He sounded urgent, worried – why? Had she sounded different? She had made him laugh, hadn't she? Or was it him? Was there some sort of danger about which he wished to keep her in the dark?

'Of course I am. And you? No polar bears?'

'No polar bears. It's not much longer. God bless. I'll talk to you again a week today, same time, be there.' There was a click, and silence, and Penny sat holding the receiver, missing the sound even of the static now that it was gone, feeling flat, loving her husband, wishing there was more than a telephone line between them, and now not even that.

Then, as she always did after these calls, she poured herself another drink, lit another cigarette, sat on the sofa and wept.

When Terence let himself in an hour later he found his stepmother red-eyed but collected, drinking a large gin and tonic and watching *The Bill*. 'I've never seen you watching that sort of telly before,' he said, fetching himself a beer and settling down beside her. 'What's happening?'

'I don't really know. I don't think it matters,' she answered.

Terence looked at her more closely. 'Are you all right? Anything up? Your hair looks very tidy.'

She smiled. 'Shall I admit something very silly to you? Whenever I'm going to talk to your father I check my makeup and brush my hair. As though he could see me. Idiotic, isn't it?'

'Talk to my father? What do you mean?'

Penny was cross with herself. 'He rang while you were out.'

'You must have known he was going to. Is that why you asked me to go and buy the supper?'

'Yes.'

'I would have liked to talk to him.'

'I know, I'm sorry. But it's so rare, and I—'

'It's all right.' Terence looked more sympathetic. He supposed she had reason to want to talk to her husband without him being there, but then, looking at her red eyes, hearing how steadily she was talking, another possibility crossed his mind. 'Did you tell him I was here?'

'Yes.'

'Did he mind?'

'Of course not. He sent his love.' That was a lie, but then there had not been much time.

'Did you argue?'

'About you? Of course not. Why should we?'

Which answer only made Terence's vague theory the more solid.

'Did you tell him you'd gone to dinner with your boss with the silly name?'

'Yes. Why?'

'Did he mind?'

'Of course not. What are you on about, Terence? Why should he? He doesn't expect me to sit here in purdah and wait for his return. He doesn't mind about you, he doesn't mind about Herbie. He doesn't mind about anything.'

'He doesn't worry about you?'

'I don't know. I shouldn't think so. He knows I can look after myself. Why should he worry?'

'There are two reasons a man might worry about leaving

his wife all alone.' Penny thought Terence sounded pompous, but she waited to hear what he had to say. She had made John laugh, after all, at the idea of his son looking after her. Perhaps she could turn this scene into a joke, make a running saga out of the idea of his hopeless son taking responsibility for his stepmother. 'Money, which I assume is all right.'

That did make Penny laugh. 'And what, dear boy, would you do about it if it weren't?'

He flushed, his lips twisted and suddenly there was no sign of his good looks. He looked like a petulant small boy with a weak mouth. Penny had never seen John look like that. Terence was definitely his mother's son as well as his father's.

'No, all right, I was just making a point.'

'And the other cause of worry?' Penny wondered if she should be angry, but she did not have the energy.

'Infidelity, of course.'

'You really are the end, Tel. Do you honestly think John thinks I'm having an affair with either you or Herbie? Grow up, it's not like that in the real world.' Still she was more laughing than angry.

'You're patronising me again.'

'Terence, don't go all uppity on me. You've been living here almost a month. You must know I'm not having an affair with you. I've seen Herbie once in that month so it would be a pretty sad affair if I were. And his wife and golfing cronies were chaperoning us. You're imagining things. You read too much. Or watch too many soaps. And, anyway, my affairs are my own business.'

There. She had said it. Her affairs were her business. All right, maybe it was not Herbie (she was lying when she said she had seen him only once, she saw him five days a week, there were plenty of opportunities). Maybe she was discreet, but she would give herself away eventually. Terence was very glad he was here, protecting his father, rather than discussing him with a second-rate children's book writer. Here he was useful. He could not defend him from polar bears or ice floes or whatever dangers lurked around at the Pole, but he could defend him from an unfaithful wife.

Penny put her drink down carefully on the coffee table. 'Terence, I'm sorry,' she said. (Why should she apologise? It was he who was in the wrong.) 'Speaking to John always jangles my nerves. Let's go out for supper. I fancy a pizza. Why don't we walk up to the Gate and go to Pizza Express? It's on me. Come on, it might be fun. If we sit here I'll drink more gin and we'll argue. John sounded pleased that we were here together, and we haven't made the most of it. I've been working too hard recently. Let's go out for supper and we'll plan some fun. I need some fun. I'm only thirty-one.'

'So you keep saying,' he said, and smiled at her. 'And don't worry, I do understand. Yes, let's go out. I'll get my jacket.'

She had apologised so she knew she was doing wrong. Maybe there was hope for the future. He would keep an eye on her. Poor girl, she was like Mother really. Needed keeping an eye on, that was all. Funny how he had left Ireland to avoid looking after one woman and found himself with another needy female. They were all the same, really. Lucky there were men like him around them to help.

The two of them set off up Ladbroke Grove, the street-lights following the hill, the car head-lamps shining out of nowhere as they crested the slope, then bearing down into their eyes. Penny slipped her hand into the crook of Terence's arm. 'Poor John,' she said softly. 'Do you know, I think London's more romantic than anywhere in the world, even the North Pole, don't you? There's so much more possibility here than in the middle of a frozen sea.' And Terence, resolving that in the light of her apology he would not cause any more dissent, agreed, and squeezed her arm, and felt manly.

Chapter Five

The meeting was over quickly. Penny had found Philip Veysey talked nothing but sense, did not seem inordinately fond of the sound of his own voice, and any criticisms he had made of her ideas were entirely constructive. She had expected an entirely different man. Against all the odds his first novel, a bleak story of a marriage breakdown in a culture of joblessness and despair, had not only been well reviewed but had sold well. His publishers – which often used Parkhouse and Langabeer PR – were keen to build on this early success and had given Penny a generous budget to ensure that he was more than a one-hit wonder. Penny had expected a cocky 'artist', full of views about his own importance and how she should do her job. She had found a gentle and humorous man with trenchant views. She smiled and stood to shake his hand. 'Thank you for coming in. I'll get this all typed up and send it over to you. There's plenty of time to make changes if you want, but this is a good framework. I'll ring you in a couple of days.'

Veysey stood too, and Penny noticed yet again that he was only marginally taller than she. She had expected him to tower over her, but his grey eyes were easy to meet.

'Do you have time for a drink?' Veysey spoke abruptly, as though he was expecting a refusal, and Penny liked him for it. He was a bit of a star, after all, he must be used to women saying yes to him. Her hesitation was not because she did not like the idea, rather because she was surprised at how much she did like it. 'Of course, if you're busy.' He did not tail off, nor did it sound like a question. It was just a statement, but one that expected an honest response.

'No, no. Perhaps I should say I was rushing home to work, but I'd love to have a drink. It's been a long day.' *And I like your intelligent smile*, she stopped herself from adding.

They walked round the corner to the wine bar that ran an account for the office. Despite her instinctive warmth towards Philip Veysey, it did not occur to Penny that this was anything other than a wind-up-the-meeting friendly drink; it would not hurt to know the man a little better. She might find herself spending a week on the road with him, accompanying him on his author tour. It was always easier when she knew what to expect.

The walk, and the business of finding a table and ordering wine, broke their mood of complicity, and as the glasses and bottle were put down in front of them Penny found herself wondering why she had said yes. It would have been easier to pour herself a drink at home.

'Are you any relation to Izzy Brunel?' Philip asked, as he poured the wine.

'Yes. He's my brother-in-law. Do you know him?'

Philip smiled. 'Not really. I was at school with him, but I'm a few years younger.'

'You were at Wellington?'

'Yes.'

'A public-school boy?'

'Of course. Aren't we all?'

'We?'

'The "middle-class left-wing poseurs who claim an under-standing of the underclass, all patronising compassion, no experience". John Osborne was a public-school boy – is there anything more middle class than that ironing board?'

Penny smiled. 'So you remember your reviews.'

'Of course. And love and hate with equal passion those who are kind or cruel.' He took a sip of wine, lit a cigarette and changed the subject. It was deliberate, Penny was sure. He did not want her to walk down that track.

'Which of the brothers is your husband?'

'John.'

'Ah.'

'Ah?' It was the kind of response that usually pricked Penny to anger, but not this time. Veysey intrigued her. His 'Ah' did not mean 'Cor. I'm impressed by your famous husband.' She knew that much.

'It's difficult,' he said, looking straight at her. 'That sort of marriage.'

Penny took a handful of cashews and looked at Veysey seriously. 'You sound as though you've had some experience.'

'Not of marriage, but of a relationship when one half is on the road. And when one half is very – sought after.'

'How do you mean?'

He hesitated. 'I used to – well, I would say live with – except she was barely ever there – Rose Winterton.'

Penny couldn't help but raise her eyebrows and looked at Veysey with new eyes. For a couple of years Rose Winterton had been the darling of the West End, until she had been adopted by Hollywood. She was beautiful in a quirky, sexy way that quite saw off the conventional beauty of other Hollywood stars, and managed to combine a patrician English hauteur with a warmth and humour that had the entire western world eating out of her hand. She was also a brilliant actress. 'I see.'

'Do you?'

Penny thought she did, but something didn't quite add up. 'But, Philip, let's be honest, aren't you pretty – what was your phrase? – sought after?'

'I suppose I am now, a bit. But not in her league. And, anyway, then I was nowhere, struggling with my first novel and working as a publisher's reader and copy-editor to pay the rent. However much you love someone, it's very hard feeling left behind.'

'I'm not,' Penny said quickly. 'I mean, obviously I am in that I'm not walking beside him, but I don't want to be. I have my own career here. I wouldn't give it up, not for John, not for anybody.'

'Maybe for yourself?' he suggested, taking her completely aback.

'For myself?'

'There may come a day when something, I don't know, larger comes along and you don't want to work any more.'

Penny flushed angrily. 'I suppose you mean babies. I wouldn't have thought it of you. Hadn't you heard that women can work and have children?'

He smiled. 'I have. And I didn't mean babies, actually. Although, of course, that might be one thing. Shall we have more wine? Or would you like dinner?'

Penny made herself relax. She did not know why she had felt so nettled at Veysey, and liked him for not really apologising, or explaining himself, or rising to meet her irritation. 'I don't know. It's a little early, isn't it? But, yes, let's have some more wine. Thank you.'

'And by the time we've drunk it it will be a decent enough time for dinner.' He gestured at the waiter.

'What happened with you and Rose?' She wanted to be the one asking the questions.

'Oh, well, you know, the usual heartbreak. I suppose I blame the telephone more than anything. It wasn't jealousy, or loneliness, or envy that undid us but the telephone.'

'How? I would have thought it kept you together.' But as she said so she remembered the countless fragmented conversations, split up by static, interrupted by echoes.

'The time thing, the different moods. She wanted to talk about parties she'd been to, full of names I'd heard of but people I didn't know. She'd ring after she'd got in from somewhere, and I'd be getting up in the grey winter rain without her, and there was all this sunshine and wine in her voice, and I was full of sleep and some half-witted manuscript I was editing. Or I would ring her with news of our friends and she'd be more interested in gossip about a lot of people with initials for middle names who might or might not be going to make our fortune. Maybe if we could both have sat down in the same time zone, seven in the evening, say, with a drink to hand, we could have pretended we were in the same room, talking after work, like other people. I tried to be interested in her life, and she tried to be interested in what had been our life but was increasingly becoming only mine, and it just didn't work.'

He looked into his wine glass, eyes hooded from Penny, and she thought she had never seen a sadder mouth.

'I'm sorry. You sound as though it still hurts.'

He looked up, forced a wry smile. 'You know, we split up two years ago but, yes, of course it still hurts. It always will to some degree. I don't think anyone ever forgets their first real love. And it's almost worse when it ends with tiredness and gentleness. Not even enough emotion left to be angry with. Anyway, that's why I hate the telephone. I only ever use it for business, and even that I prefer to do face to face.' He smiled again, a real smile this time, lighter and happier. 'Don't you?'

Penny thought of her tears after her own disjointed telephone conversations, of John's polite attention when she told him about Herbie, or the secretary's latest fashion gaffe, or Beth's latest boyfriend. She remembered the gaps in the conversations when maybe she should have asked for more detail about the ice-caps, or polar bears, or John's state of mind. She gave a little shiver that was nothing to do with cold, but something to do with fear. She looked at Veysey, hoped that his broken heart would mend, and smiled back. 'Yes, it's much better. Let's ban the telephone.'

If Terence had been a stepson of a more conventional age — ten, say, or even fifteen — he would have been easy enough to entertain. Penny would have to be sure someone was at home with him after school, would have to cook supper and breakfast for him, would have to change his sheets and encourage him to bath. At the weekend she would have taken him to the cinema, or to football matches, or arranged that he should go skating with friends. Whatever boys of that age did.

It dawned on her, after Christmas and New Year had been and gone, as John neared his polar goal with (as far as he reported to Penny) no out-of-the-ordinary adventures, that she was not doing her duty by her stepson. She was providing him with shelter, food and drink, but that was all. She never suggested that it was time he moved on, allowed herself to show no curiosity at all about his movements either during the day, while she was absent, or in the evenings when he was out, and she turned down his vague offers of money. She knew how little they were worth and would rather not be reminded of his uselessness by his occasional pretence of being a functioning adult. Yet, if she were honest with herself, she knew something was missing.

'If he were a dog, I'd walk him,' she told Beth one day over a bottle of Sauvignon in a bar in Frith Street. 'If he were a cat, I'd buy him catnip. If he were a parrot, I'd talk to him. But I'm blessed if I know what to do with a twenty-something man who behaves like an adolescent.'

Beth offered Penny a cigarette, and lit one for herself. 'I don't see why you've got to do anything for him. Like what?'

'Like maybe find him a job, except I think he'd be livid if I suggested it. And, after all, what sort of job? He's too old for anything under the work-experience banner.'

'What's he done before?'

'I don't know. Everything. Sold ties, painted houses, looked after people's houses. Worked in bars, on farms, on building sites. He's never started anything you'd call a career, but he's worked enough not to be given too hard a time by his father. In theory he's willing to turn his hand to anything, but in practice he just sits staring into space.'

'Sounds like he's getting you down.'

'Oh, I don't mind. But, you know, I do feel slightly answerable to John. What do I tell him? I haven't even admitted that Tel's still here.'

'Why not?'

'He hasn't asked.' Penny was aware this sounded a little feeble, so she added, 'I mean, we have so little time to talk . . .' There was a pause. Penny poured herself another glass of wine. Beth's was still half full. Suddenly truthful, Penny said, 'I suppose I don't know which of us John will be cross with, and I don't want it to be me.'

'Cross with?' Beth looked interested. She had never thought that Penny might be frightened of John.

'Well, you know, I am his stepmother.'

'Yes, but he's almost your age. You're not responsible for him. From what you say, I hardly think John can be said to be responsible for him either.'

'Of course he is. He is his son.'

'Yes, but he was kept away from him in his childhood, in his formative years, whatever you call them. John can hardly be held to blame for how he turned out.' Beth looked over Penny's shoulder at the other customers in the bar. She was becoming bored with the trials of Terence.

'What he needs, I'd have thought, is some fun,' Penny mused out loud.

'Fun?' Beth switched her attention back to her friend. This sounded more like it. 'What kind of fun?'

'Well, you know, fun. If he met some people more like himself, people more or less his age, creative people, whatever . . .'

'Is he creative?'

'Well, he must be something. He's obviously not hard-working.' Despite herself, Penny laughed. 'He says I sound sixty when I talk to him sometimes. He brings out the grown-up in me.'

'The maternal instinct?'

'No, the grown-up.' Penny was firm.

'You were saying fun. Why don't you give a party?'

'A party?' Penny was horrified. 'I never give parties.'

'Maybe you should.' Beth poured them both some more wine and waved the empty bottle at the barman for a replacement. 'You know, maybe it's not only Terence that needs shaking up.'

'What do you mean?'

Prickles out, on the defensive, fingers gripping the stem of the wine-glass. Give-aways all, thought Beth, who was trying to train herself to be observant in case she was ever going to write a novel. 'Well, I certainly do,' she said carefully. 'I reckon we all do. I reckon everyone over about twenty-five does, come to that. You know, it's always the same – leave school, get overexcited about going to university, have a good time there. Then you come to London, get overexcited about that, new job, more money, new friends, more freedom. Next thing you know it's five years down the line and you're stuck. Job all right, friends all right, nothing new. Don't you ever long for something new?'

'No, not at all,' Penny said quickly. 'But it's different for me. I've got John. I'm very happy with him, I don't want anyone new.'

'I didn't mean that. I just meant a change, a shake-up. I don't know. I just feel that nothing ever happens.'

'You sound like people at the beginning of children's books. They always used to say something like that and the next thing you knew they'd found a phoenix or an abandoned gypsy child or something. Shall we have something to eat?' Penny felt uncomfortable. She did not like conversations like this, felt threatened by other people's emotional truths. Life was for jokes, after all. For work, for jokes, and for love. At the moment it was all work, but so what? Soon enough the jokes would come back. And the love would come home.

'Yes, let's. I feel a bit pissed, if I'm frank. About this party ...' Beth did not in fact feel as drunk as she was pretending, only drunk enough to try to force her way past Penny's natural reserves.

'Which party?' Penny was studying the menu, although she didn't feel hungry.

'The one you're going to give for your stepson. As I see it, you've two options. Either jelly and ice-cream and good advice, or all your beautiful unmarried friends who are dying to take up with a toy-boy. Come on, Penny, none of us has met him yet. We're going to begin to think he has eight heads or something, that he's some mythical monster from the blue lagoon.'

Penny laughed. 'A party. OK, why not? What do you reckon? Dinner for eight or drinks for thirty?'

'Drinks for thirty, of course. Dinner for eight's hopeless. You never get enough men.'

'Four of each is conventional.'

'Yes, but think how low the odds are of meeting the man of your dreams when you probably know at least one of the men already, and three other women are fighting for the same three!'

'Well, I'm spoken for.'

'Oh, come on, you know what I mean.'

'You, Beth, are going to turn into one of those come-and-marry-me lunatics we all used to laugh at.'

'Five years ago. It's different now. I told you, I need to see some new people. Everyone at work is a woman or a homosexual. Anyway, I'm not talking marriage, I'm talking *fun*.'

Fun. Penny wondered about fun. She knew what Beth meant, of course, but she wondered about the word. Did she have any fun nowadays? She enjoyed herself, of course. There were people to laugh with, things to do, jokes to make. But *fun*?

'Why do we want fun?' she asked, talking as usual more to herself than to her companion.

'Why do we want *fun*?' Beth looked at her as though she were mad. 'Well, it's part of the human condition, isn't it?'

'The human condition?'

'Yes, you know. Love, hate, feel happy, feel sad, feel envious, feel proud, feel like fun. And I'm in the feeling-like-having-fun stage. Aren't you? Or does all that stop when you get married?' She looked at Penny with a degree of curiosity, and even perception, that Penny did not like at all.

'Of course not. Although maybe fun changes when you get married.'

'The deep, deep peace of the double bed after the hurly-burly of the *chaise-longue*, that sort of thing?'

'Don't look so disbelieving. Wait and see.' (Too quick, too defensive, she thought, and restrained herself from any further barbs on her friend's single state.)

'All right. But *chaise-longues* aside, when are you going to give this party? I've got my diary with me, come on, let's fix a date.'

Penny had felt bullied, but she had given in with good grace. Sometimes there was no other way. Apart from anything else, maybe Beth was right, maybe she did need a little more fun. And if she invited a whole group at once, who knows what invitations might come her way, what new permutations of friendship might arise? Hating drinks parties, she had decided on asking about twenty people for supper. Hating cooking, she rang up a caterer and ordered a Greek dinner to be delivered at seven o'clock on the evening of the party. Hating her friends to know how much disposable income she and John really had, or how she chose to dispose of it, she said she wanted no waiters, but had all the food transferred from the caterer's dishes to her own. She was quite happy to imply it came from an upmarket supermarket, would not stoop to pretending she had cooked it herself. In a world of people putting on fronts, she and John did not need to pretend. They were strong, separately and together, and they were independent.

Terence was very happy at the idea of a party. He wondered whether to suggest asking some of his pub friends, but decided against. It would be more interesting to see Penny performing on her chosen territory, with her own chosen audience. He wondered whom she had invited in the way of men. Would her boss with the silly name be coming?

He hung around the kitchen pretending to help. He was useless as always, but Penny was glad of the company.

'Why this sudden social whirl?' he asked facetiously, and did not miss Penny's quick grimace of annoyance.

'I don't know what you mean. I see a lot of people.'

'Maybe, but not here. Have I been cramping your style?'

Penny was not quite sure what he meant, but played along. 'A little, I suppose. I haven't wanted to bother you. But then I thought perhaps you needed a little entertaining.' She was not sure why, but knew she had given the wrong answer. Once again she felt that Terence was checking up on her. Still, she had decided to give the party, she was in a good mood – almost looking forward to it, now that it was upon her – and she was not going to allow Terence to upset her.

'Look, can you check there are enough glasses in the sitting room, ashtrays and all that kit? There are some more bottles of fizzy water in the cupboard under the stairs, and while you're there check the tonic. Thanks. I'm just going upstairs to tart up a bit.'

Terence idled through to the sitting room and glanced cursorily at the drinks table. It seemed all right to him. Not much beer, but perhaps that was in the fridge. Back in the kitchen, he found the beer supplies satisfactory, and helped himself to a can of Boddington's. Going upstairs to tart up, indeed. It just went to show that she was feeling at home with him. What a slip of the tongue. Even his mother never talked like that. Although, God knew, she did it. On impulse, he picked up the telephone and dialled the number in Ireland. The telephone was answered almost immediately, by a man. 'Pip? Is it?'

There were muffled gigglings. 'Of course it is. Or was last time I checked.' (More giggles and the faint sound of a slap.) 'Who's that, then?'

'It's Terence.'

'Oh.' Terence could almost hear Pip pulling himself together, sitting upright, clearing his throat, mouthing some silencing comment at Rowena. 'Oh, Terence. It'll be your mother you're wanting.' It had been a mistake to telephone. Terence almost ground his teeth with irritation at Pip affecting the Irish intonation. Not the accent yet, but it would not be long. He had seen all the signs before. And then, just when the interloper had thought he had cracked it, that Rowena was his for as long as he needed her, something would go wrong, the irritations (on one side or the other) would begin to grow, the huge eyes underneath the fringe and the makeup would begin to ooze salt water ever so gently (too much and the eyes would look red, the kohl and mascara would run, the effect would be ageing rather than appealing) and Pip, like so many before him, would disappear to wherever he had come from, leaving Terence to pick up the pieces. Oh, shit.

Meanwhile his mother was on the line, breathy, giggling, still in the throes of her newest love. (Oh, God, they hadn't been, had they? They can't have been making love, not at this time of the day, not when he was about to go to a party full of his stepmother when he had to keep his mind clear?)

'Terry?' she repeated.

'Mother.'

77

'Oh, and it's Mother, is it? Why did you ring and disturb us if you were going to be cross with your poor old mother?'

Oh, Lord, at all costs he had to stop this kind of conversation. Penny would be down in a minute. He just did not have time or energy for it. He'd been silly to ring. 'Of course I'm not cross, I just wondered how you were.'

'I'm well, my darling. Very well. You're not thinking of coming home, are you now?' Still the Irish, which meant danger. And the faintest hint of alarm in her voice. Did she not want him back, then?

He took another swig of the beer. 'No, no. I'm still at Penny's. I thought I might stay here until John comes home. I don't think it's going to be much longer now, and she seems to be liking the company. We're having a party tonight.'

He liked the 'we'. It gave him gravitas, made him head of the house, made him feel involved. That would teach his mother to be making love at seven thirty on a weekday evening when all right-minded people were in front of the telly or on their way out.

'Oh, are you, now? Well, that's nice.' She did not even sound interested. Perhaps it was time he went home after all, but he had not yet finished his job here. He had to be sure before he left that Penny was pure. He wanted to be able to look his father in the eye, and not be in possession of a secret or even a doubt about his stepmother.

'Yes, we've invited a lot of friends. Greek dinner, we're having. It looks delicious. I'm having trouble waiting for everyone to arrive.' He laughed gaily, but his words had not been without a hidden spring of malice. One of Rowena's most traumatic love affairs had been with a Greek man she met on holiday in Kos when Terence was about thirteen. They had even left Ireland for him, but it had not taken long for the young man to tire of his ageing Circe, and Rowena and Terence had been back before six months were over. For years afterwards Rowena would not eat lamb, said it made her sick, she had eaten so much of it in Greece, scraggy, fatty stuff, and all that spinach ...

'Greek, how nice. It's been a long time since I had a good Greek meal. Not many Greeks have settled in Cork after all.' She spoke light-heartedly, the accent back towards Roedean. Terence wondered if she was as carefree as she pretended, or whether she, too, was playing games. He felt suddenly tired. What did it matter, after all? Somewhere, someone was waiting with whom he could have a pure relationship, with whom he could face the truth without fear. There was his father, of course, but he needed more now, someone of his own. Someone he did not have to share.

He could hear Penny walking around upstairs, knew she would be down soon. 'I've got to go, Mother. I'd better get tidy before the guests start arriving.'

'All right, Terry, have a good time. Ring me when you can, there's a good boy. Don't forget your old mother.' He heard the dismissal in her voice, knew she was saying the words she always said without really thinking. But for once he did not mind. He was going to shave and brush his hair and do his father proud. Perhaps tonight he would meet someone who would change his life. In his heart he knew that no one in the Percy, or the Ladbroke Arms, or any of the other pubs where he spent his money, was likely to do that for him.

Penny was surprised at how much she was enjoying herself. She looked around the room, checking with her usual professionalism that everyone else looked happy, but her mind was not really on the job. Helen, looking remarkably eccentric, was in earnest conversation with Peter Drake, a friend Penny had made through work – he headed the publicity department of a huge drinks company. They made a pretty pair, Penny noticed, with satisfaction. Beth had cornered Terence, and was flirting for England. Sarah was talking to Giovanna, Penny's assistant, whom she had invited out of duty. Giovanna was good-looking in a big-boned, Italian way and both she and Sarah looked as though they were waiting for something more exciting to come along in terms of party conversation, but realised it was better to be talking to someone than no one.

The real reason that the party was a success for Penny was that her two star guests had turned up, relatively sober and charming, and seemed to be throwing themselves into the crowd. Melzi, the film-maker-turned-novelist, and Philip Veysey were her wild cards. Penny had told herself that this party was for Terence, and for Beth, who had bullied her into it and clearly felt in need of meeting fresh blood, but looking at the laughing, drinking faces around her, she admitted she had been lying to herself. She, too, had felt like having fun, and being seen to have fun. She had been outraged at Beth's suggestion that her life was without its highs, wanted to prove that she had glamour in her life, that she still knew how to laugh ...

And she enjoyed Melzi's admiration. There was nothing wrong in that, was there?

She remembered their first meeting. For once, she had been almost unsure of herself. Most of the people or products she was paid to promote were already fairly high-profile – it was mostly a question of keeping the profile high, or limiting damage after unfavourable publicity. Her company charged high enough fees to ensure that it worked only with the big names. First-time novelists were therefore an unheard-of product. For pleasure, Penny read Anthony Trollope and Angela Huth, Jane Gardam, watched films like *Brief Encounter*. She saw films like *Trainspotting* and read Veysey's books because she worked in PR, lived in north Notting Hill, knew media people. Those were the films and books she should be aware of to survive. This did not count as pretending, just as part of existence. If anyone asked her, she would admit to *The Eustace Diamonds* or even Wilkie Collins, it was just that she did not volunteer the information.

So, when she had met Melzi for the first time, it was not as a natural admirer. She had liked the idea of him, liked the fact that it was a different kind of job, that he was notorious rather than famous. She supposed that as he was Italian she would be called on to flirt a little, although Giovanna, who had dealt with him on the telephone, said he sounded businesslike. Penny had seen photographs of him and had been prepared for his height and his ugliness, but no photograph could capture the easy charm or the naked sexual appraisal in his eye. Here was a man who dealt in drug-dealing and small-time gang warfare on one side, and who on the other wrote about the countryside around the Italian lakes with a sureness of touch that managed to show love without sentimentality, who could describe Italian food in a way that put the ever-greedy Carluccio to shame, who dealt with religion and love and sunshine as easily as he dealt with back-streets and abortions and shame. What was she to make of him?

Much to her discomfiture, he had asked her the same. 'What will you do with me, Miss Brunel?' he had asked, as he looked at his menu on their first meeting. 'I suppose you have seen my films, read the novel. What do you make of me?'

She looked up from her menu, startled. She was meant to be handling this interview, not he. Usually people were slightly in awe of those who, in a sense, held their careers in the palms of their hands. 'Mrs,' she corrected. 'It's Mrs Brunel.'

He smiled. 'Of course, Signora. Accept my apologies. It

was not that I did not think you could be married, more that in the modern, business world . . .' And she wondered why she had corrected him. She never did normally, didn't mind a tad what she was called. But instinctively she had felt that he should know she was married.

'Penny, anyway. Call me Penny,' she said.

'And to my question?'

'What do I make of you? Well, I'm not sure yet. That's partly why I asked you to lunch. I felt that I should try to know you a little, rather than accept either of the two faces you have chosen to present to your public.'

'My two faces?' He looked a little angry at that, which pleased Penny. She would show him she knew a thing or two about pretending.

'I have been hired to promote your novel. Not you, not your films, but your novel. Nevertheless it would be silly to pretend that the films do not exist. The reason you are high-profile is because of the films, which is why your publisher has hired me.'

He chuckled suddenly, a rich, foreign-sounding chuckle. If Penny had had any doubts about whether she would like this man, she lost them then. Anyone who laughed like that was aware of his soul, she knew instinctively.

'They were very taken aback by the novel, I must say. Polite, but taken aback. They had paid me a lot of money, you see. Wanted to commission Damien Hirst to do a cover picture,' Melzi said.

'That wouldn't really do,' Penny said carefully, then met his eyes and they both laughed. Later, whom she knew him better, she would ask him whether he had written the book as a joke, as an elaborate tease on the whole media, promotional, advertising world in which she was involved. For the moment she must still go carefully, but it would not be long before they were friends, she was sure of that. In fact, by the end of lunch Penny knew she had not met a client with whom she could get on as well as this for a long time. He made her laugh, he flirted but was not threatening, he was alternately serious and humorous, almost teasing. The lunch flew by and Penny asked for the bill with a certain regret. For once she was not at all sure how well she had been doing her job: she had been enjoying herself too much to make a proper action plan, and she had drunk enough to leave her head too fuddled for any chance of working effectively in the afternoon. There was a faint tussle over the paying of the bill. Suddenly Melzi was all old-fashioned Italian gallantry (or chauvinism – Penny often thought the two were closely linked). 'Please, you know this is a business lunch. I'm on expenses,' she insisted, and he looked at her with big brown eyes and said sadly, 'There should be no discussion of money between friends.'

For a moment she was taken aback, then she saw the laughter behind his eyes and grinned. 'Don't tell me you're an actor too,' she said, then added, 'Well, do, actually, I need to know all that sort of stuff.'

'Do you ever forget your work?' he asked, suddenly serious.

She looked at him, nervous that perhaps she had been wrong, that he was going to make some sort of a play for her and spoil everything, but no, the frank look in his eye held no hint of flirtation now, just curiosity. 'Of course I do,' she said firmly, remembering Beth and fun and then, without thinking, blurted, 'I'm having a supper party next week, just a few friends. Why don't you come? If you want to, I mean – well, obviously you're probably busy.'

She heard herself babbling like a schoolgirl and wondered what had happened to her, until he interrupted her by saying gently, 'I don't know if I'm busy – you haven't told me the day,' then listening, and accepting, and leaving her with a formal handshake and a nod that was almost but not quite a bow. As she walked down the street back to her office Penny found herself thinking of boring Giovanna and conventional Sarah (who were already invited) and disliked herself for realising that perhaps they weren't quite up to Melzi and that she would probably have to invite some more amusing people. 'Why did I ask him?' she wondered aloud. 'Oh, Lord, well, it's done now and I'll have to make the most of it.'

That was the line she took with herself about Melzi after the first lunch.

And then here he was at the party, looking amused, talking not to Veysey, invited so that there was another media star, but bearing down on Giovanna and Sarah. 'Of course, he probably spotted Giovanna's Italian,' Penny muttered into the oven, as she took out another dish of stuffed vine leaves, but came back into the sitting room to see him talking in English to both the girls. 'He must be being kind to spinsters,' she thought aloud.

'Spinsters? What an old-fashioned word,' said Veysey, taking a vine leaf and pushing it whole into his mouth. 'What a nice party.'

'Is it?'

Veysey looked surprised, then looked at the gathering and laughed. 'You're right, I don't know if it is. Yet. But I think it's going to be. It's got that air. Everyone looks as though they've come here to have fun, so they probably will.'

'Fun. Why do people keep using that word all of a sudden?'

'Do they? Or do you just think they do?'

'What do you mean?' Penny thought she was going to enjoy this conversation. Veysey had a fierce look on his face that she liked. He had stopped the social chit-chat and was thinking. That was what people were for, to think and make their friends do likewise. There was no point in giving a party for guests who just said they were enjoying themselves without thinking about it. Good manners were often just another form of pretence – although, of course, they had their place. She brought her attention back to Veysey.

'Words are always there, all the time, floating around us. They enter our consciousness beyond their level of usefulness, mere information givers and gatherers, when in fact they follow our subconscious to where it already is.'

'Are you thinking of getting pretentious?' Penny asked, with a smile to soften the rudeness of her question.

Veysey barely looked at her. His eyes were still fierce, his thoughts still totally engaged. 'I don't think so, although maybe I'm not expressing myself properly. You say everyone is suddenly using the word fun. Obviously what is happening in fact is that you are suddenly noticing it. Because you are suddenly preoccupied with fun. Or the lack of it.' His face cleared, his eyes on her face were looking beyond the evening makeup and trying to see the Penny behind it. 'Am I right?' He, too, smiled, but Penny saw he was concentrating on her in a way that made her uncomfortable.

'Sorry, not pretentious. Psychobabble instead,' she said lightly. 'Have another drink?' He held out his glass, holding her gaze. 'You're unfair, Penny,' he said. 'You stop me making polite conversation and mock me when I move on to something more serious. Let's just say that if you do ever want some fun, give me a whirl. I'm rather good at it.'

'Despite the "brave, breaking bleakness of your vision"?' Penny quoted from an early review of Veysey's work, which now was splurged across the front cover of all his books.

He laughed. 'Perhaps because of it. I only pretend to be

brave and bleak, you know. Really I'm the life and soul of the party, never away from a dance-floor or gambling-den. My mind is filled with frivolity. I know the names of all the Spice Girls' mothers, for instance, and every number one Elvis ever had, in date order.'

'You should work for a tabloid.'

'No, that would be giving the game away. Now, introduce me to that goddess over there, would you?'

With a flicker of irritation she followed his gaze. Helen. Well, fair enough. If ever a woman deserved to be called a goddess it was Helen. And, much as Penny loved her friend, she did not feel threatened intellectually by her. She nodded and made her way across the room, followed by a smiling Vesey. Could he really read her mind or was he only good at looking as though he did?

Terence leaned against the door-jamb, watching. He saw how his stepmother worked the room. There was no doubt that she knew what she was doing, and did it well. It was not just her undoubted good looks that made all the men want to talk to her, or her clothes, which were clearly expensive, well cut, skimming her body in understated allure. To be fair to her (and Terence kept telling himself how much he wanted to be fair to her) Penny was almost underdressed for the party compared to some of her friends. Helen was in a shimmery silvery material that made her look like some sort of ancient warrior, Beth looked pretty tarty in her tiny A-line skirt and high ankle-strapped shoes, the Italian assistant had clearly tried hard to look as though she knew about clothes but her swirling layers of contrasting cloths made her look enormous. Only Sarah looked to Terence as a woman should: quietly dressed, she wore a navy blue two-piece suit with a striped shirt. She looked what his maternal grandmother would call 'tidy', feminine but unthreatening. It was a shame no one much was talking to her, he supposed, but maybe she liked it that way.

He shifted from one foot to the other and took a swig of beer from his bottle. He was nearly moved to go over and talk to Sarah, but when he came to it could not quite be bothered. What could he say to her, or she to him, that would in any way interest or enlighten either of them? No, he was better off here, standing between two rooms and watching.

The men were more interesting to Terence than the women, and Penny's reaction to both was most interesting of all. Never had he been made more aware that Penny was by nature a man's woman. She had girlfriends, knew how to treat them, but her antennae were clearly more alive to the men's needs than the women's: her smiles were more frequent and more disarming for the men, her laugh lighter, more infectious. Oh, they liked her all right.

Terence had seen her in heavy conversation with the novelist fellow – he rather wanted to meet Veysey, but in a moment, when he was ready, not now – had seen her lightly touch Melzi's arm as she talked to him. (Wasn't that a bit fresh? According to her she barely knew him.) Terence had seen a look in her eye that he recognised from his mother as she threw a remark over her shoulder at a balding man in a well-cut suit. He did not like the look from Rowena; it seemed almost as disgusting from Penny.

How could she do it? How could she laugh and flirt and drink, be alternately flippant and earnest, yearning and yearned for, when her husband was so far away, so alone? Was she not aware that John was in danger for every minute of his absence? She should lock herself away, go into a semi-mourning (except for work, he would allow her that, he didn't see why she should live entirely off his father's money) until John returned. Then was the time for parties, for entertaining, for triumphant happiness and a flaunting of her good looks. Not now.

Terence emptied his beer bottle and moved into the dining room where the drinks were laid out. He had thought he would enjoy this party, had looked forward to it, but he felt out of his orbit. Oh, Penny's friends were warm enough (especially the women), but he felt as though he were on show. 'Look what I've got, this amusing stepson, almost my age, but luckily I'm too attractive to worry about appearing old. Do be kind to him, he's a bit of a wastrel, but we're very fond of him in the family.' But Penny was not like that – was she?

And the friends themselves, all achievers, all with hopes and aspirations of which they were more than happy to tell him. Were they interested in him? No. They asked about his father and told him about themselves. Only Beth had made a real effort, teasing him, laughing, pushing him to tell her what he did, what he had done, what he hoped to do. And what did she mean by that? Had Penny set him up, told Beth to find out when he planned to leave, what he planned to do with his life? Or was Beth just nosy? Terence did not like to have to explain himself, any more than he liked to be ignored. It made social interaction rather difficult sometimes.

He hesitated by the whisky bottle. But no, he did not drink much as a rule and whisky would not be a good idea. He poured himself some wine, and turned back to face the party. He saw Beth making for him across the room. A pretty enough girl but he did feel he had done his duty by her.

'Supper's ready,' Penny said at his elbow, and was startled to see how coldly he looked at her, until he remembered, and smiled. 'D'you mind helping? Just to carry the stuff through from the kitchen and put it on the table.'

'Of course not,' he said, but he did, felt like a child being fagged. She wouldn't ask *Melzi* to help, would she, or *Veysey*, or any of her *smart* friends? He heard his voice echoing in his head, knew he was being childish, was almost pleased with himself, and felt vindicated when he saw that the only other two people who helped were earnest Sarah and the assistant.

As plates were being filled, guests finding corners where they could perch to eat one-handed, glasses balanced with plates, spinach and wine spilt on the carpet (Penny had known all this would happen, wanted the eating bit over with as soon as possible, felt it intruded on the conversation, flirting and jokes) the doorbell rang. Terence, bored, curious, near the door, answered it. A man stood alone on the doorstep, holding a gift-wrapped parcel and a bunch of flowers. 'Oh, have I the wrong house?' he asked, trying to shut the door and look at the number nailed on to it again. 'Penny Brunel?'

'No, you're right enough,' said Terence. (Who was this man? Why was he so late? What was with the presents?) 'I'm Terence Smith Stourton. John's son.'

'Of course, excuse me. I'm Herbie Langabeer. I work with Penny. May I?' he took a small step forward.

Terence remembered his manners and stood back to let Herbie pass. 'Is your wife coming in?' he shouted rudely at Herbie's back, leaving the door ostentatiously open. 'She's parking the car, is that it?'

Herbie turned, looking surprised and rather foolish with the parcel and the lilies in his arms. 'Christine? No, I'm afraid that at the last minute something came up and she couldn't come. I'm on my own.'

I bet you are, thought Terence, as he slammed the door and followed Herbie down the narrow corridor to the dining room. He wanted to see the meeting between Penny and her 'boss'.

Penny, overseeing the dishing out of food, looked at Herbie

almost in surprise. 'Happy birthday,' he said, holding out the flowers and parcel.

'Oh, but it's not,' she said, and laughed, and took the offerings.

'I'm sorry,' he said, and Penny was surprised to see how ill-at-ease the normally suave Herbie appeared. 'Christine seemed to think . . . Anyway, she sent this, I bought the flowers, and she sent her apologies, she's er, not feeling . . .'

'Don't worry. Who's going to complain about being given a present?' Penny said. She had not expected either of the Langabeers to turn up, knew that Christine would not and did not think Herbie would be allowed out on his own for anything not related to the company. In the kitchen, she searched around for a jug for the flowers and opened the present. It was a tapestry kit, rather large and she knew quite expensive. 'For heaven's sake!' she said to herself. 'Is the woman mad?'

Terence, hovering in the corridor, smiled to himself. Clever move, Mrs Herbie, he thought, and ambled into the kitchen. 'What've you got there then?' he asked, laying a friendly hand on Penny's shoulder.

She shook it off, saying, 'Look what Herbie's wife has sent me. Apparently she thought it was my birthday. A tapestry kit. I ask you! And honestly, even if I were into tatting, look at this pattern!' Hundreds — or so it seemed — of penguins danced over a kitsch ice floe. In a blue sky hung a pale shadow of a crescent moon. Penny's astonishment, her genuine outrage at the tastelessness of the picture, made Terence laugh.

'Is it all right?' asked a gentle voice from the doorway. 'She said she thought that as you were alone so much in the evenings it might help pass the time.'

Penny turned, immediately contrite. 'Thank you, what a nice idea. It was very kind of her. I'll write, of course. It's just' — she could not help but laugh again – 'it's just ... Don't you think there is something intrinsically funny about penguins? I mean, look ...' The laughter had a hysterical edge this time, she was in danger of losing her self-control.

Herbie looked perplexed, which only made her laugh harder.

'Come on, Penny,' Terence said, 'they're only quite funny,' and now Herbie joined in with the laughter and Terence, forgetting that only a moment before he had been mocking this man's wife's taste in soft furnishings, felt livid, excluded, a child again at a grown-up party. He turned and left the room, in search of something to eat (he was feeling a little drunk) and more convivial company. Perhaps he should go back to Ireland. He could not wait for his father for ever.

'Got any dice?'

Terence looked round in surprise. A man he did not know, had not been introduced to, wearing an expensive-looking rumpled suit with no tie and looking as though he were having a little trouble in focusing, stood before him.

'Dice?'

'Yes, you know. Poker dice. It looks like there's a bit of a poker school getting itself up. Except, of course, we need the dice.'

'I don't know. I doubt it.'

'Well, normal dice, you know with dots on. Got any of those?'

'Dice with dots on?' What was this man talking about?

'Yes, dice with dots on. I thought you were the son or something. Don't you know?'

'Yes, I'm the son, no, I don't know about dice with dots on. Or Monopoly or anything else like that.'

'I'll ask the lovely widow, shall I? She must know.'

'She's not a widow,' Terence hissed. 'My father is alive and well.'

'And carrying the white man's burden, I suppose,' sneered the stranger. 'Well, good on him. Meanwhile, where are the dice?'

'I know she's got Perudo.' It was Sarah, who had detached herself from Giovanna at last and was looking at the dice-seeker with a degree of interest. 'Will that do?'

'Very eighties,' he jeered, 'but, yeah, why not? Will you get it? And I'll bring some wine over. Thanks, mate,' he said, with no apparent irony. 'Catch you later.'

'Who is that?' Terence asked Sarah.

'Glenn Fraser. He's a consumer-affairs reporter for one of the tabloids. I've met him here before, once or twice. He looks as though he's overdone it a bit tonight, but he's usually good fun. Perudo might settle him down. I'll go and find it. Why don't you come and join in?' she added kindly.

It was the kindness of strangers that he hated most. 'I don't think I will. I'll watch. And maybe try to stop the tabloid journalist from sucking back too much more drink.'

And so he did. He stood back and watched as a group settled down to Perudo, shouting and laughing at each other. At first, conversation went on around them – Fraser, Sarah, Helen and two other men. But then the idea took seed. Melzi took Helen's place and Vesey suggested poker. Cards were produced, tables cleared, and before long almost everyone was involved.

'Interesting, isn't it?' Penny stood beside Terence, sipping a glass of mineral water.

'What?' Terence had been asked to join in, but still felt sour at being excluded.

'You're not being very nice this evening,' Penny said, 'but that isn't what I meant. I meant about cards, gambling, what-have-you. Look at them. They're not even gambling for money, but their blood is as hot as if thousands were at stake.'

'People gamble for all sorts of reasons,' he said absently. 'Only people like John don't need anything extra. Everybody else has to feel they're living dangerously sometimes.'

Penny looked at him with more interest than she had shown in her stepson for some time. 'What do you mean?'

'Everyone needs passion in their lives. Wine, women, song – that's all it's about. Passion. And for some it's drugs. Or gambling.'

'And you?'

'Me?'

'Yes, what are you passionate about?'

He looked at her closely. Sometimes she was a very stupid woman.

'For God's sake, Penny, send the lot of them packing!' he exploded.

'Terence?' (Well, he had stopped her laughing at least.)

'Excuse me.' Herbie backed out, went in search of a drink, poured himself a glass of wine and, seeing Giovanna and Sarah standing together looking silent and desperate, crossed the room to make conversation with them. He did not know what was happening between Terence and Penny but he did wonder whether another evening at home with the gin bottle and a daintily served dinner might not have been more peaceful than all this north Notting Hill emotion.

'Terence, what do you mean?' Penny spoke quietly now, still holding the despised tapestry, her face tense with fury.

'Well, look at them all.'

'Look at them?'

'Yes, look at them. What's going on in any of their heads that's worth one second of my father's life?'

'Are you drunk?'

'Every time you don't understand me you ask if I'm drunk. No, I'm not. Or not so that it makes any difference. What's this party for? What are these people doing? Sitting around in your sitting room – my father's sitting room – eating your food, drinking your drink, thinking about themselves. Their own boring lives – oh, they may be very successful, they may have power in one sense. That one over there, the one who wanted the dice, started the game, can you really believe he should be trusted to get an old lady across the room, let alone make decisions that change people's lives?'

'Tel, have you gone mad?'

'No, I haven't. Penny, don't you see? I'm just trying to make you see.'

Her face crumpled, and for a moment he thought he had reached the part of her that he needed, the part that would listen and understand, the part that must have made his father fall in love with her – because John did love her, Terence knew that, could never question it.

But then, 'I thought you wanted fun!' she said, and it sounded to him as pathetic as his mother's whines about another lost love.

'Fun! It's *them* who want fun. Look at them!' He gestured through to the sitting room, where the noise level rose with every throw of the dice. 'Fun with you. You know that, you must. They sniff around like a pack of dogs after a bitch on heat, bees round a honey-pot if you prefer. They don't care about John, about your wedding ring. They're all just waiting for you to make some move, some little nod in their direction. And then they'll have you, one after the other. They'll be civilised about it, on the surface. They'll buy you dinner and theatre tickets and flowers – that's started already, I see – but they're no different

94

from animals, not really, for all their fine words and fine jobs and smart clothes. Not one of them is an honest man.'

Penny was completely white. Taken off-guard by Terence's words, by the strength of his feeling, she wanted to throw him out of the house, but something held her back. Manners? Family feeling? The fear of her friends knowing of what they stood accused? *The fear that Terence was right?*

'You look ill, Penny, are you all right?' Penny whirled round at the gentle voice behind her. Helen stood there, her arm stretched out in front of her. 'Someone's spilt wine on my dress. I just want to put some cold water on it.'

The dark stain on the shimmering material looked like blood rather than wine, and Penny felt a surge of sickness. This party had not been a good idea. The Greek food was too rich, too greasy, the company too disparate. She had been mad to suppose Terence would enjoy himself or add to anyone else's enjoyment. 'Excuse me, no, I don't feel too good.' She took the excuse Helen offered her and fled through the kitchen. She wanted to be alone for a moment or two, to think. She felt a pair of eyes on her back as she ran up the stairs, but did not turn. For once she did not care what anybody thought, she would make her excuses later.

Helen held her sleeve under the cold tap, squeezing it gently, waiting for the water to run clear. She did not speak and Terence, watching her, wondered how much she had heard. He moved closer to her, stood behind her. He felt the tiny movement away from him. He felt that she was repelled by him, and that it was nothing to do with anything she might have heard. The thought gave him a surge of power – he who never felt powerful – and he took another tiny half-step towards her, crowding her, pushing her closer into the sink.

'What are you doing?' she asked, without turning.

'I wondered if I could help.'

'No, you didn't.'

'No, I didn't ...'

'And you weren't about to try to kiss me, either, were you?' Now she did turn and Terence realised that she was an inch taller than him, that she had to look down into his eyes. He no longer felt cruel and strong, only foolish, and he took a step backwards.

'No.'

'They're not all after her, you know.' He could not understand why her voice was so gentle. He disgusted her, he had tried to bully her. What was happening? He felt weak, out of control.

'I'm not drunk.'

She looked at him closely, not moving away now, and somehow preventing him from trying to leave. The noise from the dice-players reached a crescendo. 'Perudo!' someone shouted, but it seemed a long way off. 'No, I don't think you are,' Helen said. 'Not with wine at any rate. But something else. Why are you so angry?'

'Look at them, listen to them ...' but the anger was dissipating now, and he just felt very tired.

'Are you angry with Penny's friends, or with Penny? I thought she'd been good to you. She's very fond of you.' (Helen was not quite sure of the truth of this statement, but did not think it would hurt.)

'She's all right.'

'Or is it your father?'

Terence flushed and turned away. 'You're all the same.'

'Who?'

He was not sure, floundered. 'Pop psychology, buzz-words, you've all read too many magazines.'

She laughed. 'I never touch them. They lie around in the

waiting room for my clients, but I don't need to read them. I see all I need to see in the raw.'

'Waiting room? So you're a psychologist?'

'No, I'm an aromatherapist.' She hesitated, eyeing him.

For once he did not mind. He had a feeling that this Amazon knew something about truth. More than Penny for all her frank looks and honest talk.

'Stay there a minute.' She went away but was back a second later, holding two cold beers. She swung herself up on to the counter and sat, ankles crossed, looking down at him. 'You don't have to be your father, you know.'

'I don't want to be him.'

'Or like him. Or, at any rate, different from yourself.'

'What is all this? Who do you think you are?' He wanted to leave but could not break away. It was not so much her beauty that mesmerised him, although he could not ignore its effect, as that he could not believe that such beauty really wanted to concentrate on him. He knew he had been at his most unattractive, and knew, too, that most of the men in the sitting room would be only too delighted to have Helen's undivided attention. So, he may not have the right clothes or job or conversation, but he was the one Helen was sitting with, alone in the kitchen. 'It's my party and I'll cry if I want to, cry if I want to, cry if I want to.' He thought the words had just run through his brain, but he must have sung or hummed, for Helen said, 'Do you want to? Cry?'

He didn't answer but he did not feel sulky any more. He had forgotten about Penny.

'Why don't you go and bring him back?'

'Who?' He was genuinely startled. 'Bring who back? From where?'

'Your father, of course.' Her eyes shone as brightly as her

silver tunic. She looked almost other-worldly. 'Don't sit here bemoaning him and taking it out on Penny. Go and get him.'

'He trains for months to be fit enough to tackle the ice. I can't just walk out there and say hi. I'm not a penguin.' He suddenly remembered Penny's penguin tapestry and smiled, but Helen drew him back into their moment.

'No, I'm not suggesting you go to the Pole or wherever he is this time, but get closer to him. That's your problem, isn't it? Not being close enough to him. Go and meet him half-way, physically, and then who knows what will happen? You can't just sit here and wait for him. What will you achieve by that?'

Terence felt himself being drawn towards the idea, but he resisted the suggestion that he had been no use until now. 'I'm looking after Penny,' he said. 'Looking out for her interests. Letting men like that,' he nodded towards the raucous noise from the sitting room, 'know that there's a man around to protect her.'

'And putting a lot of ideas into her head that weren't there before.'

Terence flushed, and Helen, watching him, noticed with interest how much less like his father he looked when he was angry. He looked almost brutish, big and aggressive but still with that weak mouth. He was right to be worried, of course: he was so much less of a man than his father.

'How could I get there? And where? I don't know his movements, I don't have much money.'

'Those, Terence, are mere details, and I leave them to you to sort out. All I'm saying is, this is not the place for you. Not any more.' She swung herself down from her perch, straightened her tunic, looked approvingly at her ankles. 'I must say these shoes do all kinds of favours to a girl's legs,' she said, and looking straight at Terence, added, 'Think about what I've said.' She edged past him, knowing she should kiss his cheek but unable to overcome her physical distaste for him. As women with alcoholic fathers recognise a drunk (however sober he may appear), a woman fathered by a bully has an almost feral instinct for another bully. Helen was prepared to try to help Terence because she loved Penny, and in her half-thought-through way she believed in the hope of a better world. But she saw what he was, and she could not touch him.

Terence looked at her straight back, her long shining hair, the silver platform sandals retreating from him and wished he knew what to think.

Chapter Six

Penny woke in the morning filled with unease. She lay on her back for a while, looking up at the ceiling, wondering why she felt so unhappy. Then she remembered. She had not come back downstairs after she had fled. Terence could make her excuses, he had caused the trouble. How could she face all those men she had invited in perfectly good faith now that she knew what they thought of her?

She had laughed with John over the years at her peculiar position, half wife, half widow. 'Do you know how many men have told me that they've had vasectomies since I married you?' she would say. 'It's the most unattractive come-on I can think of, but it doesn't stop them.'

'What are they telling you?'

'That they're safe, I suppose. Half the time I think they're not even aware they're doing it.'

'Sad, really.' He rolled over in bed and, leaning up on one elbow, looked down at her.

'What?' Every so often, even after years of marriage, she was struck again with amazement that he loved her, that he still wanted her.

'That to sell themselves men have to undersell their virility. We seem to have come an awful long way from the animal world.'

'I suppose thirty years ago women boasted about being on the pill. It's the same thing, really.'

'You might be right. I don't think I like the idea of all those nutless men coming after you.' He had moved his hand towards her under the covers but Penny had slipped out of bed, suddenly angry with him for his calm complacency. He was right, of course. She was inviolate, would wait for him for as long as it took. One day he would come home and stay.

Now, lying in bed, faintly hung over from all the cigarettes she had smoked the night before, she remembered that conversation and was angry again. Angry with Terence for not trusting her. Angry with John for trusting her. Angry with herself for being so naïve. Were they really all after her? She thought of Melzi's liquid looks, Veysey's fierce eyes, as he told her to consider trying to have fun with him – 'What did he mean by that? Is Terence really right? Do they really think they're in with a chance?'

She sat up, reaching for her dressing-gown. A bath, then she would face the mess downstairs. She would just have to be a little late for work today. 'Shit. Lunch with MacLaing,' she remembered. 'That won't be any fun. And I haven't done my homework.' MacLaing's whisky had noticed a huge dip in its sales in Scotland and the West Country. They had been unable to work out why, until a poll commissioned by Penny had discovered that it was rumoured the MacLaing family was anti-blood sport. As a result not one of the huge West Country shoots or local hotels was prepared to buy any MacLaing product. It was up to Penny to work out a cost-efficient damage-limitation exercise. 'And I'm not sure I can deal with my own life today,' she said, to her reflection in the mirror. Late nights and self-pity told on her skin nowadays. 'I'm getting old,' but the eyes that had looked at her last night had told her she was attractive. The mouths had not spoken, but the eyes ...

'Shit,' she said again, and poured a generous slug of Jo Malone essence into her bath. 'And then there's Terence. Shit. Well, I'll deal with him when I get home. He won't be up.'

A quarter of an hour later she came downstairs to find Terence up, shaved and dressed, sitting at the tiny kitchen table eating toast and making some sort of a list.

'Good morning.' If her tone was icy, it passed him by.

'Morning, stepmother,' he said cheerily. 'Good party last night. Helen's nice.'

'Yes, very pretty. Very in demand,' Penny said sourly, and switched the kettle on. 'Oh, Terence, you could at least have emptied the dishwasher.'

'I'd only have had to fill it up again,' he said reasonably, pointing at the stacked plates and dirty glasses that littered every surface. 'And I've been busy.'

'Doing what?' she asked sourly, unloading plates as noisily as she could in a doomed effort to shame him into helping.

He won the battle of wills, of course. He probably did not even realise that he was engaged in a silent tussle with her. For the first time since he had walked through her door, he was preoccupied with something. Her curiosity finally overcame her. 'What are you doing?'

'Making a list.' He looked up at her frankly.

He seemed better-looking than usual today, she thought, or maybe it was just that she was feeling old and tired. 'Shopping?' Facetious and ineffective.

'No.' He put down his pen, finished his toast and – perhaps most extraordinary of all – tidied his plate and knife into the dishwasher. Never mind that she had not quite finished emptying it of its clean load. 'It's been good of you to have me stay for so long, Penny. Thank you. But I think it's time I moved on.'

She could not help the surge of relief she felt, but hoped she managed to disguise it. 'Oh? Where to? Ireland? Of course, you're welcome to stay as long as you want.'

'No, not Ireland. You're right about Mother. It's time she stopped using me.'

'I'm not sure I said exactly that . . .' (Had she? She couldn't remember. She wasn't functioning properly yet today.)

'Whatever. Anyway, I've decided to go and fetch Dad. John.' He looked at her and laughed. 'Well, now I have surprised you.'

'Fetch him? From where?' For a mad moment she thought John had rung, that she had missed him, that Terence was off to Paddington or Heathrow. 'Tel, what do you mean?' She shouted the question to cover the frightening thought that had risen unbidden. *No*, she had thought, *I don't want him back, not yet. I've some things to do first.* And then her conscious mind had overtaken, pushed back that treacherous impulse. (But what had it meant? Why did she not want him back yet? What was it she had to do?)

'No, I don't mean fetch, do I? I mean find.' Penny looked at him, her perplexity only increasing. 'Yes, she said find.'

'Who said find? What do you mean?'

Terence was looking earnestly at his list as though it would answer all her questions. 'Now, then, presumably there's some office in London. Or somewhere.'

'What kind of office? What are you talking about?' She took a deep breath. She must calm down.

'I don't know what it's called, but you know, some centre. Where everything happens. For Dad. Money raised, press questions fielded, all that kind of thing.'

'Well, yes. Chris Bellew. The office is ten minutes away — in the North Pole Road, believe it or not.'

'Then I'll go and talk to him first. About how to set about it.'

When John and Penny married she had decided she could no longer represent him professionally and had handed him over to Chris, who now represented him exclusively. He was fund-raiser, sponsorship securer, press officer, media organiser and public-relations officer all in one. Small and ugly, staggeringly unfit and theatrically camp, he and John made an odd pair. Penny often suspected that Chris was more than a little in love with John but did not mind. If his unrequited passion meant he worked harder for the object of his affections, then all the better. He would come to John — or Penny if John was away — with news of some big sponsorship deal as though he were Hercules laying the result of his labours at the feet of his beloved. Penny might have created the legend that was John Brunel, but Chris had done nothing but enhance it and — and she supposed this was part of the point — made it ever more a commercial property. Both John and Penny trusted him implicitly.

'Set about what? Tel, you're going to drive me mad. Please, tell me what's happened? Have they rung? Have you heard from him? What is going on?'

He looked at her more thoughtfully now, and she wondered if he had read her mind, seen the hesitation there.

'I've been sitting around too long. Of course I'm not going to fly to Canada or somewhere and start walking. But I do need to do something. I want to join the task force or whatever they're called. I want to be involved. I want to understand what he does and why he does it. Then I might not mind it so much.'

Penny turned her back on him, switched the kettle back on,

slowly made a pot of coffee. Terence sat still, his list in front of him, watching her and waiting. 'That's very honest of you,' she said finally.

'Aren't I always? No, don't answer that. And, Penny, I'm sorry about last night.' She wanted to accept his apology, but could not, not yet, and then was surprised to hear him continue, 'I was perhaps a little over-emphatic.'

'You mean you still mean it?'

'About those men? Yes. I'm not sure whether I mean it about you. But you do seem to be waiting for something.'

'For John to come home.'

'No, not that. I don't know what it is. You're like a woman suspended in time, Penny. I thought you knew it, but now I'm not sure you do.'

'You're muddling me up with your mother.'

He denied this with his hands, pulling a face. Penny realised she did quite like her stepson after all. 'No. She's stuck in a decade, in some kind of timewarp. I don't mean that. You're like one of those insects floating in amber, or a poached egg floating in jelly. Stuck and waiting for something to happen, something that will release you.'

'A poached egg in jelly! I'll take that as my epitaph.'

'You don't need to, you know. I think maybe I was a poached egg too, but now I'm going to try not to be. And the first step is to find John. Will you tell me where the office is?'

They sat together, drinking coffee, ignoring the mess around them. Penny still did not understand where Terence was going, or why, and was not sure that he knew either. But she knew that if the dream-filled night had aged her skin, something else had happened to Terence. Maybe he was growing up at last. Or maybe he was about to stop pretending.

And if he thought that working as a gofer handling communications and PR in his father's office was going to help him, let him try.

Penny decided to give up smoking. It was no use denying that she was too old to keep going at the same rate and cigarettes left her feeling ill and sore-chested every morning. She had the last ones during a sticky lunch with MacLaing, and deliberately left her half-full packet on the restaurant table.

She was already feeling scratchy when she let herself into her house at the end of the day, prepared to find the old Terence lolling around thinking about himself. 'Don't be unreasonable,' she said to herself, as she closed the door behind her and realised she was irritable at the house being empty. 'Thank God he's found himself something to do, and long may it last.'

The telephone ringing shrilly made her jump.

'Hello.' A pause, but she could hear someone breathing.

'Hello?' Still silence apart from the light breath. 'Listen, buddy, if you think you've picked some easily frightened hysteric you can think again. Either say something or fuck off, now.'

'Is Terence there?'

It was a voice she almost recognised, but not quite.

'No, he's out. Who is it?' Again, she knew she was being unreasonable minding that the call should be for her lodger, but could not help herself. Again, there was silence. She wanted to hang up but curiosity kept her on the line. 'Can I take a message?' she said.

'Is that Penelope?' No one called her that except John and her brother.

'Of course.'

Another pause, a breath, then, 'This is Rowena speaking.'

For a moment Penny could not imagine who that might be, then, 'Rowena Smith Stourton.' Terence's mother.

'Terence's mother?'

'Yes.'

'Well, I'll tell him you called. I don't know when he'll be back.'

'But he will be?' Penny could hear the faint note of anxiety.

'Yes. At least, I suppose so.' And then she could not help but add, 'I think he's started a job today.'

'A job?' The voice sounded guarded now, not as pleased as Penny would have assumed the mother of such a listless son should be at such a piece of news. And some malicious impulse, some awareness that no mother can like being told news about her child by an almost-stranger, made her add, 'Yes, he was asking me this morning about John. I think he feels he would like to be more involved in his father's life. So I gave him the name of Chris Bellew, the operations manager, and he was going to the office to try to get some work.'

The voice that answered was icy now, Home Counties clipped with none of the fey intonation Penny had half recognised at the beginning of the conversation. 'Don't you think John should be making the effort to become involved with Terence rather than the other way round? I would rather you did not interfere with my son. I have already lost his father to some madcap romanticism about ice, I don't want my son to go too.'

'Rowena!' The gentle amusement of her tone would, Penny knew, enrage her opponent far more than any expression of anger or self-defence. 'I assure you it was entirely his own idea. The poor boy's been looking rather lost since he turned up here all those weeks ago and I'm only too pleased he's found an interest.' Penny did not often play the bitch – it was not a role that came naturally to her and not one she enjoyed. But she was tired and tense and miserable, and for the first time she admitted to herself how much she disliked this woman who had so briefly been a part of her husband's life. She bit back any retort of the feckless Rowena's 'loss' of a man she had never in any sense possessed.

'Working in an office is no kind of life for a boy – a man – like Terence. I can see you would not understand that, but Terence is an artist. He has the soul of a poet. He's Irish, you understand.'

'Not on his father's side. Nor, I thought, on yours. Except by upbringing. But he's not Greek, either, is he? Despite his time there when he was a boy.'

'What do you mean by that?'

'Nothing at all. I'll ask him to ring you.'

Penny almost apologised, but wanted the conversation to end. She knew she sounded like all the women who had patronised her, thinking that by belittling her they were defending their husbands from her predatory attacks. Perhaps her life would have been easier if she had been the kind of man-eater they all imagined her to be. Perhaps a series of affairs would have toughened her up, but other women's suspicions had done that. 'At least if I'd been bad I'd have had fun,' she said – fun, that word again.

'What?'

'I said it would be bad if he had no fun,' she improvised. 'Rowena, I must go.'

'No. Just a minute.'

Penny wondered if Rowena were drunk or high or something. The voice changed so much from minute to minute. Was the woman outmanoeuvring her? She had always been sure that no one could play games as well as she, and did not wish to be disappointed now. 'What is it?'

'I think it's time my son came home, back to Ireland. I don't know what you've been playing at, but be assured John would not like it. Terence must come back, I need him back. There's nothing for him in London. I've given him enough rope, but I will not have him disappearing off and getting involved with John's rubbish. If John wants to see him he knows where to find him. Terence should have more pride than to hang around after him like this.'

'Terence is twenty-seven years old. I can't send him home like a parcel. Furthermore he's not hanging around after John. I've explained he's got himself a job. And I've not been playing at anything. Tel turned up on my doorstep and I gave him a bed.'

'Which one?'

The audacity of it took Penny's breath away. Terence's confused imaginings and suspicions were bad enough, but this! There was no point in pretending she didn't know what Rowena was suggesting. 'Don't judge other women by yourself, Rowena. Your blatant sexuality drives your son away from home time and again, and neither he nor John is looking for another woman like you. I am his father's wife, we are family. You may fuck your close relations. I don't.'

She hung up, trembling with rage. A quiet click behind her made her turn. Terence was at the front door, shutting it behind him. From his face it was obvious he had heard at least her last words.

'Rowena?'

She nodded. 'I'm sorry, Tel. You shouldn't have heard that. I probably shouldn't have said it.'

'Yes, you should. Someone should have said it to her years ago. I'm sorry. What did she want?' He looked very young and very sad, and Penny wanted to put her arms around him and comfort him, but Rowena had planted a poisonous seed and she did not dare.

Instead she led the way to the drinks tray and silently poured them both gin and tonic. 'I think she wants you to go home.'

He nodded. 'So Pip's probably gone.'

'She didn't say. Maybe she just doesn't like the idea of your being at home in your father's house.'

'Or your house.' She met his look unflinchingly but did not agree. 'I've always known she was manipulative, but it hasn't stopped me being manipulated by her. I think maybe now I can learn to resist. God knows, it's time.'

Penny longed for a cigarette. What a nightmare that all this had happened on the day she gave up. With an effort, she said, 'What happened with Chris?'

'Chris?' He looked at her, distracted, still seeing his mother's big eyes and long fringe. Then he brought his mind back from Ireland to London, to the present. 'Chris. Oh, he was great, very welcoming, like you said he would be. But he didn't seem to think there was any excuse to send me off to meet John. Said it would be different if I were a blond leggy sixteen-year-old, but he didn't think there'd be much copy in a drop-out or never-quite-dropped-in-twenty-seven-year-old going off to see Daddy. Well, he didn't exactly say that, but it's what he meant. But he said I could come into the office regularly, no pay at first, unless something came up ... I suppose I couldn't really have hoped for much more. But, well, it does mean I'm not going to be able to afford to rent somewhere else either so, um, would you mind very much if I stayed on a bit?'

He looked so woeful that Penny almost laughed. But the last thing that the new Terence needed was mockery. 'Of course you can stay,' she said, 'as long as you need.' And this time she risked a short hug before going back to her gin and turning on the television.

'Penny Brunel.'

'Penny, hi. I wanted to thank you for the party. I was right, wasn't I? It was a good one?'

A moment of panic. Penny got frustrated with people who did not announce themselves properly on the telephone. Then, of course, Veysey. 'Philip. Hello.' An awkward silence followed. Should she apologise for disappearing half-way through or had he not even noticed?

'I hope you're feeling better.' He had.

'Yes. I'm sorry about that. I don't know quite what overcame me. But I thought it better to slide off. I didn't want to break up the party.'

'I'm surprised you slept. It all got very rowdy.'

'Well ...' She tailed off. Now what? He had thanked her, her mind was on MacLaing and she wanted to get back to her spreadsheet. She had been concentrating on her computer. She hated it when she was rung socially at work, but with someone like Veysey it was difficult. He was a work contact, too – she could not quite treat him as she would a friend.

'Actually, that's not just why I rang.'

A little more of her attention went towards Veysey and away from MacLaing. Perhaps she should be wearing her working hat after all. 'Yes?'

'I wondered if I could buy you dinner one night – next Tuesday? Or any day next week, really.' And there, bang, her mind was totally alert.

'Dinner?' she repeated feebly.

'Yes, dinner. How about it?' He sounded relaxed enough,

as though it were totally normal to ask other men's wives out to dinner.

'But we do lunch.'

He laughed, and she felt her heart relax a little. That laugh could not hide an ulterior motive. 'Well, yes. So far our friendship has been restricted to the occasional mostly working lunch. And, of course, your supper party. But, you know, when people make friends all kinds of things happen. You dance with each other for a while—'

'*Dance?* We can't go dancing.'

'I didn't mean we should, although I can't see any reason why not. I was speaking metaphorically. You know what I mean. You curtsey, I bow, we do a stately little promenade, another bow, another curtsey. And then, if we like what we see, maybe we do a little waltz, leading on to a polka. And who knows? We might end up doing the tango.'

'The tango.' Wasn't that meant to be erotic? Penny was feeling muddled. Her hand went out automatically for the cigarette packet, which was no longer there. The first few days of not smoking had left her with a worse morning chest and head than usual. But she tried to play along. 'I see. So where are we now?'

'I'd say you asking me to your party, which was not related to the office, which I had been expecting, put us up to waltzing and if you come out to dinner we might be hopping along to the polka. So what do you say? Can I mark your dance card?'

Penny was confused. She was enjoying this, but it was outside the rules. She was happy to flirt, always had been, but somehow expected to be the one to open the bidding. And now here was Veysey, asking her out to dinner, talking a lot of nonsense about the polka, and she was enjoying it, did not feel threatened, or challenged, just realised he was right, it was time to have some harmless fun. And what could be more harmless than dinner with a friend?

She made her decision. 'I'd love to, and Tuesday would be fine. But don't expect me to tango. I can't be doing with all that South American stuff. The polka is a jolly little dance and will suit me just fine.'

And she hung up, and smiled, and went back to her spreadsheet with the warm feeling that comes of having something to look forward to.

'You can't, Penny! You can't possibly!'

'Why on earth not?'

Sarah and Penny were sitting in an Italian restaurant, sharing a bowl of mussels and drinking Oyster Bay Sauvignon. Sarah had rung Penny during the day, saying she wanted to talk to her and could they have supper? Penny felt that she had seen enough of Sarah recently and would rather have sat at home and watched a girlie video over a plate of pasta and a glass of Rioja, but sensed that Sarah really wanted to talk to her. Her friend had not yet broached whatever subject was bothering her and to fill a silence Penny mentioned her date with Veysey. 'Did you meet Philip Veysey the other night? The novelist. Beaky nose, fierce eyes. He rang today and asked me to dinner.'

'Oh, yes? Which one was the wife?'

'The wife? He doesn't have one. I don't think he's planning on cooking, he asked me out.'

'What? Just the two of you?'

Penny's heart gave an unaccustomed lurch. She had assumed he meant just the two of them, and realised that she very much hoped he had. 'I suppose so,' she said nonchalantly, sucking a mussel from its shell but keeping an eye on Sarah as she did so.

'Don't you mustn't do it!'

'Why on earth not?'

'It's obvious. Married women don't go out to dinner with men on their own! It gives all the wrong messages.'

'What, he'll think that by agreeing to eat spaghetti bolognese with him in a public place I'm really saying I'm gagging to go to bed with him? Don't be silly.'

'A spaghetti house? I suppose that's all right.'

'Actually I was hoping for the Connaught. I should think he can afford it.'

'But that's a hotel.'

'I've lived in London all my life. I know the Connaught is a hotel.'

'Penny, I don't think you're taking this seriously. Even if he doesn't think you mean to go to bed with him, everybody else will. You can't possibly go to dinner alone with a man in a place where there are beds. It's just not done.'

'You're not joking, are you?' Penny looked at Sarah in amazement.

'No. It's just not — I don't know, not—'

'Proper?'

'Yes, proper.'

Penny carefully poured more wine into her glass. She did not want to lose her temper with Sarah, but she felt a red flush of anger rising behind her eyes. She knew Sarah was prim and proper, knew that she was only not a virgin by the narrowest of margins (which was pretty much of a feat) and that she was as frightened of sex on her friends' behalf as she was on her own, but she had not realised quite how deeply entrenched in the past Sarah was.

Or maybe not. Maybe everyone thought like Sarah. Maybe she *had* agreed to go out to dinner with Veysey because she was hoping to go to bed with him (but that was not the case, not at all, she just liked the man, dammit).

'Sarah, you do know that people can – make love in the afternoon, don't you? That you can go out to *lunch* with a man and then go to bed with him? Or even skip lunch altogether and go straight to the bedroom.'

Sarah looked affronted. 'Of course I do, I wasn't born yesterday,' she said, so primly that Penny's anger retreated. 'But that's not the point,' Sarah went on. 'It may sound old-fashioned, but it *is* important, it *does* matter. Whatever you do, you have to go through the form, you have to be seen to be doing the right thing. I can't understand why you don't see it, but you must feel it. Your reputation, Penny, it's vital. What are you without it?'

Penny thought for a moment, distracted by a memory teasing at the edges of her brain, then, '"The purest treasure mortal times afford/Is spotless reputation; that away,/Men are but gilded loam or painted clay" ... How does it go? Something something "Mine honour is my life; both grow in one;/Take honour from me, and my life is done."'

'Exactly. Who said that?'

'Shakespeare. Richard II. Isn't it funny how memory works?'

'Don't change the conversation. Penny, everybody admires you. Everyone says how marvellous you are, managing on your own. Everyone tells John how amazing you are. You can't want there to be doubtful silences about you when he next comes home, can you?'

'I don't want to be admired. I'm not marvellous. I get on with my life. What's the difference between us? You're on your own because you're not married, I'm on my own – sometimes—'

'Often.'

'Regularly, because John has to go away. We both get on with it.'

'You must be lonely.'

'So must you.' She could not resist it, but Sarah's primness was really too much. She would not be patronised by this sexless spinster, no matter how old a friend she was.

'I can go out to dinner with men without anyone caring.'

'So can I. John wouldn't mind a bit and it's nothing to do with anyone else.' At least, she had always supposed John wouldn't mind. Oh, help, that was something to brood over later. 'And at least they do ask me,' she added, knowing that the last remark was nothing but unpleasant.

'And they do me too, actually,' Sarah said quickly, and the sudden flush on her neck showed that this was why she had asked Penny out to dinner. Lord, oh, Lord, she finally has a boyfriend, Penny realised, but could not understand the prickle under her skin at the news. She couldn't be jealous, she who had John, of some dull accountant that Sarah had picked up on singles' night at Sainsbury's. ('I must stop being bitchy,' she muttered, only just under her breath. 'What is the matter with me?')

She made herself take a deep breath and an interest. 'Sarah! Who is he?' Back into role-play. Girlie-girlie let's talk about boys. She restrained herself from squealing. Neither of them was sixteen any longer. Thank heavens.

'He's called Robert, and he's a policeman.'

'A policeman! Well, that's a turn-up for the books. How did you meet him?'

'I was a witness of a car crash a month or so ago – didn't I tell you about it? Anyway, he took my statement and he *says* he recognised me at once, although of course I didn't him – but he was wearing that tall hat. She giggled and looked happy, and Penny could not help being envious of the sheer folly of early love. 'He was at Exeter with us – well, not quite with us, he was a couple of years below us, but claims he recognised me. Anyway he certainly knew my name because straight away he said, "Exeter," and we started talking and forgot about the car crash – at first, I mean, of course we did it all properly soon enough.'

'You would,' Penny said absently, sopping up the mussel sauce with bread and wondering if Sarah was going to offer another bottle of wine or whether she should just order a glass and have done with it.

'Of course. And he asked me out and did again, and so it seems, well, it seems . . .'

'As though you have a boyfriend,' Penny finished for her. 'Well done. So is it the real thing?'

'Oh, I don't know, it's early days yet. We'll see how it goes.'

'You seem keen.'

'I am. I think I am. He likes me, that's important.'

'And you him?'

'Of course.'

Sarah looked at her plate, could not meet Penny's eye, then waved at a waiter and asked for another bottle of wine. Penny's heart sank. This was going to be worse than the folly of new love, she sensed.

She waited a moment, giving Sarah a chance to say what she wanted to say without prompting. Why was she finding it easier to give her heart to listening to her friend when she sensed the other woman was unhappy, not happy? It was not that she wanted anything but joy for Sarah – although she did wonder if her friend was capable of real, bone-shuddering head-swimming joy.

Sarah took a breath. 'He's very keen,' she said.

'And that's not good?'

'He's talking about marriage. Babies. All that stuff. A mortgage in Putney.'

'Already? You said yourself it's early days.'

'I know. But he – he's almost overwhelming.'

Almost, Penny noticed, with a sinking heart. 'Isn't marriage and all what you want too?'

'Yes.' But Sarah would or could not meet her eye.

'So?'

'So I suppose I was hoping it would all come with – you know, like in the films ...' She gave a timorous little laugh.

Say the word, *say* the word, Penny urged her silently. 'With?' But still Sarah wouldn't, so Penny said it for her: 'With love.'

Sarah sighed and finally looked at her. 'Yes. Is that very silly?'

Penny thought of John and how, in the early days, she had felt the breath stop in her throat for love of him and feared that she could actually, literally die of love. 'No,' she said gently, 'it's not silly at all.'

'I didn't think I was the kind of girl men fell in love with, I suppose that's the problem. Now I just suppose I'm not the kind of girl who falls in love. It's not that I don't want to, it just doesn't seem to happen. And Robert – I can't understand why I don't. I mean I do, I like being with him, I'm very fond of him, I suppose I *love* him, I just don't ... it's just not ...'

'Is it Doctor Hook?' Penny asked herself. 'That song – "sorry when I kissed you, you only heard me whisper, you never got to hear those violins", something about not making it more like the movies for you ...'

Sarah managed a shaky smile. 'That's why men love you. You remember Shakespeare and soppy songs. I don't remember anything except mortgage rates and how to make mincemeat. Useless, really.'

'But Robert loves you,' Penny reminded her.

'I know. Oh, what shall I do?'

Penny paused. She was still not quite sure what question she was being asked. 'Do?'

'Well, do I marry him or not?'

'Hey, I can't possibly answer that question for you. You know I can't. Whatever I say will be wrong.' She knew the answer, though, or thought she did. But she could not ask the questions that would make Sarah realise what she was doing. *Does he make your heart sing? Are you suddenly stricken with weakness at the thought of him? Does he make you laugh? Cry? Do you feel you and he are the same person?* And then she heard what Sarah was saying, and thought perhaps Sarah did understand, or was struggling towards comprehension.

'I'm not in love with him, but he is a good man and I know that we will be – content, I suppose. Probably happy. He's very easy to be with, very kind. We have so much in common. And I'm nearly thirty-three. I do want babies and a mortgage in Putney.' *But does he make your heart sing? What if you meet someone in ten years who makes your heart sing? What then of your policeman and your babies and your mortgage in Putney?* 'I think I've been hoping for too much. I don't think I'll ever love anyone like you love John. I just don't think I'm made like that. What was that you were saying about violins? I don't think I ever will hear them. You know me, perhaps I just don't have a heart.'

'But you do, Sarah, of course you do.'

'Then maybe it's my soul that's wonky, whatever bit of you that goes overboard.' She paused, and Penny sensed she was making her mind up as she spoke. 'You know, it may be settling for half, but I think I'm never going to get more than half. And this half will be good, I'm confident of that.' She looked straight at Penny then, and Penny could see the courage growing as she spoke. 'It's no good pretending, is it? Well, of course I'll pretend to everyone else, and maybe with enough pretending it will start to become true. But I'm not going to pretend to myself that it's anything other than what it is. A marriage of affection and convenience, and you know we will live happily ever after.' She took a swig of wine, looking relieved, then added, 'After all, you married for love, and you're not really very happy, are you?'

And Penny, looking at the friend who for so long she had pitied for her lack of emotional imagination, suddenly felt as though she were drowning.

Chapter Seven

She felt as though she were surfacing from a deep dive, head swimming, bright stars exploding behind her eyelids, her face turned upwards, gasping for air. She sat up sharply, frightened of whatever dream she was escaping, not sure what it had been. What time was it? The alarm radio was already on: she could hear the measured tones of the news-reader. Then suddenly she was fully alert. *'What?'* she shouted at the radio, and then, *'John!'*

'Radio contact was re-established after a few hours, but rescue teams were already on the way. The explorer, who has conquered the most distant parts of the globe, seems to have failed in his third attempt to reach the Pole on a solo trip. It is believed that he succeeded in saving himself from the ice, but conditions are making it difficult for the support plane to land. We will have more news of that story in our next bulletin.'

Penny turned off the radio and sat up in bed, arms hugging her knees, head spinning. 'Perhaps it's someone else,' she said, but knew it could not be. There was no other major expedition on the ice at the moment, no one else trying to reach the Pole alone, no one as newsworthy, as interesting, as heroic as John. What had happened? Why had no one rung her? She should not have heard like this, half asleep, dragged up from some dream by the news of her husband's – death? And then she remembered. She had switched off the telephone – something every wife with a travelling husband knows never to do. But she had been tired, so tired. 'Where is he? John!' and, as she had so often before, she struggled to send her love around the world, to make him feel it wherever he was and be comforted and make him want to come home.

But for some reason it was too hard today. She felt too anxious, perhaps, too bound up in worry for him to be able to send him any strength. 'It's not that my love is weaker, John,' she said, tears streaming down her face, 'I promise, it's not that.'

As soon as the telephone was plugged into the wall it rang. Her mother, worried. Penny could not admit to her that she knew nothing. Her mother was too quick to judge, she would never be allowed to forget that she had left the telephone off on such a night. From now on every time her father had a cold her mother would be ringing to make sure the telephone rang in case he died in the night. Penny brushed her mother aside and hung up.

Again, before she had time to call Chris, the telephone rang, Patrick this time, from Exmoor. 'I've been trying you since six, since I heard the news. What's happened?'

'You know more than me, then. I'd switched my telephone off and only caught the second half of the news. What have you heard, Patrick?'

'They seem to think he fell through the ice. He managed to radio back to the support team and then they lost contact.'

'The bloody fool!'

'What?' Patrick sounded alarmed.

'He told me only idiots ever fell through the ice. Said it was almost impossible. Only Little Johnny Head-in-Air does that, he said. Oh, God.'

'Penny, stay calm. Ring Chris. He'll know more. Then get back to me if you can. I'll let you go.'

Patrick hung up, not bothering with soothing platitudes. Penny was grateful to him, almost loving him although they had little in common except John. Both loving John so much (Penny sometimes suspected John meant more to Patrick even than his wife and sons), they sometimes sparred, jostling like jealous children for a parent's precious time. But now Penny blessed him for understanding, and leaving her alone to do what she must.

Terence. The thought hit her like a hammer-blow between the eyes. Oh, God, Terence. He barely listened to the radio, sometimes had a commercial station playing in the background while he made himself breakfast. He was keen and eager in his new non-job, might already be up. He must not be allowed to go to the office without first hearing the news. God knows what it would do to him in his fragile state.

She pulled on a dressing-gown, tears forgotten, and ran downstairs to the kitchen. Terence, in boxer shorts and T-shirt, was just making himself some Nescafé. The radio was silent. 'Thank God.'

'Thank God?' He turned and looked at her with scorn. He was white-faced and unshaven. 'Thank God what?'

'Tel, it's John, your father,' she began, only fleetingly concerned at his appearance. 'There's been an accident.' She spoke quickly, as though the radio would spring into life of its own volition, breaking its news into the room before she had a chance to speak. That had happened in her bedroom, after all.

'I know. And you're thanking God for it?' There was an Irish touch to his voice, which Penny knew meant trouble.

'No – no! Don't be mad. I thought you hadn't heard – I heard on the radio, I didn't want you to hear the same way.'

He studied her, his eyes piggy in his bristly face. 'So what do we do now?'

'I'm going to ring Chris. Presumably you're going in to work?'

'Work! Don't patronise me. I'm useless. Not worth a salary. I can't help John there or anywhere. I don't know why I ever fooled myself. It's just another place where I'm not needed, where I'm in the way. I'm going back to Ireland.'

'Terence, I don't have time for this now. Do what you want, you always have. But in fact you might suddenly find yourself very useful at the ops centre. More so than you've ever been in your life before. You won't know until you go in. But, frankly, that's up to you.' She turned towards the telephone then, changing her mind, went back upstairs to her room. She wanted to be alone to make this call.

She tried the office first, guessing that Chris would have gone in as soon as he heard.

He picked up the telephone on the first ring. 'Penny. I've been trying and trying to reach you. Your mobile was switched off and no one was answering at home.'

'I'd switched them off. Chris, what's happened?'

Talking to him, Penny felt calmer already. Like every good agent, part of his job was to nanny his clients. She felt the security blanket settle around her shoulders and could begin to convince herself that everything would be all right.

'I'm keeping in touch with base camp. They've sent a plane to pick him up if he needs it. By all accounts he's all right. Wasn't in long enough to get soaked right through. I can't quite understand why he lost radio contact but he sorted it. You know John. Cheer up, it means he'll get extra chocolate rations.'

The support team only dropped supplies every five days, and Penny knew how John craved chocolate by the fourth day. The most iron-willed of men, the one place he always let himself down was over the chocolate. He had never once managed to make his supplies last the full five days.

'He's going to be livid,' Penny said miserably. Now that she was reassured about his safety she began to worry about how John would be feeling. 'I hope he manages to go on.'

'I know you do, pet. We all do. Look, I'd better go, but I'll keep you up to date. What about Terence? He's not here yet – I thought he'd be in early.'

'Tel, oh, Lord, Chris. He's cutting up rough, says he's not needed and he's going back to his blessed mother.'

'Going back?' Chris sounded alarmed. 'Now, look here, flower, you tell that boy to get himself over here fast. I think he could be useful. And don't you worry. We'll get your John home to you safe.'

Penny hung up, yelled down the stairs to tell Terence that Chris had some plan for him, and ran herself a bath. 'But I don't want John home,' she said, as she poured lavender salts into the hot water. 'Not yet, not until he's finished this job. Oh, Chris, if only you knew.'

She heard the front door slam. Terence. She hoped he had gone to Chris, hoped he would be back this evening. She felt so cut off from John, from caring about him, that she instinctively wanted someone who loved him in the house with her tonight.

She lay in the bath, chin under water, eyes closed, willing the heat to relax her, to stop her thinking. She tried working out a shopping list: 'I'd better get some more coffee, Tel goes through it very fast. And we'll need cheering up tonight, so I might make a bit of an effort for a change and cook something good. Or try to.' But on and on in the back of her mind came the thoughts about John that she wanted to push away. 'Pork, perhaps, he likes that. There's that easy thing with cream and mustard. And I'll get an M and S nursery pudding, sponge or something . . .' She tailed off. It was no good. She was going to have to face herself.

Her marriage could only be more perfect if she saw more of her husband. She was (of course) as much in love with her husband as ever. Not just loving, but *in love*, yes. If she were honest, she was beginning to think about babies, but that was a conversation she could have with John when he was next home. He had never ruled them out – 'Despite Tel, who would have been enough for most people. But it's not babies, is it? Or his absences. I really don't want him to come home yet.' She listened to the mind's echo of her voice saying those traitorous words. And said them again, to see what they sounded like. 'I really don't want him to come home. Yet.' It was no softer the next time around. And where at first her words had sounded tentative, this time there was a ring of conviction.

'It's only because he'll be so disappointed if he comes home because he's failed.' Disappointed and bad-tempered. 'And bad-tempered.' She was almost beginning to enjoy saying the unsayable. Perhaps she should try it out on some other people and see what they thought. But no, that would be disloyal, and disloyalty was a fault she abhorred almost above all others. 'But I might as well admit it to myself. It's true. He's horrible when he comes home after a trip that's gone wrong. Horrible,' she repeated. 'Of course I understand it, the disappointment and the sense of failure and all.'

She reached for the soap, topped up the bath with hot water, lay back again. She was going to be late for work but Herbie would understand. She wondered if war widows had spent a lot of time being late for work. 'Probably not, they didn't have enough hot water,' and she giggled to herself, then felt shock at her sudden lightheartedness. 'John could still be in danger,' she reminded herself, really thinking that it was time she repainted her toenails, especially if John was on the way home. 'Now is not the time for jokes.'

But why not? Why should any moment not be the time for jokes? John was in some sort of danger most of the time he was away from her, but it was an entirely self-inflicted danger. 'And I really don't think he'd want me never to laugh. Although maybe not at jokes about war widows.'

She stared at the ceiling, thinking not about John, usually the focus of her thoughts at such times, but about their marriage, and realised that the two were separate. Of course John was a hero – half the women in England were in love with him at a distance – but he was a bad-tempered hero. Not always, very rarely publicly. But bad-tempered. Perhaps it was her fault. 'Or his mother's fault,' she reminded herself. 'Perhaps she spoiled him.' Although, with four sons so close in age, that was unlikely. Penny wriggled her toes again, reached out for the soap, sank back into the water. She liked being alone in the house, liked the silence around her, the faint noise of a lorry juddering down Ladbroke Grove occasionally reaching her to remind her there was a world out there. 'A living, breathing world, hustle and bustle. How can John stand it, his silence?' She had often wondered that, but never actually asked him. She would when he came home this time, force him to talk to her about his ice-bound world.

When she first knew him she had been interested in the physical practicalities of his life – how he trained, what he ate, whether he took books with him on his voyages, what food he missed. But only now, lying in her hot bath, waiting to hear how and where he was, did she realise that she had never asked him

– and he had never volunteered to tell her – about how he felt, what he thought about as he lay with the wind blowing and the ice hissing around him. 'Do you miss me?' 'Of course I do.' That was as far as it went. The telephone calls proved he was alive, but told her little about his state of mind. She talked, gossiped about their friends and families, told him details about her daily routine – she thought he would like it, that it would make him feel closer to her, but perhaps she was wrong – and he told her very little. She had always assumed that it was because there was not much to tell, or at any rate not much he could tell without worrying her. Perhaps she had been wrong.

When they first knew each other it had been she, not Chris, who was his nanny. As his PR representative she had to look after him, had to make allowances for him, had to stand back and let him take the floor. That had been part of the job. But it was also the way she was. For all her aggression and know-how in her business, she was old-fashioned in her attitude to men. 'But I've always liked that about myself. I've always thought that kept me sane, different from all those crazy women in sharp suits who want to rule the world. PR is just another way of looking after people, isn't it?'

The water was cooling. She pulled out the plug and lay in the bath as the water swirled away beneath her. Had it felt like that for John? Had he felt the suction of the water beneath him? Felt it slip away from him? Or had he been too cold, too frightened, to feel anything?

Wrapping herself in a huge white towel, Penny tried to feel something herself. Sorrow, fear, love. Where had it all gone? All she felt was a detached interest in her lack of emotion and a longing for a cigarette.

The shrilling of the telephone interrupted her. 'Good thing, really, I'm getting silly,' she muttered to herself, as she picked up the receiver. 'Hello?'

'Hello – Mrs Brunel? This is Sheena Vickery, I'm ringing from the *Daily Express*. I am *so* sorry about your husband's accident.'

'Are you really?' Penny asked coolly. 'Well, thank you.'

There was a brief pause. 'Yes, well. Of course it must be a horrible shock for you. I understand that you represent him, and I wondered if you had anything you'd like to tell us about his return.'

'You're out of date, Miss Vickery. I don't represent him any longer, and no, I have nothing to say about his return.' She drew a breath, forced herself to slow down. She of all people should know not to antagonise the press. 'I'm sorry, I don't mean to be rude. I'm a little shocked, I'm sure you understand. I have no firm news at the moment, and if you don't mind I'd like to keep the line clear. Let me give you the number of the ops office; Chris Bellew's in charge and I'm sure he'd be delighted to talk to you.' She rattled off the number, sweet-talked the journalist a little more in the hope of forgiveness (knowing it was not Miss Vickery but John who should forgive her) and tried to hang up.

'One other thing, Mrs Brunel. I wonder – would you be interested in being interviewed for us? I think yours is a very interesting story, would reach out to our women readers ... you know, the woman left at home waiting, how you pass your time, your relationship with your husband, what you think about his putting himself in danger ... that sort of thing. And then maybe we could do pictures of you meeting him, perhaps with the kids?'

If there had been any hesitation, the last decided her. 'Miss Vickery, I don't wish to tell you how to do your job but I suggest that at the very least you do your homework before you approach your next subject, or victim. I pass my time with work and friends, I think about much the same sort of things as any other woman, my relationship with my husband is entirely our affair and he puts himself in no unnecessary danger. I have no "kids". I am sorry, but that is as much of an interview as you will ever get from me. If you need to know any more about John's trip and his return, ring the number I gave you. As I said, I want to keep the line clear. Thank you for your interest. Goodbye.'

She dressed quickly, surprised to find her hands shaking as she did up the zip at the side of her dress. Why should she talk to some strange woman about her relationship with her husband? For the titillation of a lot of bored housewives who fancied John from afar? If she wanted to talk to someone she would talk to her friends. 'Well, I wouldn't, would I?, but I would if I were a talker,' she said, to her reflection, as she brushed her hair, put on some makeup, tried to paint herself back into herself. 'Does some idiotic woman, some half-wit with a degree in journalism from some technical college in Bournemouth, think she can trick me out? Can find out stuff about me that no one knows?' She liked the sound of her voice raging against the absent woman, the voice on the telephone. She was filled with anger, and thankful to have an object at which it could be directed.

Chapter Eight

Herbie's hands were shaking as he pushed the letter back into its envelope. He laid it neatly on the centre of his blotter and looked at it thoughtfully. He supposed its contents had not come completely out of the blue, but he had pushed any thought of decision-making to the back of his mind. Until now. And there it was. In black and white, the words still stark in front of his mind's eye even though their treacherous import was safely hidden by the crisp white of the envelope.

He knew already what he was going to do, of course. Maybe that was why he had been able to ignore the question so effectively for the past few months, ever since the feelers had first been put out in his direction. It was just a question of how he was going to tell Christine.

Herbie had worked for Parkhouse and Langabeer PR (originally just Parkhouse PR, of course) for ninety per cent of his career, and had been the managing director for the last ten years. PR was a young man's business, he knew that, and he, at fifty-one, was no longer a young man. In fact, he was already significantly older than most of his peers in the public-relations world. He knew that others in the firm — notably young Bruce, who had only been with them for three years — were looking at him in a pitying way, waiting for him to leave, give up his fat salary and control of the company in favour of someone else. He knew, too, that most of them feared that because of the family connection he would hold on to the job to the bitter end, until with increasing incompetence and old-fashioned ideas he had run it into the ground. One of the reasons for him to leave was that if he did not the firm would be likely to lose some of the younger, more thrusting account-holders to other firms.

The other reason to leave was inside the envelope. Communications director to the largest of the privatised rail companies, one with huge amounts of money behind it but a terrible record of lateness and cancellations. The job would be an enormous challenge, which he welcomed. He did not feel old yet — not mentally old, anyway. Emotionally old, yes. But not mentally. He was sure he could do this job well, would love having one enormous project rather than a turnover of one-offs.

And, of course, there was the salary. He had never dreamed he could earn so much money honestly. That might mollify Christine, of course. She could go on that cruise she had been talking about. Take a friend, maybe — he was not sure he wanted to go and, anyway, he would be too busy. She could spend some money on the house. Not that she would want to. It was her museum to Mummy and Daddy, especially Daddy. How he wished he and Christine had a child who wanted to move into it so that they could buy a flat in St John's Wood, but he knew there was no hope of being allowed to move.

He wanted to accept the offer immediately but knew he should tell Christine first, make her understand that really he had no choice. He dreaded that conversation more than he could have imagined possible, and knew that he should get it over with as soon as he could. He knew his weakness was cowardice, moral if not physical. Sometimes, deep in the night, he knew that if he had been a braver man he would have left his wife years ago, but he could not bear to hurt people's feelings, even though his were hurt daily by the emotional emptiness of his life. He sighed, buzzed for his secretary, asked her what his commitments were for the day. A couple of meetings with potential clients in the morning, then nothing until the fortnightly house meeting at four. No excuse not to go home in the middle of the day, have lunch with his wife, break it to her then.

'I'll be out of the office in the middle of the day, Dawn,' he said. 'I think I said I'd have a sandwich with Penny at lunchtime, she wanted to talk over the MacLaing account with me before the meeting, but will you tell her I've had to go out? I'll see her at three thirty, if she wants. Apologise to her.'

'Oh, Mr Langabeer, I don't know if she'll be coming in. Haven't you heard?'

'Heard? Heard what?'

'It was on the radio this morning. Her husband has fallen through the ice on his way to wherever he's going this time. They don't know where he is, or something. I couldn't quite follow the story, I didn't realise it was him until half-way through. Anyway, it sounds bad.'

Dawn, a middle-aged woman with an overdeveloped bosom and overdyed hair, spoke with the triumph of someone who has predicted disaster for years. Herbie hoped that Penny would manage to avoid her.

'Oh, Lord, how awful. Has she rung in?' he asked.

'No, but you wouldn't expect her to, would you? I told Giovanna to cancel her appointments, but she won't until she hears from Penny herself. I don't know why she wouldn't take my word for it.'

Herbie's heart sank. He knew he was being selfish, but he did wish that either John had fallen through the ice or he had received confirmation of the job offer on a different day. The idea of the personal assistants engaged in their own power struggle today was almost more than he could face.

'Perhaps she didn't take your word for it because she knew that I would come to work.' Dawn jumped and turned to the door where Penny, pale-faced but otherwise just as normal, stood watching her with an icy expression. 'Oh, Penny, I'm sorry, I didn't mean ...'

'I'm sure you didn't. Could I have a word, Herbie?'

Herbie stood up, his face crumpling with concern so that Penny almost felt she should be comforting him. 'Of course, Penny. Dawn ...'

'Yes, Mr Langabeer. Penny, I'm so sorry about Mr Brunel. If there's anything I can do ...'

Penny did not even grace Dawn with a look, and the older woman backed out of the room, muttering inanities.

'Penny, how awful. Dawn has just told me. Is he all right?'

Penny sighed, sat down in the chair opposite Herbie's and shook her head. 'I don't know. We think so. Chris is still waiting for news from Canada. There's nothing I could do except wait too, so I thought I'd come in. I hope you don't mind.'

'Don't be ridiculous. But, of course, if you need to, go at any time. Giovanna can rearrange your meetings.'

Penny smiled wanly. 'She's a good girl. I must admit I don't know how you stand Dawn. I know she means well, but she drives me mad.'

'I'm not at all sure she does mean well.' Herbie was as

surprised to find himself realising that truth as Penny was to hear him say it. 'But she's the kind of woman I know how to deal with.' Penny thought of Christine, and Herbie struggled to correct himself. 'In offices, you know. They've always been around. I would feel much less at ease with one of those young, thin, fashionable secretaries that other people seem to have. I suppose that's why Bruce thinks I'm too old for the job.'

'Does he?'

'You must know he does. He's good, Bruce, works hard, pulls in the clients, delivers the goods. But he thinks the difference between us is age, and I know it's not just that. It's that Bruce, for all his well-cut suits and public-school education, is not quite, well, not quite ...'

'A gentleman,' Penny finished for him.

'Well, that sounds a bit old-fashioned but, yes, I suppose that is what I mean. Oh, Lord, Penny, I'm sorry. You don't want to talk about Bruce. I wish I could do something for you, something practical.'

'Herbie, you're an angel but there's nothing anyone can do. In fact, talking to you about Bruce is about as good a therapy as anything. When you can't do anything about your own troubles you might as well listen to other people's.'

'Do you mean that?' Herbie eyed the envelope, which seemed to have grown in size as they were talking. It sat there on his desk, always on the edge of his vision, dominating his thoughts, and he wished he could ask someone's advice. Here was Penny, dark eyes huge in her pale face, hands fidgeting (she must be longing for a cigarette), saying she would like to listen to someone else's troubles.

'There's something hanging over me somewhat,' he confessed. 'I know I can trust you.' It was more of a question than a statement, and Penny gave him a brief nod of encouragement. 'I have to go home at lunchtime today, to see Christine.'

'Herbie, I—'

'Oh, no, no, it's all right, I'm not going to talk to you about her, at least not like that. No, it's work.'

Penny sat back again. She did not think she could have borne to discuss the state of someone else's marriage, not when she was so confused about herself, about her hero . . . To think that Herbie had once been Christine's hero, she thought, looking at her boss's puzzled face. Maybe his kindness had been heroism enough for her. It was a comforting thought.

She listened as Herbie, hesitantly at first then with more and more confidence, told her about the job offer, about how he was going to take it – but how should he break it to Christine, what should he do about the company, should he sell, should he become non-executive director?, how he wished he had some plan before he faced his wife. Penny, listening to him, nodding, commenting, being soothing just by being there, wondered again about his marriage. What must it be like to be married to a woman who held the purse strings, who in a sense was his employer but who took no interest in the company that made up so much of her life? Could their marriage be an equal partnership? Was any marriage? Hers and John's, she supposed. But for the first time she realised she was only supposing: she did not really know.

'I'm sorry, Penny, I've gone on too long. Thank you.'

'I haven't given you any answers.'

'I didn't expect you to. I think I needed to practise my speech before I talked to Christine. You're a good listener.'

'Am I?' Penny was pleased. She had always thought of herself as the talker, John as the listener. That had been one of the things that had first attracted her to him, his silence, his essential stillness.

'You are. Oh, heavens, look at the time. I've a meeting in ten minutes, I must look at the file. You won't say anything to anyone, will you?'

'Of course not. I'll wait for an announcement. Good luck with Christine. She may surprise you, may be delighted. Perhaps she'll want to become more involved with the company if you leave it. Well, no, maybe not. But, Herbie, congratulations. It's a wonderful job. Don't lose sight of that as the heavens break over you, will you?' On impulse she leaned across the desk and kissed his cheek.

As she left the room, she turned and smiled at Herbie, who was still wearing his puzzled look. 'And don't worry about Bruce. I can deal with him. I'll rather enjoy it.'

After a lot of thought – his mind had been entirely elsewhere during his two meetings that morning – Herbie decided to play the whole thing as a huge celebration. He was not sure it would wash with Christine, but any sourness on her part would put her in the wrong. If he came in looking apologetic he would be handing her a weapon before she even knew what ammunition she had.

So he opened his front door with a cheery shout, a bottle of Bollinger in his hand. It had not occurred to him that Christine might not like to be surprised, that this was the first time in all their marriage that he had ever come home unexpectedly, that for a woman who thrived – or perhaps just survived – on routine his return would be enough of a shock for one day.

Automatically he turned into the sitting room. The curtains were drawn, the room smelt stale, of last night's whisky. For a moment he was surprised not to find Christine sitting on the chintz sofa, looking at the space where he would shortly appear. But of course not: it was twelve thirty, not six thirty. Maybe she was out to lunch. Or shopping. He should have rung after all.

He wandered through to the kitchen, surprised to find the breakfast things still stacked on the side, post scattered across the table, a half-drunk cup of coffee cooling. The cup was skew-whiff on the saucer, a disgusting layer of skin collecting over its lip. Herbie felt suddenly sick. He put the champagne into the fridge, feeling a little foolish. Where on earth was his wife? Why was the house so messy?

'Christine?' he called again, less cheery this time, even less confident of a welcome. He thought he heard movement upstairs and stood still, head cocked like a spaniel concentrating on a pheasant. 'Christine?' But this time it was almost a whisper.

A picture flashed across his mind. Christine, frilly nightdress rucked up, one large pale breast exposed, white legs akimbo, arms flung wide (Christine had never been a toucher, had never once held him as he made love to her. Why had he suddenly realised that, after all these years? Why *had* her hands remained so resolutely her own, like a tart's lips?), some strange man's hands holding her face as he— Was Christine upstairs with a man? Could she, after all, surprise him? He was frozen for a minute, but knew he had to find out, had to go upstairs and see for himself.

He did not creep, nor did he stamp. With measured tread he climbed the stairs, paused outside their bedroom door then opened it. And, no, Christine was not in bed with a man. She was lying almost as he had imagined her – frilly nightdress creased around her, arms flung wide, the breast mercifully covered, but alone, snoring slightly, mouth open, the room in semi-darkness.

Herbie was disappointed. His first, sharp emotion was not of relief but of regret. A man would have given him a way out of this house, out of this marriage. He could have begun a new life today. Instead he had to face Christine, find out why she was asleep in a filthy house in the middle of the day, tell her that eleven years after Daddy's death he had had enough of being in Daddy's shadow and was finally preparing to be his own man.

He sat on the bed and watched her. He wondered how he had let her down so far. Perhaps he had just cut off from her too soon. He remembered her when he had first seen her, pretty, shy, unsure of herself. She had been at a drinks party given by her father when Herbie had joined the firm. 'We're like a family,' old man Parkhouse would always insist. 'Families welcome new members with a party, and so do we. You must meet everyone straight away.' And there at the party was his daughter, his only child, ignored by everyone else including him, hovering around the edges of her father's sitting room, not even allowed to pass round the canapés as waitresses had been hired for that purpose. Her mother, laughing, bold, beautiful in a brittle, social, heartless way, had held the floor, introducing Herbie to his new colleagues and their wives, who had all indeed been friendly and welcoming and made him feel that perhaps he was joining a family with whom he could be happy. And all the time he had been conscious of the pretty girl in the corner, quietly talking to a friend at one moment, mostly just watching and looking as though she wished she were elsewhere.

He managed to make his way across the room to her. 'Hello, I'm Herbie Langabeer. You must be Christine Parkhouse. Your father talks about you a lot. I'm glad to meet you.'

She had looked up at him, ignoring his outstretched hand,

and although she smiled at him it seemed to him that she was on the verge of tears. 'Hello. Daddy said he was very pleased with you, too. Glad you've joined the firm, he meant.'

'Do you work there?' he asked, immediately aware that the question must give away that her father had in fact barely mentioned her.

'No. I did for a little while. Daddy was encouraging, but I'm not sure I was very good at it. I'm not really sure what I'm good at, to be honest.' Her eyes looked up at him, so blue and so confiding. 'I'm going to do a cordon bleu cookery course. I think that'll be fun. Then Daddy says we'll see.'

Had it been her look of gratitude that had pierced his heart, that had led them to be engaged within a year, before the end of the cordon bleu course? Had it been a relief to see one person in the room who was not showing off, not trying to make an impression, trying simply to be?

Looking at his wife, a fine thread of spittle hanging from her lower lip, her still blue eyes shrouded by the thinning lids, the discontent visible in the puckers between her brows, Herbie felt only pity. At least he had his outside life, his job, his friends, his music. She had nothing except bridge and dinner parties. No wonder she crept back to bed when he was gone. No wonder he could not walk away from her. The neediness that so encroached upon him now was the very thing that had drawn him to her originally. She had not sinned, had not changed. He had only himself to blame.

'Christine. Christine.' He was gentle. The pity would not last, but for now at least the kindness was as felt as it had been twenty-one years ago, downstairs in this same house. 'Wake up, sweetheart.'

She stirred, 'Herbie?' and sat up, looked at her watch, at him, quickly around the room, and he was shocked to see fear in her eyes. 'Herbie? What are you doing at home? Is everything all right? I'm sorry, I felt a little ill ... What's the matter?'

To his shame, he felt his irritation return. He stood up, walked to the bathroom, turned on the bath taps. 'Have a bath and get dressed. I'll wait for you downstairs.'

In the kitchen he looked at the dirty cups and plates before deciding it was not up to him to do anything about them. Instead he took the champagne and a couple of glasses into the sitting room, where he drew the curtains, opened the windows, even plumped the sofa cushions. Then he poured himself a glass of champagne and sat down to wait.

Chapter Nine

By the end of the day, the worst of the waiting was over. John had been reached, had been picked up, had been checked for physical damage, had been given new supplies and had been put back on the ice. A link was to be set up that night so that Penny would be able to talk to him. She was half relieved that the expedition was to continue and half furious. For the first time it occurred to her that John's single-mindedness was as much born of selfishness as of bravery. Chris had offered to be there with her when John rang, but she had turned him down.

'What you could do, if you want to help, is keep Terence with you,' she had said. 'Invent something for him to do, keep him out of the house until after I've talked to John. Is that all right?'

'Of course it is. I'll take him out for a drink. Do you mind?'

'Mind? No, why should I?' She did not notice Chris's brief moment of discomfort: only later, replaying the scene in her head, did she pick up on it, but maybe by then she was superimposing her knowledge on to the past. At the time she was concerned only to talk to John without being watched by

Terence. She did not want Terence to pick up the telephone, did not want him to talk to his father first. Did not, if she were honest, want him to talk to his father at all. Not yet, anyway. Not until she had brooded a little more on her new uncertainties.

At seven o'clock, hair brushed, pale pink lipstick in place, John's favourite Chanel scent sprayed on her neck, she sat waiting in North Kensington for the call from the far north of the globe. The irony of it was not lost upon her; nor was the fear that, once again, this link would be no link, no substance, just echo.

'Oh, God, what's wrong with me?' she said, and despite her good intentions fetched herself a glass, ice, lemon, gin, tonic. 'Everything was going swimmingly, everything was fine. What went wrong?' And into her mind came a picture of Terence, leaning against the door-jamb, his good-looking face twisted with an inner meanness she did not understand.

'Why does he look at me like that? I've only ever tried to be kind to him,' she muttered, and despised herself for the self-pity she heard in her voice.

For the fiftieth time that day she longed for a cigarette. Well, John would be pleased she'd given up. That was something.

At last. The telephone. 'I remembered to switch it on,' she said, and stood, looking at it, unable for a moment to pick it up. Then, 'Hello?' She heard herself echo back, unsure, unwelcoming. What was the matter?

'Penny? It's John. Don't sound worried, it's all right.' He sounded jubilant, almost laughing. 'What a bloody fool, eh? Little Johnny Head-in-Air. I said I'd never do it. Well, that taught me.' He paused, must have heard his own echo, must have heard the fizz, but no answering voice. 'Penny? Are you there?'

'Yes.' Her voice was a croak. Could he feel her disloyalty? 'Are you all right?'

'Of course. Didn't Chris talk to you? I'm fine. I got myself out pretty damn sharpish, I can tell you. To be honest I felt the ice going under me, managed to fall sideways so I didn't go right in. I was out too quickly for it to go through more than the outer layer. Honestly, I hardly felt a thing.'

'Were you frightened?' That was against the rules. She was never meant to ask him questions like that, just make jokes about bloody polar bears and/or penguins. But suddenly she had to know.

For a moment she thought the link was broken. Then, 'Well, yes, for a minute or two I was. After I'd hauled myself out I just sat on the ice and wished I had some chocolate. Even some whisky. And then when I found out I'd lost radio contact − I just hoped they'd notice I'd gone quiet.'

'I was frightened, John.' And, yes, she had been. But had it been for him, or for herself? She remembered waking that morning, remembered the spiralling into consciousness. Yes, her immediate fear had been for John, for his actual life. But she also remembered − although she wished she did not − the long, luxurious bath, the hoping that John was safe but that he would not come back.

'Are you coming home?' she asked, knowing the answer as she spoke.

'Of course. I always do, don't I?'

'You know what I mean.' What was he doing, joking? She was meant to be the joker in the family. What was he hiding? 'What's going on?'

She had not meant to ask the question, but he took her concern to be with the immediate, the particular, nothing wider.

'I'm going on with the walk, Penny. It would be madness not to. There's all that money, all that sponsorship. It will take too long to set up the whole thing again. I promise you, I'm safe, and I'll look where I'm walking.'

'It's got to stop.' She had never thought she would hear herself say those words, was not even sure she meant them.

'Stop?'

'This – ice-walking. We've got to start real life.'

'Penny. This is real life. This is my real life, and yours. You know that.'

Her hands clenched on her glass. 'I've given up smoking,' she said, to stop herself saying anything else.

'Good, well done. You are brave,' he said, with no apparent irony. 'Penny—'

'No, not now. Of course not now. I'm sorry. We'll talk when you get back. Watch where you're walking.'

'Of course. I love you.'

'Thank you,' she said, finding herself unable to answer, *I love you too.* 'Thank you. Good luck,' and she hung up as she heard him say goodbye.

She had meant to tell John about Terence's mission to find him, about his working in the ops room. She had meant to make him laugh about Chris shyly asking if he could take Tel out for a drink – they laughed at Chris behind his back, she hoped not unkindly, at his hero-worship of John. 'Well, he won't be able to hero-worship Tel, will he?' she had meant to say, laughing gently, mocking Terence and Chris at the same time. No one, after all, could hero-worship poor old Tel. But the conversation had not taken that turn, and, besides, something about Terence was beginning to make her uncomfortable. Not because of his mother's hints – every bone in her flirtatious body told her she was safe from any unwanted attention from her stepson – but because of something else. That picture of him watching her came into her mind again. 'If he's not careful I'll give him something to watch,' she said, pouring herself another drink and wondering whether to give in to an evening of *Men Behaving Badly* or to have another long, hot bath.

The telephone rang again, breaking into her thoughts. She wished she could turn it off more often.

'Hello?'

'Penny, it's Beth. I've just seen the news. Is everything all right?'

'Beth, thanks for calling. Yes, it's fine. I've just talked to him.'

'And are you all right?'

'Of course.'

'Of course. You always are.' Was she admiring or mocking? It was hard to tell.

'I think I'm a bit jumpy, though. It doesn't help that I've given up smoking.'

'Oh, you poor thing. Look, would you like me to come round? Or shall we go out somewhere? Is Terence there?'

'No, he's not back yet. I suppose he will be soon, though. Don't worry about me.'

'I'm not worried. I'd love to see you. Come on, there's no point you sitting on your own there and me sitting on my own here. I could do with some company myself.'

'Are you sure?' Penny was touched, surprised that Beth sounded so eager, but ready to be swayed. Beth was right: what was the point of drinking alone? Suddenly she felt ravenously hungry and said, 'OK, yes, what the hell? Let's go and eat something. Delicious and expensive. On me. Oh, Lord, perhaps I should let Tel know where we are—'

'Don't.' Why did Beth sound so keen? A week before she

149

had been desperate to see more of the handsome stepson. Beth must have heard the eagerness in her own voice and added, a shade more calmly, 'I'm having a bad-hair day. I don't want to have to make an effort. Come on, girlie night out. I want to talk to you.'

'All right.' She pushed down a faint feeling of guilt. Terence was not yet home, he was having a nice time out with Chris, he did not need her. Or, if he did, he should have told her so. She told Beth where they should meet, and hung up. It had been a rough day. She would enjoy some good food and wine, and the company of her friend.

Considering that she was officially the one in need of comforting, Penny found herself spending a lot of time that evening reassuring Beth, who was discontented with her life. She wanted a new job, and a lover. 'I mean, honestly, I'm too old to use the word boyfriend and I haven't even got one.'

'Yes, but "lover" sounds as though it's someone else's husband.'

'It probably will be. You know my luck. Oh, don't worry, not yours, but some other sad woman who thinks everything in her garden is rosy.'

'Other?'

'You know what I mean.'

'Yes, I suppose I do.'

As though remembering her duty, Beth looked more closely at Penny. 'Is your garden rosy? Apart from your husband falling through the ice, that is.'

Penny fiddled with the stem of her wine-glass. She hated talking about herself, yet had been a little irritated that her friend had only told of her own troubles, not asked after hers.

And yet now that Beth was asking, she felt the old barriers go up. She shrugged. 'Yes, it's all right. I get a bit fed up sometimes, but who doesn't?'

'And Tel?'

Penny tried to laugh. 'You're not still after him, are you?'

'No. You were right. He's too young. And there's something about him ... I don't know. It's odd that he can look so like John yet *feel* so different. Do you know what I mean?'

'Yes. I think it's that he's unhappy. Or unfulfilled or something. You can't say that about John.'

'And you? Are you fulfilled?'

Penny looked up sharply. It was unlike Beth to try to dig beyond the outer layers. Penny had often thought of her as all surface, and with no depth of her own she showed no interest in other people's. Perhaps she was wrong. 'I suppose so.'

'Which usually means no.'

'Oh, you know what it's like. Something like this – like John's accident – it always makes you brood a bit when the danger's over. You see the possibility of a huge change, and it frightens you.' She did not add that when the possibility was gone, you realised that maybe you did want some change, that it might not be so frightening after all. Not John's death – never that – but something, some sort of shake-up. 'Are you going to have a pudding?'

Beth shook her head, then changed her mind. 'Oh, why not? Lemon tart, please. So you do or you don't want a change?'

'I don't know. There's no point in change for change's sake.'

'Oh, yes, there is!' Beth was emphatic. 'Do you know, I sometimes think that if I have to look at one more fashion spread I'll blow my brains out. I never thought I could be bored of clothes, but the idea of spending the rest of my life writing about the length of hemlines and the shape of white shirts drives me to despair. I want another job and I don't care what it is. News, maybe, or feature-writing. Anything – even women's features – but not fashion. And definitely not beauty.'

Penny laughed. 'Then it's not change for change's sake. What are you doing about it? Are you putting out feelers?'

Something changed. Beth faltered, could not quite meet Penny's eye. 'Oh, I don't know. Something will come up. It usually does if you're greedy enough. Talking of which, where is that tart?'

Christine did not know if the tranquillisers or the champagne had been responsible for the rather agreeable feeling of blankness that had overtaken her after Herbie's abrupt departure. In any event, the house-tidying had passed in a blur, and by the time he came home from his office she was ready as usual, sitting in the pretty chintz chair, holding a magazine, waiting for her gin.

Herbie had been expecting something different – to find her back in bed or maybe not in the house at all. But he had reckoned without his wife's blind adherence to routine. His heart sank when he put his head round the sitting-room door and saw her sitting so still, so expectantly. Well, if she was hoping he had changed his mind she was to be disappointed.

The scene at lunchtime had been dreadful. Christine had appeared downstairs half an hour after him, in fairly good order. To anyone else the smile would have seemed warm, the cheerful welcome artless. But he had seen the stupefied sleep upstairs, seen the filth surrounding her, and he knew what an effort this renewed patina of appearances had cost her. It aroused no tenderness in him, though, only curiosity and a faint disgust.

And so he poured her champagne, told her his news and

waited for her reaction. Christine did everything slowly, so it did not surprise him that it took five minutes or so for the news to sink in. He had expected her to moan and weep and reason in the gentle voice that brooked no contradiction. He had not expected the hysteria that overwhelmed her. 'So what was it all for? All Daddy's hard work – all yours, come to that. My sitting here waiting to entertain your important clients but only ever being brought your friends. Or your colleagues. It's the Mirabelle for the big clients and home for the little ones, the ones that don't matter, because I was going to let you down, wasn't I? I had nothing to say, just a housewife, waiting at home with the dinner night after night? I suppose you wish I was different, had some kind of career, something to talk about. And now you know how I spend my days, but what does it matter? I've always kept my side of the bargain. Everything's always been ready for you, hasn't it? You have no right to complain.'

'I never have complained.'

'Oh, not aloud, I know that. But in your heart. Don't you see? I never pretended to be any different. I was never going to have a career. I had one laid on for me, and I didn't want it. I wanted to be a wife, and a – and a – carer. That's what I thought I was promising to be. You knew what you were getting. But it wasn't bloody enough, was it?'

He realised with a shock that he had never before heard her swear, barely heard her raise her voice. 'Christine—'

'Christine nothing. You can't do it. I – I *forbid* you to leave Parkhouse and Langabeer. It's what it's all been for all these years. So we could pass it on.'

'To whom? Who are you planning to pass it on to? Christine, we have no children, no relations. *There is no one.*'

'There will be!' The look in her eye frightened him.

'Christine, there won't be. You must know that. We've been

married twenty years and there's been no baby. Now you're forty years old – it's less likely every day.' And we have not made love for two years, he wanted to add, but could not bring himself to be so cruel.

As always she skirted round the hateful truth, veered off in another direction. 'Anyway, you can't sell. It's mine. You can't sell. I won't let you. And I won't let you leave either. What do you mean, it's a good job? You've got a good job.'

'With, as you make abundantly clear, my wife as my employer.' Never mind that in fact he held thirty-nine per cent of the shares to her forty-one, with Penny and Bruce, the other two partners, holding ten per cent each. There was no point in telling her that. To her it was Daddy's company, her company and always would be.

She gasped and looked him straight in the eye. 'How dare you?'

Herbie felt a rush of adrenaline. What heaven it was to argue, to shout, to stop being polite. Why was this the first time it had happened?

He stood up, refilled her glass (he could not help having good manners, perhaps that was his undoing) and said, very calmly for someone who had just discovered the joys of confrontation, 'Well, as you are my employer, I would like to hand in my notice. I've been offered a better job. I will, of course, formalise this notice in writing and will remain with Parkhouse and Langabeer for two months, or until you appoint someone to take over from me.'

It had been a mistake to fill her glass. She hurled it at his head with a strength that surprised them both. The stem clipped his temple and the glass smashed on the door behind him, spraying the champagne in a wide arc as it broke. 'And I suppose you want that bitch Penny Brunel to take over from you!' she shrieked.

'This is what it's all about, isn't it? You know it's the only way she can get promotion – give her your job. This is just another way of being kind, isn't it? Oh, you and your kindness. I've had enough of it. I saw the way you looked at her when she came to dinner, saw how eagerly you went off to her birthday party. You couldn't even pretend to be sorry I wasn't going, could you? And it's not as though you never see her. You're with her day after day, staring at her with those hangdog eyes. Well, she didn't even look at you. She took more interest in that fairy from the fashion-house you insisted on inviting along than she did in you. At least he made her laugh! Well, she can't have your job. Not if I have any say left. Anyone rather than her. How could you trust her to run a company? She can't even run a house. Can't even keep her own husband at home. So she's not that clever, is she? I may not be clever enough to run a company either, but I'm clever enough to stay at home where I belong and to keep my husband there too. That's more than she's ever managed.'

Herbie was not even sure if Christine was aware of him leaving the house. As he closed the front door behind him, he heard her screams following him. Well, she could scream all she wanted. He may not be man enough to walk out on the marriage, still could not bear to hurt her any more than she had already been hurt, but nothing was going to stop him leaving the company. At the very thought of it his spine straightened, his shoulders went back, his chin was raised. He even smiled at a passer-by whose glance met his and who smiled back in some surprise.

Yes, he would leave Parkhouse and Langabeer. He would be free.

Or so he had thought as he slammed the heavy door of his BMW at a quarter to three. At six thirty, seeing the ice and lemon laid out as usual, he was not so sure.

✳   ✳   ✳

This time the bad news came not via the wireless, but from Terence. His crisis seemed to be over. Chris had talked him into staying, he was taking calls, handling the press, reassuring the sponsors. He had written a press release that trod a careful line between hard fact and optimistic cheerfulness. Chris told Penny that Terence was genuinely useful, and Terence seemed more relaxed in his new rôle, less watchful, cleaner even.

Until the morning, two days after John's accident, when he marched into Penny's bedroom without knocking at half past seven and threw the *Daily Express* down on to her bed. 'What the fuck are you playing at?' he shouted, spraying spit at her in his rage. His mouth was so twisted, his face so engorged with rage that she put her hands up, frightened for one mad moment that he was going to hit her.

'What do you mean? What have I done?' She sat up in bed, wishing her dressing-gown was within reach. Half asleep still, she felt at a terrible disadvantage lying in her bed with this monstrous anger blowing around her.

'Done? You've really done it, really betrayed him this time, putting your sordid little secrets out for everyone to read about! How much did they pay you? Or did you do it just for the hell of it?'

'Do what? Terence, honestly, I—'

Perhaps he believed her ignorance, for he calmed down briefly, picked up the newspaper again, turned to an inner page and pushed it back at her. 'Read this, then, and tell me you didn't have any part in it.'

Penny sat up straighter, picked up the paper. As she read the headline her hands began to shake.

*   *   *

HERO'S WIFE WANTS CHANGE
When the ice-walking has to stop

'What the . . . ?' she gasped, giving Terence a quick look. She went back to the page.

> On Wednesday, a nation woke to hear that John Brunel, one of the last remaining great English heroes, had fallen through the ice on his latest adventure. Brunel has conquered areas of the ice-caps that make even polar bears nervous, but it looked for a moment as though his story might finally be over. On this attempt to walk alone to the North Pole Brunel has met with the usual share of adventures, but details of the dangers overcome are never released until he is safely home. Why? Not to protect the feelings of the millions of housewives to whom he is a heart-throb almost as great as the singer Daniel O'Donnell, but because, safely in England, guarding the home fires, are his wife, Penelope, and cat, Spindleshanks.

'What the hell is this?' she asked. 'Daniel O'Donnell? What are they on about? Does Chris know about this?'

'Go on,' Terence said. He was calmer now, his face grim rather than livid. As she read he paced the room, but kept his eyes fixed on her face. 'It gets worse.'

Penelope is a successful career woman in her own right, the only female partner in the PR firm Parkhouse and Langabeer, one of the oldest firms in the business. She is in fact credited with discovering John Brunel and taking him from his lonely life as an explorer to the heights of his television celebrity. But now she has had enough. She has told friends that she is thinking about starting a family, and perhaps because of this her reaction on hearing that John had met with an accident was one more of rage than of concern.

'He is lucky enough to be fulfilled, now it is my turn,' she says. Hers is, of course, a problem as old as the feminist revolution, that of balancing career with that old biological clock, but with her husband so far away from home her well-appointed Notting Hill house feels a little empty in the evenings. 'Why should I always have to drink alone?' she asks.

And so it went on. A whole page of drivel. Speculative, impertinent, inaccurate drivel. By Sheena Vickery, it said. Sheena Vickery. The woman to whom Penny had given the brush-off on the telephone. She had refused to be interviewed, yet this was presented as an interview. There was a photograph of her with John at their wedding, and another more recent one, taken at some press launch. No new one, of course. But the readers were not going to spot that. The piece looked for all the world like a proper interview, rather than something cobbled together from cuts and old press releases.

'But it's more than that, isn't it?' Penny looked up at Terence and spoke as though he could read her thoughts.

'What?'

'More than just a cuts job. Someone has talked to this woman.'

'Not you?'

'No, Terence, not me. Don't be ridiculous.'

'You know how to use the press.'

'Yes, I do. And this isn't how. What good could this conceivably do me or John or anyone? This woman rang and asked me for an interview. I refused. It was the morning of the accident, I was – I was all over the shop. I realised I was putting her back up, I tried to undo it. I obviously didn't succeed.'

He stood still and looked down at her. Doubt and belief chased each other across his face.

'Beth.'

'What?'

'Oh, my God, it was Beth.' She remembered joking to Beth about wanting a baby, remembered how eager Beth had suddenly been to talk to her about John. She had been set up by a Fleet Street pro and her old friend Beth, who had picked up the bill although Penny had paid for dinner. 'I'll get it on expenses,' she had said cheerfully, without actually offering to pay. Penny hated it when Beth did that, although she had been assured that all journalists did the same. It seemed to her that claiming on expenses was one thing, making money out of them another, and letting your friends pay then claiming the money was little less than stealing from your friends. As usual she had looked the other way as Beth pocketed the receipt. And this time it was almost a legitimate expense (or would have been had Beth bought dinner). Because Beth, greedy for Fleet Street and all it had to offer, had gone home and rung up an expectant Sheena Vickery and sold her friend for – how much? A couple of hundred pounds. If that. The story did not even have Beth's name on it.

Penny closed her eyes to force back the tears. She would not let Terence see her cry. But by God she was going to see Beth cry over this.

Chapter Ten

Penny nodded at Dawn, waved through the glass wall at Herbie, smiled at Giovanna and walked through her own glass door into the comparative privacy of her office. No one had yet said anything to her about the newspaper piece but, then, she had not given anyone a chance. She flicked the cord of the blinds and they tumbled full length with a clatter of plastic, shutting out the rest of the office and giving her an illusion of privacy. First of all she must ring Chris, although she supposed Terence was already at the office spitting venom. She sighed. It was time Terence left her house, but she was oddly reluctant to make him go. He was a part of John, after all, even if not the better part. Much as she hated his self-pity when he talked about his childhood, she did feel he had been treated shabbily and in John's absence she felt she owed him a roof over his head. Yet his being in the house every morning made her realise how much she enjoyed its emptiness when he was not there. Occasionally she had wished for the sounds of another human being when she woke, but having Terence there made her realise how little she needed anyone else. 'Except John,' she said quickly to herself. 'Of course, it's different when John's here.'

She rang Chris quickly, before she could begin thinking. She recognised Terence's voice answering the telephone and, for some reason, made a vague attempt to disguise her own. She had talked to Terence enough about the *Daily Express* for one morning. Her vague attempt at a northern accent cut no ice with her stepson, though. 'Penny? Hi, I'll put you through,' he said, remarkably calmly.

'Penny, how are you?'

As always Chris's voice, with its lingering traces of a Durham accent, immediately comforted her. 'Pretty cross, actually. I think it's one of my best friends who sold me down the river,' she said, and somehow just saying it made her feel better about the betrayal. In the end Beth had betrayed herself, after all, not Penny. Penny had done nothing wrong.

'Aye, well, don't worry about it. We've decided dignified silence is the best tack. The Vickery woman rang here this morning, looking for a follow-up, but obviously we didn't give anything away. Tel says it was some woman called Beth who made a play for him at a party you gave. Hell hath no fury, eh?'

'I think he flatters himself. She wants to move out of fashion journalism into newspapers. I suppose she just couldn't resist the opportunity.'

'Do you think it'll do her any good?'

Penny hesitated. 'Probably. Other journos love that sort of thing. They call it investigative but they mean immoral. I haven't decided yet how to deal with her. I think I'll leave her to sweat for a while. I don't think she's done this sort of thing before so she'll be feeling pretty terrible. It'll get easier for her, of course, every time she does it. But she'll feel bad about this one for the rest of her life. At least, I hope she will. I don't think she's bad enough to feel no shame.'

'Well, don't worry about it, pet. All I've done is issue a press release saying Mrs Brunel does not give interviews, not mentioning the *Express* by name. I think that's the best policy. And look on the bright side. John won't be reading it.'

'You'd be amazed. If there's bad news someone always manages to give it you. I can just see some passing polar bear saying in a sympathetic voice, "Awful that piece in the *Express*, wasn't it, John? Still, I'm sure they misquoted her." It'll probably just happen to have a copy under its arm, or wherever polar bears carry their newspapers.'

Chris chuckled. 'Well, I'm glad you're so chipper. Tel here is looking like a wet weekend. Are you two getting on all right?'

'Not now, Chris. It's a long story.' Now was not the moment to go into Terence's history, but that was not the only reason Penny hung back. Somehow it jarred that Chris should call Terence Tel. To her knowledge, she and John were the only people who ever used that nickname, and it felt wrong to hear it used by anyone else. Even Chris. Maybe especially Chris. She wondered quite what was going on there. 'Chris, I don't know if I've ever thanked you properly for taking Terence on,' she said suddenly. 'It's only been a few weeks, but he seems happier already. More confident.'

'No, I should be thanking you,' he said. 'He's a great lad. It's been good getting to know him. Anyway ... John's back on course, so we can all relax. It won't be long now.'

'Long until what?' Penny said to herself, as she hung up. Something was going to happen, she felt it in the air, but what?

She reached for her diary but the telephone rang immediately. 'Melzi on the line for you, Penny,' said Giovanna. 'He's been waiting a while – but he doesn't waste much time, does he?'

'What do you mean?'

'That he's the most outrageous flirt it's ever been my privilege to deal with. Nice enough, but we both knew he didn't mean a word of what he said. It's you he was waiting to talk to, after all.'

'So you're tired of the ice-walking?' came the voice with its undeniably seductive tones into her ear.

'Don't believe everything you read in the papers. You should know that as well as anyone.'

'I do, of course. But I must admit to being the tiniest bit disappointed.'

'Disappointed?'

'I was hoping the ice lady was melting, just the smallest bit, and maybe I could persuade you to come out to dinner with me. Business, of course.' Penny could not help but feel warmly towards him. But then she felt panic-stricken. Veysey – when was their date? In all the drama about John she had forgotten it. Had it been last night? She felt guilty, miserable, disappointed. He would not ask her again if she had stood him up. For once she did not even consider the implications it would have for their working relationship. She realised how much she wanted to see Veysey again. With one hand she reached for her diary and flicked through the pages. Tonight. The wave of relief that swept over her left her feeling almost nauseous. 'Thank heavens,' she muttered, and was brought back to earth by the sound of Melzi laughing again.

'Thank heavens? That it's business?'

'Oh, no, I'm sorry, I was wandering. I'm not – very pulled together at the moment.' She turned on the flustered-woman act, knew that it would wash well with Melzi: she was probably acting exactly as he expected – although there was more to him than that, wasn't there? He was not the stereotypical Italian man he played at being. She reminded herself that Melzi was as much an actor as she was, and wondered what he was really after.

'Mario, I'd love to. But I must say I don't know what you mean by "ice lady" – I think maybe I should take offence.'

'I wouldn't. I just liked my idea – the man with his heart full of passion walking across the ice for the woman he loves, the woman staying behind, an ice maiden, untouched by his heroism. I might write a novel about it one day.'

'Don't.' She knew he was teasing, but her voice was sharp. 'You can't write a novel about people you know.'

'Ah, but I don't know the ice-walker.'

'No, and you won't know me either if you start on that tack.'

'Then I'll be able to write the novel,' he said triumphantly, and she relented.

'All right, you win. Dinner? Why not? When?'

She felt quite reckless. Veysey tonight, Melzi next week. She was longing to tell Sarah about it and see her reaction. Meanwhile she must pull herself together and do some work.

'How could you do it?'

'I didn't. What, anyway?' Beth knew she had given the wrong answer. She had been rehearsing her response ever since she had said goodbye to Sheena Vickery, but it had made no difference. She had panicked, and given herself away.

Helen did not seem to have noticed, though. 'Didn't you?' She sounded uncertain for a moment. 'But, then, who did? Penny swears it was you.'

Beth thought quickly. Thank heavens her first self-justification had been over the telephone, so Helen could not see her. After this conversation was over she would at least be fluent in whichever line she chose to take. A pity it was Helen, though. There was something about Helen that wrung the truth out of one. 'Me who did what?' She would try the innocent for a little longer, but knew it would not wash, not entirely.

'You must have seen the *Express* this morning.' Helen sounded weary. 'A socking great piece about Penny, claiming to be an interview. Actually it's cleverer than that. It doesn't actually claim to be an interview, but it certainly implies that it is one. A lot of stuff about her sitting room, as though they were cosied up there together.'

'Who?'

'Her and this woman called Sheena Vickery.'

'Oh.'

'You do know her?'

'Yes. A bit.'

'And you haven't seen her piece? I thought you got all the papers at the office.'

'I do, but no, I haven't, not yet.' She had been avoiding them, dreading what she would read, wishing that she could undo what she had done. She sighed. Oh, shit.

'So there's this interview, all about Penny wanting babies and not wanting to drink on her own. It goes on about her handsome stepson living with her, in this really *suggestive*, almost smutty way. It says she's had enough of John travelling, wants him home. And all this stuff about her cat, you know, trying at one minute to paint a pathetic picture of a grass widow alone with her cat, some kind of Mrs Slocombe figure, then the next she's this cut-and-thrust aggressive superwoman with a toy-boy who just happens to be her stepson. It's awful, Beth, really dreadful.'

Beth could not trust her voice for a moment. It sounded worse than she had imagined. Then she made an effort. 'Would it sound bad to someone who didn't know Penny?' As though that would make it any better.

'Well, it wouldn't sound good. That it doesn't feel like Penny is one thing – you know how she never opens up to anyone, she'd hardly pick a *journalist* to start with, would she? It's more that it makes her sound like not a very nice person. And she is. I'll tell you what it sounds, it sounds really jealous, really resentful. I bet this Vickery woman fancies John something wicked. Or wishes she were as successful as Penny. I mean, being a feature writer on the *Express*, making up stories about people who are better than you, it's not much of a life, is it? Beth?'

'Yes?'

'Look, do you want to read the piece and ring me back?' She paused, suddenly remembered why she had rung Beth in the first place. 'Beth,' she said more calmly, climbing down from her high horse, 'you said you did know this Vickery woman.'

'Yes.'

'Oh, Beth, you didn't, did you? What on earth possessed you?' She had been so angry, but now there was sorrow in her voice, which was much harder for Beth to bear.

'I didn't mean to.' She sounded as miserable as she felt. 'I honestly didn't.'

'So what happened?'

'Sheena rang me, asked me out for a drink. I haven't seen her for a while. She was a junior here on the magazine – did ring-arounds, ran errands for people, the lowest, most starting-off sort of job. She made me laugh, we'd go out for lunch sometimes. She always said it was just a starting point. She's ambitious, she wants – oh, everything. You know, a column, to be a pundit, to be allowed to air her views. She never minded the crap she had to do at the magazine because she said it had a point, it was all part of her journey. In a way

I admired her. You know, I whined and moaned when things got dull. I worked hard, but beefed about it. And she was right. She got a job on the *Express*, more of the same stuff. Ringing Lionel Bloom and asking him whether he preferred Bovril or Marmite, ringing Chris Evans and Tara Palmer-Tomkinson and asking them if they've ever had affairs with their best friends, all the usual feature-writing crap that ties in with whatever film is making waves. But she got on with it. And in no time at all she was doing interviews. Now she does all the celebs. They know about her, they say hello to her at parties. Richard Young takes pictures of her arriving at openings now, not just of the people she's going to see.'

If she thought she was explaining herself well, Helen seemed unconvinced. 'So she's a journalist. For the *Express*. It's still pretty dim.'

'But it's *Fleet Street*. And OK, the *Express* isn't everything, but then it'll be the *Mail*, or the *Independent*. You know, it's all a ladder.'

'And you feel stuck on a different rung?'

'Yes. I was explaining to Penny the other day – oh, God, I'd better be careful, I don't want anyone to overhear. I don't want to lose this job until—'

'Until Sheena Vickery has fixed you up with another one?' Helen's voice was icy. 'And you really think she'll do that? On the strength of a few lunches some years ago and one betrayal of a friend?'

'It wasn't like that.' Beth heard herself, knew she sounded as defiant as a small child caught stealing the Bendicks' Bittermints. Now she wished this conversation was not happening over the telephone, felt that she would be able to justify herself better face to face.

'So what was it like? If you want Penny to forgive you you'd better start by explaining to me. I'm not sure she wants to see you much at the moment.'

'I don't blame her, if the piece is as bad as you say.'

'Even if it weren't, it might have been.'

It was typical Helen logic and Beth could not help but smile to herself.

'So?'

'So, Sheena rang me. She said that she wanted to do a piece on Penny and she thought I knew her. Would I help?'

'To which you said of course not, catch you later?'

'To which I said was she talking to Penny? and Sheena said they didn't want to disturb her because it was obviously a difficult time for her.'

'If you fell for that you're never going to make it as a journalist. Not the Sheena Vickery type, anyway.'

Beth ignored this. She did not like the truth in what Helen said, nor did she like her friend's acid tone. 'I told her to ring that man who's always hanging around when John's there. You know, the gay Geordie who runs his office.'

'Chris Bellew.'

'Yes. She said the line was constantly engaged and she wanted to start work on the piece straight away. Then she asked me out to lunch. That day.'

'Oh, Beth.'

'I know. And I went, and we talked about work, and I said how I wanted to get out of fashion-writing, and she said I could, she had. And she said she'd introduce me to her features editor, and then we got on to Penny, and she said it wouldn't do any harm, all she wanted was a bit of colour for her piece, and I don't know. Well, I do, it was a combination of being pleased that I *knew*. That I had something she wanted. It sounds pathetic . . . but, you know, she'd done so well but she still needed me. So maybe I was a bit indiscreet, telling her personal things like the name of the cat—'

'Come on, that couldn't matter.'

'Exactly, that's what I mean. I thought, how could that matter, but the conversation went on, and I suppose I said more than I should. I was showing off in a way. It's so easy to do, Helen, but you're not like that, you can't understand.'

There was silence, as though Helen was thinking about that, or trying to understand it. Then Beth, almost relieved at ridding herself of her guilt, went on, 'It gets worse. That evening I felt guilty, thought maybe I had said too much. So I rang Penny and asked how she was, suggested we went out for a meal. I felt sorry for her suddenly. And we did go out, I wanted to make it up to her, although she didn't know what I had done.'

'She told me she bought dinner.'

'She did, but that wasn't the point. Oh, Helen. I haven't told you the worst yet.'

'There's more?'

'Yes. Penny wound me up a bit that evening. I don't know why, she was just flashing her money around, and not listening to me. I tried to tell her, said I wanted to change my line of work, that I was greedy for more. She just wasn't *hearing* me, as the Americans say. I went home all disgruntled, probably my fault.'

'I expect it was yourself you weren't liking much,' Helen said calmly, and once again Beth resented her truth.

'It was not,' she said, stubborn as a child again. 'Anyway, Sheena rang me the next morning, saying she was trying to fix up a meeting with the features editor, when could I go in. And then she said she just wanted to check up a few facts for her piece on Penny.'

'Penny thinks you rang Sheena Vickery as soon as you got back from dinner. The dinner she had bought you.'

'I didn't! I wouldn't do that.' Beth was so grateful to have something to be indignant about that she could overlook her own guilt. For a moment, at least.

'So she rang you and then you really put the boot in.'

'No. But maybe I said a bit more. You know, I'd just spent the evening before with Penny, my mind was on her. Maybe I wasn't concentrating.'

'Beth, you're a disgrace.'

Now the confession was off her chest Beth felt much better. And with the easing of her guilt came an impulse of self-justification. 'I'm not. I don't believe a single thing I said could have harmed Penny. I don't know what spin Sheena put on it, but that's not my fault.'

'She couldn't have put a spin on anything she was ignorant of – like Terence living there.'

'Oh, for God's sake, Helen, don't go all pi on me. You've said yourself it's odd how long he's been hanging around Cambridge Gardens.'

'But I said it to you, my friend. Not to some journalist. Remind me not to tell you anything in future.'

'No one would be interested in you, anyway. You're just a North Kensington aromatherapist. Unless you marry someone famous, of course.'

There was total silence between them. Even Beth was amazed at how far she had gone. She drew a breath, preparing to apologise, but Helen was there before her. 'I was wrong. You will make a good journalist, if that's what Sheena Vickery is. Good luck in your new job, Beth. If you get it.'

And the line went dead with a little click. Beth put down the receiver and sat looking at it for a moment. 'Shit, shit, shit,' she muttered, under her breath.

'All right, Beth?' The beauty editor was looking at her with interest. 'Anything wrong?'

Beth shook her head.

'Good. Can you come and look at this spread on the new anti-cruelty makeup with me for a minute? I'm not sure we've got it right.'

'Yes, of course.' Beth pulled herself together. 'There's just something I must do and then I'll be with you. Just a minute.'

She watched the skinny woman's back as she made her way towards her office. Then, checking quickly that no one was watching her, she drew a piece of plain paper towards her, wrote her home address at the top in a neat hand and then, pausing only momentarily, wrote underneath:

To: Daily Express
Attn Sheena Vickery, Features

For, information Penny Brunel piece: £250
Expenses (receipts enclosed): dinner £75
taxis £15

payment now due
Beth Venables

She had done it, after all, so she might as well be paid.

Luckily Helen had a slot free that afternoon – it did not occur to Penny that Helen might have cancelled a client to make room for her friend: Penny never compromised her professionalism for friends. As the day had progressed Penny, nerves jangling over John and Beth and her forthcoming date, had felt less and less equipped to deal with an evening of flirting. 'Or whatever.' She muttered as she looked at her washed-out face in the mirror of the ladies' loo.

'Don't worry about it, dear, it's the strip-lighting, makes us all look ill.' Dawn, coming out of the cubicle behind her, had noticed Penny staring at herself. 'Doing something nice this evening?'

Penny flushed. She hated being seen to be vain, and hated the innuendo she sensed in Dawn's voice. 'I'm just a bit tired,' she said, ignoring the question. 'I've had a bad few days.'

'Oh, I know, it wasn't very nice that piece in the paper, was it? I'm surprised you talked to that Vickery woman. She sounded like a nasty piece of work.' Dawn was washing her hands vigorously, but her beady eyes were fixed on Penny's reflection. She paused, but when Penny gave no answer continued, 'Have we had any dealings with her before?'

'We still haven't,' Penny said, wishing Dawn was not there so she could put on some makeup.

'Oh? I thought—' Dawn faltered.

'Yes, well, you were wrong. Anyway, it doesn't really matter, does it? I know the truth.'

Dawn reached into her bag for a comb, teased at her rigid locks for a moment. 'I was only *asking*,' she said, sounding huffy. 'I only wanted to be *supportive*.'

'Thank you for that, Dawn. I thought you wanted some gossip to report back. I'm sorry I misjudged you.'

Penny made her escape, immediately regretting her lack of control. She put her head round Herbie's door. 'I'm sorry, I may have upset Dawn. I snapped her head off. I'll make it up to her later.'

Herbie rolled his eyes. 'Thanks for warning me. I was about to have a few words with her myself. I'll save them for tomorrow.

Don't worry about it, she's usually quite easy to calm down. Tell her her top suits her. That usually does the trick.'

Penny laughed, but out of politeness. She had queered Herbie's pitch for the day now, all because of her temper. He had probably been on the point of telling Dawn about his new job. Oh, God, I should go and ask him how it went with Christine, she realised, as she sat down at her desk. I can't face it, not now. Oh, shit, I must get my act together. On a whim she rang Helen, booked herself in for a massage, and felt herself relax in anticipation.

It *was* relaxing. Helen, still smarting from the only-a-North-London-aromatherapist tag, put all her skill into her strong arms and supple fingers and in minutes Penny began to feel her troubles ooze away from her. More than that, she felt a compulsion to talk to Helen, but was somehow oddly shy. She did not know how to open a conversation about herself, had never really done so before. And Helen, professionally trained in sympathetic silences, did not give her much of an opening. Penny wondered if she should have arranged instead to meet Helen for a drink after work, but knew that had she done so she would not have wanted to talk intimately. She would have turned the whole incident – the newspaper, Beth's behaviour, even John's accident – into a joke. Perhaps she was not so different from Beth: she turned everything into a joke, Beth into copy. She sighed. And her sigh gave Helen the opening for which she had been hoping.

'Are you feeling better about it all?'

'I don't know. I'm not as angry as I was, but I do feel hurt. I suppose I should have known better than to talk to her, but you know I didn't feel as though I was "talking to" her. I thought we were just having a conversation. The worst of it is, if she had come clean, if she had said, "Look, I want a change of career, an interview with you right now would sell and could help me, will you do one?" I might have said yes.'

'No, you wouldn't.' Helen's fingers continued their calming work. 'Don't tell yourself that, you wouldn't have dreamed of it. You don't talk to people, Penny. You must know that. It's odd that you gave anything away about yourself to Beth at all, not odd that she sold it to that harpy. What made you?'

'Made me what?'

'Suddenly tell her stuff – babies, and John, and you wanting a change.'

'I don't know. I certainly didn't say anything in the way it was used. But, yes, I did say stuff to her. I suppose . . . I suppose it was just that she asked.'

Penny felt tears prick her eyes at the truth of what she had just said. Had it taken so little – just to be asked?

Helen stopped, turned away and poured some oil into a palm. She massaged her hands together for a moment, giving herself time to think. 'You're odd, Penny. People talk to you all the time, I know they do. I bet you know more about each of your friends than any one of them knows about you. I suddenly think we all take you at face value too much.'

'That's the way you're meant to.' Penny's eyes were still closed.

'I don't know, I've been thinking recently. We're all a bit hard on you. We just leave you to get on with it.'

'Whatever "it" is.'

'Exactly. It's English, I suppose. We don't want to pry, so we don't ask questions. Perhaps we should.'

'I wouldn't have answered, anyway.' Penny smiled into the soft towel under her face.

'Maybe you would under the influence of my truth oil.' Helen kept her voice light, but she felt she should warn Penny how she was at last opening up. She would rather never hear anything about Penny's soul than lose her friendship.

'You could be right. I think I need to distance myself from myself to be able to talk about myself. That's why I talk *to* myself. I don't really trust anyone else enough. And it turns out I'm right. Does that make sense?'

'Just about. What I'm trying to say, Penny, is that if you do want to talk, you must know you can trust me.'

'Unlike Beth.'

'Unlike Beth. But we always knew she was silly, didn't we?'

'Of course. She's a journalist. Of sorts.'

'Of sorts. Keep her on board for the jokes, don't trouble her with confidences.'

'But she asked,' Penny repeated. 'That sounds pathetic, doesn't it?'

'Other people have asked, and you've kept your own counsel. I just wonder what changed, why you did talk. Why you suddenly needed to talk. Penny.' Helen stopped massaging, wiped her hands on a towel, looked down earnestly at Penny's glistening back. 'Penny, do you have a lover?'

Penny spun on to her back and sat up, eyes flashing. 'Helen! How dare you? You know I don't – that I wouldn't . . .' She tailed off, faced with Helen's gentleness. There was no prurience, no malice in her friend's eyes. Just a concern that brought the tears near to the surface again. 'Anyway,' she said, with an attempt at a smile, 'if there were, you'd be the first to know. Truth oil, remember?'

Helen did not smile back. She went on wiping her hands, looking down at her friend, a compassion that Penny did not like to see shining from her eyes. 'But might you be going to get one? Is there someone in the wings?'

'No.' As she said the word, Penny realised she was not sure. Was there really no one in the wings? Was she being honest with herself? 'But I have got a date tonight.' She stood up, wrapping herself in the towel, turning to find her clothes so that she could busy herself while she told Helen about Veysey. 'Not that there's anything to tell,' she added, whether to herself or Helen she was not quite sure.

'A date?' Helen waited for a lead, for some clue as to how to react.

'Yes. And one next week – with a different man.' She paused, but Helen still said nothing, so Penny went on determinedly dressing until she could bear the silence no more. 'Hey, you're no fun. When I told Sarah – and that was only about the first one – she went completely mad. Said I shouldn't go anywhere with bedrooms upstairs with him in case I got so carried away by the spag bol that I forgot myself!'

Making a joke of it, laughing at Sarah, made it easier for Penny to turn and face Helen. She was relieved to see that Helen was smiling now, putting the lids back on her jars of oil, not looking directly at Penny.

'Two in a row – I'd say it would make her less worried. Although she does take things so seriously. Who are they?'

Helen was not as good at dissembling as Penny, who sensed her friend's concern if not disapproval. 'Oh, I met them both through work, so it's a work sort of thing, really,' she said, fairly convincingly. 'They were both at dinner the other day. Philip Veysey tonight, and Mario Melzi next week.'

'Hey, go straight for the big guns', Helen said, with a real laugh this time. 'Don't waste your time on the small fry, will you?' She suddenly heard Beth again, taunting her, telling her no one would be interested in her unless she married someone famous. For a brief, unworthy moment, she wondered if Penny was only interested in fame, but pushed the thought back. Penny was too straight, too honest to be impressed by mere fame — wasn't she? 'I should watch the Italian, though,' Helen went on quickly, wanting to change her train of mind. 'I noticed him at your house. He flirted with almost every woman there — I've never seen anything like it. But I thought it was all a huge game, that he didn't mean a word of it.'

'Isn't that what flirting's all about?' asked Penny, reaching into her bag for her wallet. 'It's one of the best games ever invented and does no harm at all. Much less than rugby, say.'

'Or Monopoly?'

'Or Monopoly. Think how siblings fall out over Park Lane. I didn't speak to my brother for a week once. No, flirting is as good clean fun as you can get. As long as everyone knows the rules.'

'And Melzi does?'

'I'm sure of it. Or I wouldn't be going out to dinner with him. Oh, I don't know, I just felt low and he was quite persuasive and, to tell you the honest truth, I'm fed up of being the extra girl at the dinner party. Either that or there to balance some homosexual who needs flattering. Sarah did almost unnerve me, but what's it to her? John doesn't mind. He's never minded my flirting.'

'Well, have fun, then. Let me know what happens.'

As Penny did up her coat and let herself out of Helen's front door she thought about their conversation. She thought she had been truthful. She knew John did not mind that she couldn't help but flirt: he had told her more than once that he liked to see her perform, on her mettle, so full of a kind of energy he felt he lacked. She and Melzi would laugh and flirt and talk, and she must be careful not to drink too much, but otherwise everything would be fine.

John, so much less social a beast than his wife, would be perfectly happy in the thought that his wife was enjoying herself in his absence.

It was not, after all, for Melzi that her heart suddenly quickened. Veysey's serious grey eyes, not Melzi's come-to-bed brown ones, were the pair she was looking forward to seeing.

And somehow she did not think she had been completely honest with Helen on that score.

Chapter Eleven

Penny could not remember when she had last been so excited about an evening out. 'It's not because he's famous,' she told herself, as she wiped off her face mask. 'It's not because I'm impressed by his writing, although I am,' as she put on a light layer of tinted moisturiser. 'Nor is it because I'm sad and lonely,' as she put on her mascara. 'It's not because I'm fed up with my life. Or my husband,' as she stood despairingly in front of a suddenly empty-looking wardrobe. 'I think it's because he makes me think. And laugh. And understands the game of flirting,' as she dressed with remarkable speed. 'And because,' as she inspected herself in the mirror, 'however old you get it is still good fun making new friends. And that, Penelope Sylvia Latimer, is the truth. Brunel. I mean Brunel.'

Terence was sitting in front of the television with a cup of Nescafé when Penny came down the stairs. She nearly slunk out of the house without talking to him, but quelled the impulse. Instead she stood in front of him, asked calmly about his day, made no effort to hide the fact that she was changed, freshly made up, clearly about to go out for the evening. He half-heartedly offered to fetch her a beer, but did not ask her where she was going. She was glad. She refused to be frightened by his opinion of her but was pleased he did not cause another row. She did not have a drink before she left the house. She wanted one badly, but she had a feeling that Veysey did not drink much and she knew she wanted her wits about her. 'Whatever you do, Penny, concentrate,' she said to herself, as she checked her face in her hand mirror once more. 'Although why, I'm still not sure.'

Veysey had offered to come and pick her up, but as he lived in South Kensington and they were to dine at Bibendum it had seemed stupid to agree to his coming all the way out to North Kensington only to go back again. Instead she was to meet him at his flat where they would have a drink before going on to dinner. Penny had not mentioned that assignation point to Sarah, nor indeed to Helen. She had wondered whether it was wise, and perhaps if Sarah had not made such ridiculous speeches about restaurants with bedrooms upstairs, she would have followed her instinct and said she would meet him at the restaurant. But Penny was not a woman to be bullied, so she had agreed to go to Drayton Gardens as casually as though she were never out of bachelors' flats.

As Veysey poured her a gin and tonic she prowled around the room, pretending to admire the first-floor view, the curtains, the bookshelves, anything rather than abandon herself to him by sitting down on his sofa. He looked amused as she strode about but said nothing. He handed her the drink with a smile. 'Sit down, you're making the flat seem very small,' he said at last and, panic-stricken, she sank down on an upright chair as though she had been hit in the back of her knees. Veysey pretended not to notice, and soon Penny was wondering why she had been in such a state. It was only afterwards that she realised how he had soothed her with platitudes, with the kind of conversation that she would never have imagined having with him. Property values in differing parts of London, commuting times, the joy of not commuting, the advantages and disadvantages of working alone or with other people. For a moment she even wondered if she had not made a mistake, if she had not let herself in for a dull evening. Their conversation was at only one remove from the Young Families' discussions of good schools and the Espace versus a Toyota people-carrier that she so despised.

Veysey knew what he was doing, though. He relaxed her, and then as they walked through the streets to dinner he moved back to the interests they shared. She asked him about his writing patterns, and even teased him for the orderliness of his flat, so far removed from the inner-city grimness of his fiction. 'How can you possibly know what you write about?' she asked. 'I mean South Kensington, Bibendum, it's not exactly the mean streets of Manchester, is it?'

'I know what I'm writing about,' he said. 'There was – stuff between Wellington and South Kensington, you know.' For the first time Penny felt a door slam in her face, a clear refusal to allow her to step any closer to him. It intrigued her, piqued her curiosity. There must be some truth, then, in the rumours she had heard of his lost, junkie years, before he appeared on the scene as a publisher's reader and hopeful would-be author. She looked at him as they walked along, his step suddenly faster, his face shut.

'Perhaps I need to reread your books,' she said flirtatiously, but at once knew she had made a mistake.

'So that you can find out more about me?'

'Now that I know you as a friend,' she said hesitantly. 'Books always seem different when you know the author.'

'I don't think you'd find out any more than you did on first reading. They're written for strangers, after all, not – friends.'

He said the word almost with difficulty, then suddenly the sun came out on his face again, and the look of teasing irony was back, as he said, 'You know, writers are not unlike actors in some ways. We have to understand other people, and we have to dissemble.'

'Dissemble', she said, as they reached the restaurant door. 'Yes, I see what you mean. But don't we all do that?'

She wanted an answer to the question. She wanted to know very badly whether he did dissemble, in real life as well as in his writing. If in the end everybody did. And if everybody else did, did she? Apart from the games-playing, of course, the flirting, the acting as serious businesswoman, as stepmother (although she felt she might have lost that connection somewhere in the last month or two). But Veysey was standing back, holding open the door, and the *maître d'* had appeared and was checking their booking, and her coat was being taken and they were being seated and the moment was lost. It was only later, brooding over the evening as she drank a whisky on her own in front of her fire, that she remembered that urgency, and found herself glad that the line had not been pursued.

The gin, and the walk, had calmed her. They sat down with the menus and another gin and tonic each, and idly discussed the food. Penny felt completely safe, unthreatened. She liked this man very much indeed; he was her new friend. They read the same books, liked the same films, talked about going to the theatre together.

'I do miss the theatre. I hardly ever go when John's away,' she said. She had felt a hesitation in mentioning John to Veysey, but also a sense that she should.

'Why not?'

'I don't know. It's odd, really, you'd have thought it's the sort of thing that would be safe.'

'Safe?'

She liked the way Veysey looked straight at her, knew that he was waiting for a real answer, would not take the social line of least resistance. She found it hard to answer him, but he was not a man to be bullied by a silence.

'I'm in a bit of an odd position, really. A husbandless wife. Odder than a divorced woman because they're obviously dangerous.'

He laughed. 'Obviously to whom?'

She paused. She wanted to be truthful. 'To other women. But I'm not dangerous, I'm married, my husband just isn't around. Other women don't mind on the whole if their husbands flirt with me, because they know there's John. But *divorced* women don't get a look-in. It's famous that all they want is another husband. Apparently.'

'And the theatre?'

'I don't know, I do sometimes go with a girlfriend but going to the theatre seems to be one of those couply sort of things. Couples go and don't think to ask a singleton along. Or it's a date, and obviously that's not on. I don't see why,' she went on, thinking aloud, 'going to a cinema with a man is more of a date than say a drink after work. But somehow or other it is. I mean, people don't *do* things in the stalls, do they? Any more than they do in the pub?'

'People used to go to the cinema to *do* things, as you put it.'

'Yes, but cinema's not the same as theatre. It would be rude to the actors, wouldn't it, when they're live? It's like sweets. You can eat sweets in the cinema but not in the theatre. Do you know what I mean?'

'I never realised your life was such a social minefield. Well, I don't know, I'd go to the theatre with you any time you care to mention.'

'Yes, but you're different, you're—' She stopped, horrified, unwilling to allow herself to continue the thought, never mind the sentence.

'I'm ...?' he probed, suddenly serious.

'You're ... modern,' she finished, amazed that she could manage to come up with something, impressed that she could laugh.

He smiled. 'Modern.'

'Well, obviously you are. You write modern novels. Almost but not quite experimental.'

'Which must mean that I almost but not quite understand sexual etiquette in the new century.'

'I didn't mean that.'

'I'll tell you who does think he understands sexual etiquette, or just manners,' he continued, as though she had not spoken.

Penny felt uncomfortable. 'Who?'

'Your stepson. Maybe I shouldn't say this, but you should watch him.'

'Me watch Tel? Why?'

'Because he's watching you. And he's watching all of us.'

'You?'

'Your friends. And do you know? I don't think he liked a single one of us. Not that he tried very hard.'

'You mean at the party?'

'Of course. What is it with him?'

Penny liked that he did not bother to apologise for his question. Too many people begin by saying, 'Sorry if I'm intruding,' or 'Tell me if I step out of line, but ...' and then try to pry the pearl of your soul from its shell of your reticence. But Veysey wanted to know, so he asked. And, as an oyster shell opens with supreme ease if the right spot is tried, so Penny found she could talk.

She told Veysey about Terence, about his upbringing, the way he had arrived on her doorstep, his reluctance to leave and hers to throw him out. She told him about his sudden transformation, his so-called job and the seriousness with which he appeared to approach it. 'I could do a lot of pop psychology about him. Well, I have. But it doesn't make it any easier to deal with.'

'So you carry the can for his father's guilt.'

'John doesn't feel any guilt.' She took a sip of her Chablis, saw how Veysey was looking at her and added quickly, 'And neither should he. I've explained, it wasn't his fault.'

'Since when has that stopped anyone feeling guilty? Anyway, that's not the point. Whatever your husband − John − does or does not feel you're still the one left with Terence lurking around your house watching every move you make. I wouldn't be surprised if he weren't at another table in here, or maybe he's taken a job as a waiter so he can check on our conversation without your noticing.'

'He couldn't afford to eat here and he's too incompetent to work here.' Penny laughed, to match the lightness of Veysey's tone, but she had not liked the way in which he had spoken John's name. Had there not been the smallest amount of scorn in the inflection? She was used to hearing his name spoken with a certain amount of respect, if not almost reverence.

Her scallops, his duck breasts arrived. They tasted, approved, Penny wanting to move the conversation on. But Veysey was having none of that. 'Penny, your relationship with your stepson is entirely your business, which doesn't mean that I'm not going to tell you what I think.' Penny, who was normally so defensive, once again found herself liking his blunt intrusion. 'I could talk all that shit about friends being able to say what they think, but you might not think me enough of a friend − yet. Half of my job is watching people, but I have never seen anyone watching anyone with so much – I don't know how to describe it – so much *concentration*, I suppose, as your stepson watched you at your party.'

'He's a bit of a loner. He probably felt ill at ease. He's fond of me.'

'Maybe. But he doesn't trust you. Can't you see how complicated he is? How his relationship with his father must inform his relationship with you? Penny, he doesn't trust you, for whatever reason – it really is none of my business – and he's looking for examples to back up his instinct.'

There was a silence, in which Penny sipped her wine and looked at her scallops and felt a white rush of panic force its way from her stomach to her throat. 'He has no reason not to trust me,' she muttered, sitting opposite this man to whom she felt so drawn, but who was not her husband, was not her stepson's father.

'That's not the point,' Veysey persisted. 'I think he might be dangerous. Perhaps morally rather than physically, but you don't want that either. I think you should ask him to go. I've seen his type. He's close to the edge, not entirely safe. Penny, he's not "mean streets of Manchester", as you put it, but he could be.'

'Yet,' Penny said, looking straight at Veysey.

'What do you mean?'

'I mean he has no reason not to trust me – yet.'

Veysey looked back at her, the fierceness she had found so attractive from their first meeting back in his eyes. 'I see,' he said at last.

'I'm not sure I do.'

'Well, all the more reason to ask him to leave. While you think about it.' There was another pause while they sat and looked at each other, and then, 'Look, the waiter's hovering.

Do you want to taste my duck?' and with supreme skill Veysey moved Penny away from all thoughts of Terence, or John, or anything but the evening they were spending together.

It was only later, in the taxi home, that Penny wondered why she should dislike Terence for distrusting her. It would be more logical to dislike him for having made her aware that maybe there might be some benefit to be gained from being untrustworthy. Or, at any rate, some fun, to use Beth's word. And that maybe it should not be Terence she should be disliking, but herself. No, she should not ask him to leave. She should keep him as her guardian, her Jiminy Cricket.

The next morning Herbie called a meeting and told the office that he would be leaving in six weeks' time. Penny felt guilty that she had been so absorbed with her own affairs that she had not asked Herbie about his. She was sorry he was going, knowing that despite any protestations to the contrary they would probably soon lose touch. She was genuinely fond of him, more so after her glimpse of his home life. She knew that she had either misjudged him for all these years, or that he could not be happy trapped in such a marriage. The gentleness she liked was also his weakness. She was glad she was not married to him. (This was a new habit, this way of looking at men as if ... Would I like to be married to him? was her new mental refrain. So far the answer was always no.)

Dawn wept, Giovanna looked distressed, Bruce managed a concerned crinkle in his perfect brow, while still looking sideways at Penny. His thoughts were so transparent, his ambition so overwhelming, that Penny found herself rising to meet it, wanting Herbie's job herself, wanting it settled now, before Herbie was even decently gone and a part of the company's buried past. She laughed to herself.

'Penny?'

'Herbie, you're a peach,' she said, and kissed him. 'There, Bruce, don't you wish you could do the same?' she said, making both Herbie and Bruce blush in alarm. 'We shall all miss you, Herbie, you know we will. And you're not to abandon us. We don't want to have to catch a train to see you.'

'Of course not,' he said, looking delighted that everyone seemed to mind his leaving so much. 'We'll need to schedule a series of meetings so that I can hand over my accounts.' Here Bruce immediately perked up. 'There will, of course, also be a board meeting at some time to regularise the whole business. I'm not going to start making speeches, but I know I can leave the company entirely safe in all of your hands.'

'And meanwhile let's have a drink after work,' Penny said, as everyone scattered, gossiping about the future as they went. 'Bruce? Care to join us?'

'Oh, I'd love to, but I don't think I can ... I'll see if I can unpick my plans, it would be useful ...'

'I'm not talking useful, Bruce, I'm talking friendly,' Penny said darkly. She liked frightening Bruce: he was such easy prey. So young, so keen, so desperate.

There was a Penny hardly anyone other than Bruce ever saw – hard, ambitious, iron-willed and completely false. She was less pretty when she was in this character, but mentally she was unmatched. She wanted to show him that she understood him, that she could play at his game, but he was so solipsistic that it never occurred to him to look at the mirror she was holding up to him. He found her nerve-racking but was determined to best her.

'Well, yes, of course. I'd love to join you. I'll see what

I can do.' He set off for the telephone, clearly in a panic that Penny would steal a march on him by having the first post-announcement drink with Herbie.

In fact, with Bruce unable to extricate himself from his mysterious date ('Boy or girl? What do you reckon?' Penny whispered to Herbie), Herbie and she drank a bottle and two glasses of New Zealand Sauvignon without once mentioning the allocation of accounts, the transfer of power or anything else connected with Parkhouse and Langabeer. They mostly talked about Christine, with Herbie being more frank than Penny had ever known him.

He told her how Christine had taken the news, how after the first storm she had shown an almost frightening calm. True to his threat, he had tendered his resignation in writing over the breakfast table. 'I thought to post it might be over-egging the pudding,' he said, and laughed. 'But you should have seen her face. You know, I think – although I didn't realise it until that moment – that my leaving Parkhouse is the first thing I have ever done in direct contradiction to Christine's wishes. You see, she's been so disappointed in life that I always thought – or felt, I don't suppose I did much thinking – that everything else had to go smoothly.'

'Disappointed? She has a lovely life. She clearly . . .' Penny had been going to say 'loves' but was not sure she could, not in relation to Christine '. . . is clearly very fond of you. Enjoys her house. Entertaining.' She tailed off, not sure really what Christine did enjoy, what made her happy. 'She seemed very contented,' she finished off.

Herbie looked at her sharply. 'Contented? Not happy?'

'Well, who among us is really that?' Penny asked. Then quickly, very quickly before he could say anything: 'Are you?'

'Happy? Of course not.' Suddenly Herbie looked as though he was going to cry, and Penny found herself longing for a cigarette. 'I'm not sure I'm even contented, not really. Maybe that's partly what's made me take on this new job. I think I need a challenge. It's all been so easy for so long.'

'The new job won't make your marriage any easier,' Penny remarked, taking a shiny green olive from the bowl between them.

'No. Worse, if anything,' and he laughed again. 'In a way that's a relief.'

'A relief?'

'Yes. At least it will give us something to argue about. We're so polite. It's hard to explain. We dance around each other, instead of with each other.' Penny thought of Veysey and the polka, and could not help but smile. 'I don't know when we did last dance with each other,' he said sadly.

'Actually or metaphorically?'

'Actually is easy – we dance two dances a year, the first and last of the golf-club ball. In between I dance with all her friends and she dances with all her friends' husbands and I drink whisky at the bar with her friends' husbands and she powders her nose with her friends. Metaphorically – I don't know. She used to dance so well. Actually and metaphorically, I think. Do you dance?'

'A or M? A, not much, not any more. I don't know if that's my age or my situation. Metaphorically, all the time. If you don't dance with life, Herbie, you're lost.'

'But most people don't.'

'No. No, they don't.'

'How's John? Have you heard from him since the fall?'

Penny was startled at the change of conversation, but supposed, since they were talking about his marriage, that she had to join in. 'Only immediately afterwards. He's due to ring tomorrow, actually.'

'You must be looking forward to it.'

His words brought Penny a realisation that made her look at him with horror. 'Yes,' she stumbled. 'Yes, of course I am.'

'And your stepson?'

'What about him?'

'Does he talk to his father?'

Penny hesitated. She really did not want to have to talk about Terence again, not after Veysey last night. 'No, there's never time. Only so many minutes booked for the link ... he understands.'

'Does he? Penny, this is nothing to do with me, but I was a little worried about Terence. He seemed a very angry young man.'

Penny said nothing.

'Perhaps he was a little drunk. Or perhaps he just didn't like me.'

'He doesn't drink that much.' (Why was she defending him? But it was only right. He was John's son.) 'His mother's a bit potty. Sometimes I just think he wasn't very well brought up.'

'All right. I'm sorry. I just – I worried a little about you after I left your house. I hoped you weren't unhappy about his being there. I didn't like to say anything ...'

'You needn't have. There's nothing wrong with Terence. He's just a bit of a loner.' (Why did she keep having to say that?) 'He's all right. Hey, he's supposed to keep the baddies away, not be a baddy. He's family, remember?'

Herbie, thinking of his own family, knew he should say no more. He knew he had gone too far, but the wine and his impending departure had given him courage. Still, at least he knew he had tried. 'I should be going home,' he said, and sighed, and ordered another two glasses of wine.

Eye on the clock, heart beating arrythmically, gin and tonic in hand, hair brushed, Penny sat waiting as she had so often waited. Only this time it was different. This time her heart was beating not in longing but with a different kind of anticipation. She concentrated on the telephone, determined not to think, not to analyse, just to be.

Of course it would ring. She knew it would. John had never once let her down. Whether he was on Exmoor, in Chris's office, or in Greenland, if he said he would ring he did. 'Dependable, that's what he is,' said Penny, and smiled at how her friends would gasp and stretch their eyes at the idea of a husband who was never at home, who constantly put his life in danger for no reason other than the thrill of adventure, being classed as dependable. Sarah's policeman was obviously more dependable — but would he ring when he had promised? '*You married for love, and you're not really very happy, are you?*' She heard Sarah's voice, thoughtful, almost surprised, certainly not bitchy, not trying to score.

Penny stood up and paced the room. This was not the way to think, not now, with John about to ring her at any moment. He needed a strong, loving wife. He needed to know that she was here, waiting for him. 'You're being tiresome and modern,' she muttered to herself, smoothing an eyebrow with a wet finger as she looked at herself in the mantel mirror. 'New-style self-examination is just another way of being selfish. You're going through a mid-life crisis, that's all. Everything's fine. It will be when John comes home. Try and keep him here for longer this time. Maybe ... maybe it's the time to think about a baby . . .' She tried to imagine herself, to imagine John, with a baby. She looked at her elegant sitting room and thought of the floor covered in plastic toys, of the disagreeable noise and the agreeable sweet smell that she always associated with babies. She thought of giving up work, of having rings under her eyes, of nothing interesting to say, of not meeting people like Veysey any more. 'Maybe not a baby. Maybe a change. A change of job. A change of house. Some sort of a change.'

And then came the telephone's ring. Guilty, feeling disloyal, she snatched up the receiver. 'Penny?'

'John. Hello – darling.' Except, as she spoke, she realised it wasn't John.

'No, it's Terence.'

'Terence? What are you doing? Get off the line. You know I'm waiting for John. Is it urgent?'

'No, it's just—'

'Then ring me later,' and she hung up. What was he playing at? How could he have done it?

The telephone rang again at once. 'Penny, it's me.'

'John, darling,' this time the word came a little easier, 'how are things?'

'Brilliant. I've made up a lot of lost time. The weather's improved. I might be going to make it after all.' He sounded exuberant, elated, the John so few people saw but whom she knew and loved.

'I love you.' She said it in a rush – had not been able to say it last time, but seized the fleeting emotion and gave it voice. Yes, she did love him, her adventurer.

'Oh, good. You know, I'd think I was jinxed if it weren't going so well. Had a bad time last night, something outside the tent. Finally put my face out and came nose to nose with a bear. The extraordinary thing was, it almost smiled at me, and just

195

wandered off. I was sure it would go for the tent – I'd only just finished eating.'

'Did it have any newspapers with it?' Penny laughed, catching his mood, delighted this was so easy.

'Newspapers? What do you mean?'

'Oh, nothing. I'll explain when you get home. It's nothing serious.'

'Ah. Yes. There's something I should tell you. Chris has been doing some work on my behalf. He's been organising a bit of a tour, I hope you don't mind.'

'A tour? What kind of a tour?'

'Promotion, you know.'

'Promoting what?'

'Well, me. Obviously.'

'Obviously.' She should understand, she could hear him thinking it. She was in the game. If there was interest, you organised a promotional tour, and then on the back of it you raised more money. For the next trip.

'When?'

'On the way home. America seems interested, perhaps Canada too.'

Penny registered the ridiculous idea of the whole of America seeming interested in John (once maybe it might not have seemed ridiculous) but did not rise to it. 'On the way home? Why do you need it now?'

'Well, you know, to raise money. And, you know, he says it's time I did a book.'

'A book? But you can't write.'

'No, but other people can. You must know some writers, you do book promotion. See if you can think of anyone. We'd cut a fair deal.'

Penny's mind went blank. She did not know how she felt

about his putting off his return. Her mind stayed with writers, and the information that she had felt she should put his way. 'I had dinner with a writer this week.'

'Oh, yes? Who was he?' At least John had not assumed that it was a woman writer, that was to his credit.

'He's called Philip Veysey.'

'Any good?'

'Yes, it was fun. We went to Bibendum.'

'I meant his books. Maybe he could do mine.'

Penny felt angry. 'Yes, John, his books are very good. Very harsh. Very literary without being poncy. I don't think he'd want to do your book at all. He's a serious writer.'

'I'm serious. And I'm not poncy.'

'Of course not. The whole world knows how virile you are. Bestride-the-narrow-world stuff. But other people are good at other things, and Philip is good at writing books. His own books. And he's not poncy either. Don't ask him to write your book. He doesn't ask you to go for his walks. You walk, he writes. Those are your jobs.'

There was a silence, broken only by the crackling of the line. Penny was appalled: she had early on made it a rule never to have an argument with John over the telephone. Time spent talking was too short, time between conversations too long for misunderstandings to be given time to fester. It meant their rows always happened on his return, a day of heaven, a week of hell, reconciliation, calm, then the build-up and it all started again. She had to say something now, could not leave it like this.

'I had thought that when you came back we might go down to Exmoor, see your brothers.'

It was a sop, but he did not seem to notice. 'Oh, yes, that would be nice. Fix that up then, if you want.' If *she* wanted, indeed. 'Anyway, I'm glad you're having a good time. Look,

I've got to go. Chris'll keep you posted about the tour. Telly, couple of lectures, you know the sort of thing. But it shouldn't be long now. I'll be there soon.'

'Home?'

'No, sweetheart, haven't you been listening? The Pole. Bears, with newspapers permitting.' And he was gone.

She cried, of course. She cried because he had not minded that she had been taken to Bibendum by a man he did not know, because he had not seemed to notice her anger in defence of Veysey or her effort to please him by saying she would go to the south-west. She cried because he had not asked her to meet him in America, and she cried because she knew that, had he asked her, she would not have wanted to go. She cried because she was frightened that something precious was slipping away from her – John, or her love for John, she was not sure which it was. She did not want to find out. She just wanted to sit on her sofa and drink gin and cry.

Chapter Twelve

Helen turned up unexpectedly while Penny was upstairs changing for her date with Melzi. This time it was easier; she almost felt as though it were becoming a habit to be out in the evening with an attractive single man. It had been years, though — four years of marriage, a year before that. Fidelity in body and mind (still that, of course) but also in time. She was no longer being faithful to John with her time. 'I don't suppose it matters, though,' she said to herself, turning to check that she looked as good as she hoped she did. 'His time is not particularly occupied with thoughts of me.' A line from Roy Orbison came into her head: 'In dreams I walk with you, in dreams I talk to you'. She walked down the stairs singing, 'In dreams you're mine all of the time we're together in dreams . . .' thinking as she did so how once that had been true for her, perhaps for John, but was probably not the case any longer. Now it was television tours and drinks with Herbie, and when she dreamed, if she dreamed, John barely ever figured.

She was surprised to see Terence standing, face alight, to meet her as she came into the room.

She stopped, embarrassed, and laughed. 'I don't think I have the Roy Orbison *glissando*,' she said.

'Roy Orbison, was it?' he said. 'Pretty, though.'

Only then did Penny notice that Helen was sitting there, hands folded, watching them both with a smile. 'Helen, hello. I didn't hear the doorbell.'

'I didn't ring. I turned up at the same time as Terence, so he let me in. I just hoped you were all right.'

'Me? Fine.'

'You look as though you're going somewhere.'

'I am but I've plenty of time for a drink. What would you like?'

'White wine, if you have it. Going somewhere nice?'

'I told you. I'm going out to dinner with Melzi.'

Terence turned away from her, his smile gone.

'Oh, of course you are. I am a dope. And how did it go last week?'

'Did he take you out last week, too?' Terence asked.

'No, that was someone else. Your stepmother's certainly going it these days.' Helen laughed. 'I wish I had half so many dates. Doing anything this evening, Terence?'

He looked panic-stricken, and mumbled an ungracious refusal.

'So will I do any better if I ask myself along with you, Penny?' said Helen, accepting her glass of wine. Penny made for the gin bottle, then thought better of it and helped herself to wine.

'I doubt it. One of us will be a gooseberry and I'm damned if it'll be me. I don't think it would be at all good for Mario's character to have both of us trying to out-flirt each other. I'll set you up with him for another time, if you want.'

The two women laughed. Terence left the room. Helen

looked after his retreating back thoughtfully. 'Do you wind him up on purpose?'

'I suppose so, now. But, you know, if he's living here, it must be on my terms.'

'Fair enough. He's rather sweet really, like a savage Old English sheepdog. Guarding you at all costs.'

'From what?'

'Whatever. Melzi tonight.'

'Or you and your loose talk.'

'Loose talk! I'm the soul of reticence. And probity.'

'Me too.'

'So far.'

Had this come from almost anyone else Penny would have taken offence, but her relationship with Helen had recently shifted. She knew she could trust her, so she played along. 'So far. My virtue survived an evening with Philip Veysey – not that it was actually assaulted, if I'm honest – so I'm sure I can deal with an Eyetie.'

'Oh, Lord, I did mean it, you know. I haven't had a proper date for ages. And suddenly there you are, coming out of your chrysalis, never sitting at home watching the telly. And when you do you've a young Greek god sitting there with you. Not to mention the old Greek hero you've got travelling around the world doing romantic things for you.'

'Not exactly for me, let's get that straight. Anyway it's probably exactly because I am such a respectable married woman. They're in no marital danger from me. Do you think either Veysey or Melzi is looking for a wife?'

'God, who said anything about marriage? A cheap Italian – dinner I mean, not man – would be enough for starters. Oh, well, some day my prince will come. I don't want to cast a dampener on your evening. Have fun.'

'And be good? Isn't that what mothers always say?'

'I'm not your mother. So be good – if you want to be.'

They left, laughing, unaware of Terence standing in the little kitchen, drinking beer and despising them.

They made their rendezvous in 192 and from there walked up the hill to Chepstow Road. 'This is good Italian,' he promised her as he held open the door of Assaggi for her. 'There's a lot of stuff masquerading as Italian food in London, but this—'

'Has the spaghetti as Mamma used to make it.'

'Something like that.'

Penny had put herself into spoiled-girl mode, sat back and watched as Melzi bantered in Italian with the waiters. She even let him order for her, finding it all easier – and, anyway, it suited the role she was playing. They drank Campari while they waited for their first courses to arrive. Penny toyed with a breadstick, and watched him, and waited.

'So when am I going to meet your husband?' The question was completely unexpected.

'My husband?'

'John Brunel, the famous explorer.' He did not appear to be laughing at her.

'I know who he is. Why do you want to meet him?'

'I'm not sure I do. I think I want to know whether you want me to meet him.'

Neither was she expecting him to play the honesty game. 'Why shouldn't I? Although I'm not sure you'd get on. You're very different.'

'Ah.'

She waited. He smiled at her, and she could not help but be drawn into his eyes. She gave in first. When would she learn to tolerate silences? 'He's a very – still man. He doesn't talk much. He just looks and learns.'

'And do you laugh together?'

'Of course.' It was an instant response, made reflexively.

'What about?'

'Oh, Mario, I don't know. What does anyone laugh about? Penguins, quite a lot.'

She was pleased to see she had taken him by surprise now. Good, a point to her.

'Penguins?'

'Don't you think there's something funny about penguins? I suppose it's rude to laugh at a whole species, but they just are intrinsically funny.' She paused, remembering. 'I could almost say that penguins drew us together.'

'You and John?'

'Yes. I've never really thought of it before, but I suppose they did. When I first met him – he had come to us for publicity help, even he had realised he wouldn't get the big sponsors unless he had something of a name – all I could think about was penguins. Every idea I had involved penguins. I think he thought I was sending him up, but I wasn't. I was just fascinated that a man could spend so much time with penguins. Of course, he doesn't really.'

'Doesn't he?'

'No. I had imagined that it was like taking a dog for a walk, you know. You set off across the polar cap and a lot of penguins followed you.'

'And they don't?'

'Of course not. They're busy doing their own thing. Whatever their own thing is.' She laughed. 'I can't help it, I still think they're funny. The males keep the eggs on their feet to keep them off the snow, then put their bellies over the top to keep them warm, while the females go off and feed. Very New Man, don't you think? Or New Penguin.' She laughed again. 'Am I being very silly?' she asked, then wished she had not. It was such a *girlie* question. Worse than allowing dinner to be ordered.

'No. You're baffling me. So you laughed at penguins.' He was not going to allow her to get away with too much.

'Yes. And John said afterwards he was amazed. I looked like a businesswoman – young, but in the right kit, right hair, looked the part – but I kept laughing about penguins. He said most people want to know how men pee when they're in sub-zero temperatures. No one had ever wanted to know about taking penguins for a walk before.'

'How do they pee?' She had known that question would divert him – it always did.

'I don't know. After he said that I made a promise to myself never to ask him how he pees. And I never did. Perhaps I should.'

'Too late. You could ask someone else, though.'

'I suppose so.' She sank into silence, her lightheartedness suddenly gone. Was it really too late to find out how he peed, to find out about his other life?

'So you haven't told me if I'll meet him. Remember, if I don't I'll consider him fair game for a novel.'

'You wouldn't.'

'Why not? As you said, I don't know him. And isn't there something romantic about an explorer in this day and age?'

'Is there? I'm not sure there is. It's not really exploring any more, is it? I mean, other people have been there already.'

'Perhaps he's exploring himself.'

Penny looked at Melzi curiously. 'You don't know John. He thinks a lot, but not about himself. He knows where he is, what he's doing. He's more interested in other people.'

Mario leaned back, making way for the squid risotto that was being put lovingly before him. 'You're right. I don't know the man. But I don't believe he can be particularly interested in other people. He could never bear his line of business if he were. I think as I have not met him I can say what I think without your taking offence. At least I hope so. I'm sure he's charming, but I doubt he's interested in anyone else more than he's interested in himself.'

'How can you say that?'

'Human nature, Penny. He leaves you—'

'He has to. It's his work.'

'But it didn't have to be. He chose his work. He didn't just choose to take a few walking holidays in Nepal, climb a few of the smaller mountains in the Himalayas. He chose to spend a life on his own in a tent with or without penguins. He married a beautiful and young wife, and went on walking across the ice. Don't you see how extreme that is? You made him famous, then he married you, then he left you. I'm not sure an Italian would do that.'

'I didn't marry an Italian.'

'No. But did you really marry anybody? Didn't you just marry an idea? You have no children, you live alone, and you are eating with me. If your husband were home, would he be happy with your dining out with some strange Italian?'

Penny felt close to tears. 'What are you saying? It would be different. He doesn't mind if I go out with men when he's away. He trusts me.'

'So shall we have an affair?'

Penny felt the question like a kick in the throat. She looked at Melzi and with relief saw the laughing look in his eye. She smiled shakily. 'For a moment I thought I was going to have to take my outraged virtue home with me. Which would have been a shame as the dinner is so good.' Veysey had not suggested an affair, not even in jest, not even by implication. She wondered which was the more dangerous. 'And I don't think I could have an affair with a man who ate black risotto,' she said with a smile. (Quickly, Penny, rally yourself, get back on form.) 'Or at any rate not while he is eating the black risotto.'

'You're right, of course. That's why I didn't order it for you. I wanted to keep my options open. But, you know, it may not look very sexy, but it certainly feels it,' he countered. 'Go on, try it, do.' And he held the fork across the table to her mouth. As she met his eyes and took the risotto she felt herself treading on very dangerous ground.

Penny tried to take a taxi home, but Melzi insisted on their walking back together. The night was cold and clear, the stars out hard and bright. 'It'll take us ten minutes, quarter of an hour. Come on, it will do us good, clear our heads. I've enjoyed this evening. It would be a shame for it to end.'

Penny was easily persuadable. She, too, had enjoyed the evening, if she felt a little uncertain about where this friendship was leading. She knew that if he asked her out again she would have to start making decisions, but as long as this evening went on she was just on an innocent evening out with a new friend. As she had been with Veysey. Although Veysey already felt like an old friend, whereas Melzi . . . She was unsure. There was something so relentless in his flirting, and Penny, who understood the game so well, knew that she should watch her step.

'We're going to have to talk business again sometime,' she said, almost more to herself than to him.

'Oh, must we? I suppose you're right. Well, let's have a business dinner one night soon.'

She laughed. 'No, Mario, I mean it. I've begun to work on a plan. You're hard to deal with, of course. All novelists are — there are so many, and on the whole people don't care about them, but you are so contradictory. You know, the easy thing is to do something outrageous, like take drugs on the Prime Minister's plane, but I think we're going to try something a little less showing-off. They'll expect all that because of the films, so I think we should surprise them all and approach through dead ground.'

He said nothing and she looked up at him. He looked totally blank and she was suddenly aware of his being a foreigner. 'Come at them from the direction they are least expecting,' she explained. 'You know, the Don Camillo end of your writing.'

'And you think the great British public will have heard of Don Camillo?' He looked suddenly bored. 'You're right, this is not the moment to talk about this. To be honest I wrote the book because I felt like it. The publishers commissioned me on a whim, so I wrote on a whim. I feel I've made more than my fair share of money from it already, so I've agreed to publicise it any way they want to sell the book. But you know it was a bit of a game. The films are what I care about. They're more important.'

'Some people still think books are more important than films.'

'It depends which books, which films. In my case the book is self-indulgent, the films are what matter. The book will sell to all those ladies who holiday in Tuscany and think they read. It doesn't matter.'

They had reached Cambridge Gardens. Penny wondered whether she should wait with him on the corner, see him to a taxi, but she knew it was not worth suggesting. He would insist on walking her to her door. And then?

It was with relief that she saw the light was on in the sitting room. Terence was still up. She turned to Melzi. 'D'you want a drink? We can call for a taxi,' she added.

He smiled. 'I was frightened for a moment that the ice maiden would not ask me in. I should love something. But don't worry about calling a taxi. I can easily get one on the Grove. Or walk back. Although the walk back won't be quite the same without you.'

Terence was asleep on the sofa in front of the television. Penny looked at him and laughed. 'That,' she said, pointing at him, 'is what my friend Helen calls my Old English sheepdog. She says he is here to guard me. But not much of a Cerberus, is he?'

'More of a toy poodle, I should say,' Melzi said, looking with some dislike at Terence, whose mouth was slightly pursed as he slept.

'Should I wake him up?' Penny stepped round the sofa to the drinks tray. 'Scotch? Brandy?'

'I shouldn't bother. Brandy, please. Although then at least you'll know he's awake.'

'What do you mean?'

Terence stirred, jumped, opened his eyes. 'I must have fallen asleep,' he said foolishly.

'You did. This is Mario Melzi, you may have met him the other night. John's son, Terence Smith Stourton. Whisky?'

'No, thanks. I'll go to bed. Or perhaps not. I'll have a beer.'

He did not acknowledge Melzi's nod, stood up and lumbered to the kitchen and back. An awkward silence fell.

'So you didn't go out with Helen?'

'No, you know I didn't.'

'Helen? The warrior goddess?'

Penny nodded. 'That's the one. She turned up here earlier this evening for a drink, wasn't doing anything, tried to interest Tel here in a night on the town.'

'I didn't feel like it,' he said shortly, and then, to Melzi, 'You should try her. She's not spoken for.'

'Try her?' Penny spoke sharply. 'That's my friend you're talking about, Tel, not the number five on the Chinese menu.'

'Oh, I thought that's how you all talked. In London.'

The three of them sat for ten more minutes, making barely any attempt at conversation. Penny knew that both men were trying to sit the other out. She also knew that Terence would win. He lived here, after all.

Melzi finished his drink and stood up. 'I had better go. Goodnight, Penny, thank you for the drink.' She stood too: there was no use in asking him to stay on. She felt like a teenager guarded by a suspicious parent. She followed Melzi from the room and rudely shut the door behind her on Terence.

'Thank you, Mario, for a delicious dinner. And a lovely evening. I – I'm sorry about Terence. I expect he just woke up grumpy.' She knew she was sounding like a badly behaved toddler's apologetic mother, but was at a loss how to handle either of them.

'I enjoyed it, too.' He opened the front door and stepped out on to the doorstep. 'You should get rid of your stepson, you know. It's not that he's guarding you, it's that you're using him to protect you. From yourself. And you won't know what you want to do until you stop using him as an excuse. Goodnight.' And with a chaste kiss on the cheek and a wave he was gone.

Chapter Thirteen

Penny was not looking forward to the party. She was in too much of a state of confusion about her own life to feel comfortable celebrating another's approach to marriage. Furthermore, she knew too much about this particular engagement to be sure she should be entirely happy about it. But, then, '*you married for love and you're not really very happy*'. Every time she thought of Sarah justifying her decision she remembered those words, and every time she remembered them she had to push them aside. She could not face them, not yet.

The decision had in the end been made very quickly. Sarah's policeman wanted to marry Sarah and Sarah wanted to be married. She had said yes, and begun the pretence that she hoped she could will into reality. 'A marriage of affection, and convenience, and you know we will live happily ever after,' she had said, and here she was, the first step along the way to the mortgage in Putney and the babies.

Penny took Terence with her. At first he had seemed reluctant – she offered him bevies of girls, and dinner afterwards if he did not find one he wanted to take out (not that he ever seemed to take girls out to dinner). She thought it would be a good idea to take him on an outing, include him a little more in her life even though he had behaved so disastrously at her party. She also felt bad that all her men friends seemed to be ganging up on him, telling her to throw him out and she wanted to make it up to him, even though he was unaware of their feelings. Or unaware that they had been so outspoken. It was not until she asked him to come with her as a favour that he relented, smiled, said he would love to 'squire' her (she managed not to laugh), that she was to tell him if anyone was irritating her, and dinner afterwards would be very nice, thank you.

They sat together in the taxi, talking more amicably than they had for days ... She told him about the people he would meet, and he surprised her by saying that he had thought Sarah one of the nicest of her friends. 'I didn't know you'd talked to her,' she said.

'I didn't. I watched her at your party. She seemed to know what she was about. She was a proper woman. I can see her being a mother.'

Penny thought of Rowena, whom she had met only once soon after she and John were married, and felt sorry that Terence so obviously yearned for a different kind of mother. 'She's very conventional,' Penny said.

'Nothing wrong with that. Her bloke — what did you say his name was? — will always know where she's coming from, and where she's going to. She'll be an honest wife, and you can't do better than that.'

'You learned a lot from your watching,' Penny teased him, and he smiled.

'That's the point of watching. My mother thinks I should write novels.'

'Does she?'

'Yes, but she also thinks I should be prime minister. She's not entirely realistic.'

'I suppose that's mothers for you.' Penny thought of her own mother, who was so unimaginative, so realistic, so straightforward that only her occasionally sharp sense of humour saved her from being boring.

'No, it's my mother. She doesn't really care what I am so long as I bring her glory. I think that's what pisses her off about John.'

'What?'

'Well, if she'd stayed with him she'd have been part of something bigger than anything she can be on her own. Do you see what I mean? She knows in her heart that she's not capable of anything much so she pins it on me. Or whoever. At the moment she's hoping Pip is the next Arthur Ransome. Some chance.'

The taxi pulled up outside Sarah's house. A terraced Fulham house, like so many others. Each exactly the same as the one next door, albeit in a slightly different way, this one tiny, with the prissy feel of a house lived in only by women. Penny sighed, paid the driver, led the way to the front door. This was duty, and a duty she would carry out well. She prepared her mouth to smile, her throat to laugh, her eyes to sparkle. In an hour and a half she could be out.

Penny had no memory of Robert from Exeter, and had not yet met him with Sarah. She expected to find an earnest man with short hair and an eager mouth. She could not have been more wrong. He had red curly hair, dark blue eyes and an irrepressible smile. He looked more like one of Just William's cronies than a policeman. When he spoke his voice was gentle, with the faintest hint of an Irish brogue. Too short, too freckled, he was not remotely good-looking but the kindness of his nature and his humorous approach to life shone out of him from the first handshake.

'Penny, hello. I can't believe we've not met before. If you don't mind my saying, I feel as if I've known you for ages. Perhaps we did know each other at Exeter, but I'm sure I would remember.'

'You remembered Sarah,' Penny said, with a smile.

'I did, although I barely knew her – friends of friends, that sort of stuff. But, yes, I did remember. I couldn't believe it when I bumped into her – in the course of duty at that!'

'And you knew.'

'Oh, yes, I knew at once.' They looked at each other seriously, each understanding and liking the other.

'You'll make her happy. Congratulations.'

'Thank you. And this is your stepson, Terence. Let me get you a beer.'

Penny left the two men talking about Drogheda and made her way across the room to Sarah. After seeing Robert's radiant happiness, she expected to find Sarah in some way changed, but it was the same tidy, faintly buttoned-up girl as ever. She was smiling, talking happily enough, but she seemed distracted. She looked pleased to see Penny.

'Penny. You've met him?'

'Yes. He seems wonderful. Well done. And, Sarah, he looks so happy.'

Sarah looked worried – her normal expression, Penny realised. 'Come with me into the kitchen a moment, will you?'

Pretending to be in search of glasses, the two women went into the kitchen at the back of the house and Sarah shut the door behind her. 'He does, doesn't he? Look happy?'

'Very.'

'Penny, this is hard to say – you won't ever tell anyone what I said to you, will you?'

'About?' Penny did not want to make a wrong assumption.

'About – you know, what was that song? The violins?'

'Of course not. I've forgotten already.'

Sarah smiled. 'You haven't, of course not. You never will. But don't hold it against Robert. Or me. I won't mention it again. From now on I start.'

'Start?'

'You know – your word. Pretending.'

They looked at each other in silence for a while. Then Penny said, 'So you still don't?'

'Love him? No, not with the violins. But I like him and I trust him and I know it will all be all right.'

'It looks like he's hearing an entire symphony orchestra.'

Her words were meant to comfort, but had the opposite effect. Sarah's forehead creased again. 'I know. That's the only thing that worries me. It wouldn't matter at all, marrying under false pretences, if he didn't mind so much. You know, he really, really loves me.' She looked faintly awed. 'I never thought I could inspire such a feeling. I don't want to be unfair to him. He is such a good man. And I do love him in a non-violiny sort of way. I can imagine spending the rest of my life with him.'

Penny laughed. 'At this juncture, that's just as well.'

'So you do think I'm doing the right thing?'

Penny poured herself a glass of wine and watched the yellow liquid swirling in her glass for a second or two before answering. 'Oh, Sarah, who am I to know what's right or wrong? You know what you're doing, you're not fooling yourself about anything. He seems so nice, so happy. And, you know, I think he understands more than you think he does.'

'You mean he knows I don't love him?'

'I don't know. I have a feeling he knows your feelings don't match his. But he loves you enough to take that risk. There was something in his face ...' She thought, struggling to pin down the reason for her instinct. 'I can't explain. But I don't think you're tricking him. I think you're marrying a hero. And I think the mortgage in Putney and the babies — and Robert — will make you very happy.'

Sarah's face softened, and she laughed. 'Come on, Penny, you're the one married to a hero.'

'I'm not sure. It's easy to be a hero away from home. You watch your Robert.'

'All right. And, Penny?'

'Yes?'

'Try not to look at me, when you come to be the first baby's godmother, and think, Is she happy or is she only pretending? I'll be happy, I promise you.'

Penny hugged her. 'I know. I do know. Now, come on, you're giving a party. Out of the kitchen and go and shine.'

They pushed through the crowd of besuited men and girls in grey, holding bottles of wine up high. Terence was on the look-out for Penny, smiled and hugged her shoulders when he saw her. 'Giving Sarah last-minute advice?' He beamed. 'You couldn't have a better role-model, Sarah.' Looking at him, Penny saw he meant it, and was surprised.

So, her heart at ease, she turned her attention to the party, and found that she enjoyed herself.

Penny had suggested going with John to the West Country on his return from the Pole. At the back of her mind had been the thought that a visit might be helpful to the MacLaing account, an idea that she had not communicated to John. Two days after Sarah's engagement party, George MacLaing, the managing director of MacLaing's, announced that he would be flying down from Scotland for a week, wanted to meet Penny in London and to visit Exmoor, where the trouble lay. 'Lay on dinners,' he boomed. 'Get every owner of every one of those shoots to come and eat and drink themselves to a standstill. The big hoteliers, too, everyone involved in making this damned anti-MacLaing decision. Make sure you know everything there is to know about the Countryside Rally and the Countryside March. They'll have been the only times half of them have been to London. Learn the route by heart. If you weren't on it, pretend. Wear a stag's head if you have to. I've got three days. I want every one of them to think that we're as bloodthirsty as the best of them. Remind them about our red deer, stalking, all that stuff. I'm bringing my son. He's shot down there, he'll be able to do his bit – only thing he'll have done for the company in all his thirty-five years, but never mind. By the end of those three days I want every one of them to know the name of MacLaing, and know we are blood brothers. Can you do that?'

Penny did not like her clients to run her show – why did they need her if they knew how to do the business themselves, after all – but what he said made a certain amount of sense. And she wanted to be out of London. Away from Terence, away from Bruce's determined friendliness as he planned to take over the office, away from Veysey and Melzi, both of whom had rung her, neither of whom she had yet seen again. Exmoor was more John's territory than hers, but maybe that was a good thing. She would see his brother, and maybe Patrick's calmness would remind her of John and the reasons she had first loved him. She sensed she needed his stillness now.

Of course when she arrived at Patrick's farm, tired and tense after four hours in the car she found anything but quiet. She drove through Dulverton, stopping to buy some champagne for Patrick and Marie, and up on to the moor. It was already nearly dark, the wind blew the rain almost horizontally across the hills, and Penny could not understand her brother-in-law's passion for this bleak spot. Sheep staggered disconsolately across the road, and even the herd of Exmoor ponies gathered together in the half-shelter of a few scrubby trees looked depressed and as though they wished they were in some swish stabling in the Home Counties. She drove down the bumpy track to Windsmeet Farm, wishing she had come down the next day and gone straight to the hotel.

The children had been looking out for the car, and no sooner had she drawn up than four boys, two in pyjamas, two in school uniforms, rushed out of the house and greeted her. She realised she had forgotten to bring them anything, but irritably decided that there was no reason why she should bribe them for their affection. It was John they loved; none of them quite knew what to make of her.

They carried her bags, led her in, all talking at once, mostly about John and their ponies. Jake wanted to know if you could go exploring on ponies, Billy wondered about hunting polar bears: would you need specially big white hounds? Arthur, the smallest at five, told her he had been given a sticker for good reading that day and Isambard, the oldest, told her that he had invented a bomb with the chemistry set she and John had given him for Christmas and his mother was livid because it had killed a chicken.

She smiled wanly and followed them in, grateful to be out of the wind and rain and in the warmth of the kitchen. Marie greeted her with a hug and offered her a drink. The two women felt friendly towards each other but had little in common. Only sometimes, late at night, would they really talk — about their husbands, their brothers-in-law, the trials of their so different lives. And then they would avoid each other for a while, both worried that too much had been said, that any disloyalty might have slipped out under the influence of drink and the rarity of confidences.

'Arthur and Billy, up to bed. Aunt Penny's here now, you've seen her, and she'll still be here at breakfast – although maybe you won't want to be up as early as the boys.' Marie looked at Penny, hoping that she had not made a promise to the boys on their aunt's behalf that would not be kept.

'No, I've got to get up on time tomorrow. I've got to go and see the hotels, check everything's organised, that the whisky has arrived. All that stuff.'

'And will you be staying here tomorrow?'

'No, I really ought to stay with MacLaing. In the same hotel, that is.'

Marie smiled. 'Well, whatever you want. Of course we'd love to have you ... but this is a bonus, anyway. Arthur and Billy, you heard me. Go upstairs now. I'll come and kiss you in a minute. Jake and Izzy, go and finish your homework, then you can come back down and have a drink with us before you go to bed. If you go now.'

'A drink?' Penny was amazed. 'You start them young down here. MacLaing will be pleased when I tell him.'

'Only if he sells ginger beer. Occasionally the big ones are allowed to stay up and pretend to be grown-ups and have a drink, when someone special comes. You qualify.'

Penny smiled, more relaxed already now she had taken her first sip of gin. 'Thank you. It's good to see you all. I must admit I felt like getting away from the fleshpots of London. Where's Patrick?'

'The fleshpot of Exmoor? He's checking the stock. He'll be back soon. Have you heard from John?'

Penny felt uneasy. Of course they would ask about John, it was only natural, but she just did not know what to say. She had never felt false talking about her husband before, but she now felt she was part of some agenda she did not understand. She could only answer any questions truthfully and hope that in talking to people who loved him she would refind him. She had not liked Melzi's suggestion that she had married an idea, not a man, that she continued to love him because he was away, not because he was there. She had not decided yet whether she would see Melzi – or Veysey – again outside business, and hoped that an evening with the Brunels would help to focus her mind. As long as she still loved and was loyal to John she could see any man she chose with an untroubled conscience. It was only if her love was shaky that she should watch her step.

'My instinct's still good.'

'Your instinct?'

'I'm sorry. I was thinking out loud. I seem to do it a lot.'

Marie shot her a worried look. 'Are you sure you're all right? You look exhausted.'

'I'm tired, but I'm all right. Of course I am. And John, yes, I've talked to him since he fell through the ice. He's all right too. He sounded very confident that he would make it. He's thinking of not coming straight home, though. They – Chris, I suppose – think that he should do some sort of promotional tour on the way home, New York, Boston, combined lecture tour and visit to manufacturers to get sponsorship. It's not finalised yet, but once they decide on something it usually happens.'

'Do you mind?'

'Of course not.'

'Of course?' Marie was a gentle woman, and she knew how

the Brunel brothers rode roughshod over anything in their way to their desires.

'Well, I suppose it's disappointing.'

'You suppose? Why don't you fly out and join him? Take some time off and go and drink Bullshots in the Algonquin?'

'He hasn't asked me.'

'Well, that shouldn't stop you, if you want to go.'

Penny finished her gin and tonic and remembered the champagne. 'Look, I brought you this. Shall I put it in the freezer to get good and cold before Patrick comes in?'

Marie, peeling carrots, nodded, her eyes not leaving Penny's face. 'Thank you, that's lovely.' She hesitated, obviously unsure how to move on. 'Penny, you know—'

With a clatter of feet on bare boards the two eldest boys came down the stairs. 'We've finished. Can we have the drink now? We want to ask Aunt Penny about Uncle John and the polar bear. Has he seen any this trip?'

Never had Penny been more glad of an interruption. She poured ginger beer for the boys and more gin for herself, and settled down to be a good aunt. Never mind the present. She could tip them a fiver each in the morning.

Penny woke early the next morning with a slight headache. She had sat up late with Patrick and Marie and a bottle of Scotch (not MacLaing's, she noticed). They had talked about Izzy – the brother not the child – who was in Nepal at the moment, out of touch with his family and the rest of the world. He remained a constant worry to them, although Penny took a more *laissez-faire* approach to him than did his brothers. They had talked about Richard, the priest brother who was in China but considering returning to England and taking up a parish. 'The old priest in Dulverton has just died, but apparently you can't just apply for the job,' said Patrick. 'A shame, really, it would be good to have him down the road.' And then they worried about Kitty, Patrick's mother, who was old and weakening in her body if not her will. 'She should really live with us, but she won't,' said Patrick, and Penny, who knew she was not as good a daughter-in-law as she should be, felt how kind Marie was even to consider the idea of moving Kitty in to Windsmeet. Penny had quite a few theories about Kitty, and why three of her four sons spent so much of their lives abroad.

'You sound like a Victorian father, gathering your family around you – Richard, Izzy, Kitty. You'll be trying to tempt John down here next,' she said.

'I can sound like anything I fancy, but it doesn't happen. I wouldn't be surprised if John did end up down here, anyway.'

'If Penny wanted to,' Marie said quietly.

'Well, yes, of course,' said Patrick, but Penny felt the iron will of the Brunels under his polite tone and knew that neither he nor John would think of asking their wives' opinion on anything once their minds were made up.

'Well, there's no chance of my living here, I'm afraid,' said Penny. 'It's lovely in the summer but I don't think I could stand the long wet winters. Apart from which, what would I do all day? I would never make much of a farmer.'

'And you haven't any children,' said Marie, pouring them all some whisky.

'Was that envy, disapproval or a question?' Penny looked up at her sister-in-law, whose life was spent nurturing children and weak lambs.

Marie laughed. 'I'm not at all sure. Not a question – it's none of my business. Sometimes I long to be free, just to be able to walk out of the house without a backward look. But I'd miss them. Even if I hadn't had them I'd miss them, if you see what I mean.'

'Not really. But maybe that's why I don't have any.'

They talked about the boys and about the farm. They talked about the hunt, and what it meant to the people who lived here on the moor. Patrick told Penny about the red deer, and she was amazed at the knowledge he showed and the affection he so clearly felt for the wild animals. She had never heard anyone talk about animals with such affection but no sentimentality. But they did not talk about John. Not once was he discussed, or even mentioned except in passing. Penny had expected them to want to talk about him, especially after Marie's tentative queries on her arrival. As the evening wore on and she was left alone, treated not like a recalcitrant wife but just as a member of the family, a friend, she relaxed and forgot to be on her guard. She stopped thinking about John and stopped noticing that he was not the centre of their conversation. They were more worried about Izzy's lack of a wife or a job than John's lack of children, more concerned about Richard's lack of stability than John's brushes with danger. She stood up to go to bed feeling totally lulled.

So she was completely taken aback when, as he kissed her goodnight, Patrick said, 'Penny, John'll be home soon. Don't lose the faith, will you, now?' and left the room to take the dogs to their kennels before giving her time to answer.

Marie walked up the stairs with Penny, showed her the light switch to the bathroom (which was half-way down the corridor in a batty Exmoor way) and reminded her to leave the landing light on for Arthur. She, too, had some parting words for Penny. She kissed her goodnight and hovered for a moment in the doorway of the spare room. 'Penny, do you mind if I say something?'

Penny had no choice but to shake her head and wait, feeling

slightly drunk and very tired and hoping that whatever Marie had to say would not take too long. 'I've been in this family longer than you have. You must learn to say no, Penny.'

Penny had been expecting anything but that. 'Say no?'

'They charm you and they smile at you and they look as though they're going to give you the world but in the end, if you're not careful, they'll suck you dry and leave you a husk. They do exactly what they want – all of them. Look at the way they carry on, going all over the world, not a care, not a sense of responsibility. Nothing except charm and blind determination. You have to be as determined as they are, Penny. Or in ten years' time there'll be nothing left of you.'

Penny looked at Marie as closely as the half-light and her drying-out contact lenses would let her. 'Are you all right?'

'Me? Of course. I'm tougher than I look. After all, Patrick's here, isn't he? He may be madly trying to gather his brothers around him, but he's here. However, it was touch and go for a while. I had to make a lot of compromises, take a lot of decisions. I also learned when to say no. I mean it, Penny. I love John, you know I do – I love all the brothers. But I don't let myself be blinded by them any more. John's a remarkable man, but don't ever forget that you are a remarkable woman too.'

They heard a door shutting downstairs and the sound of Patrick coming towards the stairs. 'I'm going on too much. It's late and I've drunk too much whisky. But think about it, Penny. I know I'm right. Goodnight.'

Over breakfast Penny invited Patrick and Marie to the first of MacLaing's dinners. Strictly speaking they were not within the brief – Patrick's shoot was a small affair, basically letting guns out to his local friends, but still he was an important part of the moor social scene and Penny knew he was well respected. She also knew it would make no difference to MacLaing if two extra people were asked.

She kissed the boys goodbye and promised to send John down to them soon after he returned to England, stepped daintily through the muddy yard and drove off, waving out of her window. And today she could see the point of the moor. The night's rain had gone, leaving the air full of the sweet smell of damp earth and heather. The sky was the palest washed blue and the Exmoor ponies no longer looked like bedraggled advertisements for the RSPCA but like blow-dried tourist attractions. She stopped at the top of Winsford Hill, thinking some fresh air might blow away the last of her headache, but her shoes were too hopelessly London to walk over the rough land, so she just stood, leaning against her car and taking in the staggering beauty of the country around her.

Far away she could see the purple top of Dunkery Beacon, and before her the moorland rolled down towards the pastureland. Suddenly she could not understand why Isambard needed the Himalayas, why John was so drawn towards the wide white spaces of the ice, when there was beauty and peace and isolation like this within England. A sheep stopped its meandering for a moment and looked at her curiously. Such was Penny's euphoria that she even liked the sheep. And then, as she looked around her, no other car, no other person in sight, just herself and the sheep she saw, a few hundred yards away, a sight that made her breath stop and her heart soar: a magnificent stag, bold and proud and with a dignity entirely his own, was grazing, surrounded by a herd of about fifteen hind. And as she watched he lifted his head, holding his magnificent antlers as lightly as if they were made of gossamer, and looked directly at her. She stood still, not daring to move an inch, praying that he would trust her enough to stay where he was, so that she could watch him a little longer. He did not move either, just stood and stared, and made his decision. The hind grazed around him, trusting themselves to him. And then, after a minute or two, he began to move away, and the hind looked up, and followed him, all walking at first, then breaking into a steady trot until they had gone beneath the rise in the hill and Penny could no longer see them.

She felt as though she had not breathed while the deer were there, and took long gulps of the sweet, cold air. This, she knew now, was what Exmoor was about – not MacLaing with his whisky, not the rich outsiders who came in their helicopters, with their guns and loaders, and paid thousands of pounds to shoot hundreds of pheasant then ate and drank and went away. They were necessary, and to be welcomed. But what mattered was the air and the deer and people like Patrick and Marie who belonged.

Having taken local advice, Penny had planned her West Country campaign with care and the two days went well. The first dinner, held at a hotel just outside Dulverton, was a raucous affair that lasted until the small hours and ended up with tables being drawn back and dancing in the bar. MacLaing looked worried for a while – this was not at all what he had expected – but when he saw how his guests were enjoying themselves, how even his languid son seemed to be throwing himself into the party, dancing with land agents' wives and looking alive for the first time in years, he relaxed. Other guests, staying in the hotel or just in for dinner, seemed to be joining the party and that, too, almost put out MacLaing, until with a rare gesture of munificence he called the landlord over and instructed that MacLaing's would pay for drinks for everyone for the rest of the night. 'That'll make them remember our name.' He beamed at Penny.

'I'm not sure it will,' Patrick whispered, in her other ear. 'They'll all think they've bought the drinks. This is just a regular Exmoor night out,' and looking at him, Penny realised that he was not entirely joking.

Her big coup had been in persuading young Donald MacLaing to hunt the next day. Patrick said he would lend him a horse and look after him, but it was a decidedly green-faced MacLaing who arrived in his impeccable hunting clothes at the meet at a quarter to eleven. Penny, who had sidled off to bed at one, was feeling fine, but she was amazed at the healthy look of last night's guests who had not left until at least three. Perhaps Patrick was right. Perhaps the Exmoor farmers did regularly behave like princes in fairy stories, dancing till dawn behind closed doors, then up and working at six. The Exmoor air must have some elixir of youth in it. She breathed in extra deeply just in case.

The second night's dinner was a more stately affair, at a daintier but less lively hotel. This was held for the owners and administrators of the really big shoots – Pixton, Miltons, Charcott. Donald had been revived by a day in the wind, MacLaing and Penny had followed for the best part of the day in a Land Rover until MacLaing had admitted defeat and said he needed to go back to the Carnarvon to sleep. By the end of dinner at Langley House MacLaing had promised to take more days' shooting than even he could probably afford and everyone went home contented.

She woke the next morning with a feeling of dread. She had to go back to London. This interlude of sybaritic pleasure had done her good, had distanced her from herself and made her think of different lives, but she must go back to reality. She had stood on a high hill in ridiculous kitten heels and felt her heart sing, but now she must go back to the grey streets where she belonged. She had not rung Chris, or Terence, or Herbie. She had taken these few days a minute at a time, but the minutes had now run out. She felt time pressing upon her, felt her fate snapping at her heels. She would drive back to London and not go back to the office today. She would walk in a London park where the paths were flat and her heels did not matter and she would think about John, and saying no, and Terence, and saying no, and Veysey and Melzi and Herbie and Bruce and Chris and all the other men whose needs were overwhelming her. She would drink nothing today and go to bed early, and tomorrow she would wake up strong, the Penny they all knew. And everything would be all right.

Chapter Fourteen

The air of Exmoor had done Penny good, but there was no disguising that her world was falling apart. She was seriously questioning her marriage, she was being courted (was there really any other word for it?) by two men and found herself drawn to them both, her rock at work, Herbie, was leaving for pastures new, her stepson seemed neurotically confused about the role she had to play in his life, and indeed the role he had to play in his own life and, to add one last bathetic touch to her list of worries, her cat appeared to be seriously ill. Add to all that the inevitable gloom of a wet February day and perhaps it was not surprising that Penny lay in bed, finding it hard to face getting up. At last the telephone roused her from her self-pitying half-doze.

'Penny? It's Helen. I'm ringing in an ambassadorial sort of a way.' Helen never bothered with the formalities of telephone conversations. 'It's Beth, of course. She wants to see you.'

'So why doesn't she ring me?'

'She's frightened of you.'

Penny laughed. 'Good. But not frightened enough.'

'Yes, well, anyway. Come on, you've been friends for years, don't throw that away.'

Penny rolled over on to her side and looked out at the grey day. Perhaps she would have felt more forgiving if the sun had been shining. 'I don't think I did anything to put our friendship in danger.'

'You're being stubborn.'

'I know I am, but I don't see why I shouldn't be. Anyway, how did she drag you into it?'

'She rang me last night, came over, got in a dreadful state, ended up staying here. I promised I'd ring you.'

'So is she sitting beside you?'

'No, she's still in bed. But I knew how you felt and wanted to get it over with.'

'You're not frightened of me too, are you?'

'Of course not. I'm not frightened of anybody. But, you know, I have to feel peaceful at work, keep any personal stresses at bay or I can't do the best for my clients.'

'Oh, yes.' Penny began to switch off. Much as she loved Helen, she hated it when her friend behaved like a New Age healer. 'Are you really not frightened of anyone?'

'Of course not. You're not either, are you?'

Penny thought of herself as fearless, presented herself as someone who looked the world in the eye and dared it to annoy her, but it was only on hearing Helen's certainty that she realised, yes, she was a little afraid. Of John's displeasure. Of the look of irritation that crossed his face sometimes when she was at her most flippant (he had never minded in the old days, had laughed fondly and foolishly at her folly). As a child she had been frightened, of quite a lot of people – older children, large men, anyone who teased her. Little by little she had overcome her fear, which was probably in part why she was so good at her job. She never minded ringing anybody and asking them anything and often, taken by surprise, the grandest people would agree to do the oddest things to help her promote her cause. And now, in the face of Helen's innocent question, she found she was a tiny bit afraid of something, somebody, and that somebody was her husband, the man she loved, the better part of herself.

'Perhaps that's why. I'm not frightened of him, I'm frightened of letting myself down, of the weaker part of me disgusting or irritating the stronger, better Penny Brunel.'

'Penny? What are you saying?'

'Oh, nothing.'

There was a pause, then Helen said, 'I do think you're going potty. You're not up yet, are you?'

'How do you know?'

'You've got a lying-down sort of voice on. Do you think it's sensible to be lying in bed talking to yourself down the telephone to me? Now, what about Beth?'

'I think she's got a nerve asking you to ring up and broker a deal for her. Tell her to come round this evening after work.'

'And what can she expect?'

'Tell her I haven't decided yet.' Penny laughed, the thought cheered her up and made the day seem worth facing. 'And you can come and watch if you want. Be the Kofi Annan of North Kensington. Or at any rate come and have a drink and I'll cook us some supper. Now you're right – I must get up and get on with the day. See you tonight.'

The evening came when the ice and lemon were not laid out on the drinks tray, when Christine was not sitting tidily on the chintz sofa, and when there came no answering call to Herbie's greeting. Christine had become more and more distracted since Herbie's announcement that he was leaving Parkhouse and Langabeer. She had continued to function on auto-pilot, though, pretty much as she had for years, ever since the first consultant had sadly shaken his head and, peering over his half-moon spectacles, told her that he was sorry but he thought it unlikely she would ever bear children.

She had heard of other women who, on being given such news, had offered to leave their husbands, to give them a chance to find someone else, someone who could have children, give them a family. Christine thought that was ridiculous. After all, Herbie had married her, not any children they might or might not have and, anyway, medical science was not always right and she knew, just knew, that children would come.

Neither did Christine take the route of other childless women and invest a great deal of love in a dog or cat. No, she was married to Herbie, she would be a good wife, she would care for him, and she would be rewarded — one day — with a baby. Or two. And so she had begun the self-imposed routine that dominated her life and for so long held her together. She learned to cook. She ran an impeccably clean and tidy house. She learned to play bridge and golf, and to enjoy sitting on the edge of a tennis court watching Herbie play his amateur tennis championships. She learned to laugh prettily, to look interested, to look loving. And little by little her heart atrophied and she never laughed naturally any more because nothing was funny. She became good at shopping, good at dressing, good at putting on a front and looking the part she had written for herself. But she never read a book or a newspaper. She had little idea of what Herbie did every day, although she asked, and no idea at all of what was happening in the world outside Highgate. She had no conversation, only a low-grade level of gossip. For a while she even thought she was happy, and her heart lifted a little when she heard Herbie's key in the lock.

And then the sleepless nights began, and the returning to bed after Herbie had left the house and although she held on tight between six in the evening and eight in the morning she was finding it harder and harder to do so. She knew she had to cling on. For Herbie. For the children they would have one day. For Daddy. For Parkhouse and Langabeer. She thought she was a good wife because dinner was always ready and the house was clean and tidy, and she tried to follow Herbie's interests. She thought she gave Herbie everything he needed, and in a practical sense she did just that. She had forgotten, though, about the companionship that went deeper than sitting on the sidelines of a tennis court watching a game she only half understood and wishing she had someone for whom she could knit small blue cardigans. She had forgotten about the laughter that comes from the heart and the belly, not just the throat. And she had forgotten – if indeed she had ever known – about love. Her tragedy would come when Herbie remembered about love and laughter, but she did not wait for the tragedy as she did not recognise the danger.

Then two things happened to her. Herbie found her asleep, and he told her he was leaving – not her, but Parkhouse and Langabeer, which was much the same thing. And still she clung on, brave, misguided, stupid Christine. Still she sliced the lemons, and cooked the cordon-bleu dinners, and played bridge and shopped. Still – after her hysterical outburst – she continued with her routine, and still she did not talk to her husband, did not stand by his side and tell him everything was all right, would be all right. There might yet have been time, but still she did not, could not do it.

Herbie, distracted by the difficulties of extricating himself from the company of which he had for so long been an integral part, tried to watch Christine, to check that she was all right. 'She's back to normal,' he told Penny, over a quick lunch. 'I was a bit worried, but she seems to have taken it. She's not pleased, of course, and she doesn't talk about it, but life is back to normal.'

Penny wondered whether he was right to be so unconcerned about his wife, but she found she was disengaging herself from him as he prepared to leave, and did not want to be his confidante. She did not like Christine, recognised that the woman found her a threat, and could not find the time or energy to worry about her. Besides, she had the confrontation with Beth that evening to think about. She patted Herbie's hand, made soothing noises and ordered a double espresso.

That was the day that Herbie arrived home and found things out of kilter. His first thought was that she was back in bed again, his first reaction irritation. 'If she's trying to play some kind of game she's going to find it's solitaire,' he muttered to himself as he poured a gin and tonic. And he sat down in Christine's normal place and opened his briefcase and read some paperwork he had brought home as he drank his drink.

It was very quiet, very peaceful. But after half an hour, when he had finished his paperwork and his gin, Herbie felt irritated. He wandered through to the kitchen, where he found everything very tidy but very empty. No wife, and no sign of dinner.

Perhaps we're going out somewhere? he wondered, and looked first in Christine's neatly kept diary, which lived by the telephone, and then in his own diary, which was in his briefcase. Nothing was marked in either. Maybe she was upstairs. He made for the staircase, then paused, one hand on the banister rail, and looked up. He could hear nothing. Still, some childish impulse made him decide not to go and look, and he returned to the sitting room and poured himself another drink.

By seven thirty he was beginning to worry, and finally looked upstairs. Everything was as clean and tidy – and empty – as it was downstairs. No sign of Christine. No sign either of her presence or of a planned long-term absence. By eight thirty he was no longer worried, just angry. He did not expect Christine to behave like this, and he planned on having a good row on her return. He paced around the house, practising his speech, *inconsiderate . . . idiotic . . . can't make me behave as you choose . . . will not put up with it . . . if you want the house to yourself you can have it . . .* He thought about going out and booking himself into an hotel for the night so that she would find him absent on her return . . . and then he realised how incredibly peaceful it would be, how much he would enjoy a night away from his wife, on his own, without feeling the waves of self-pity lap from her side of the bed to his, or the waves of physical disgust that he could barely disguise creeping from him to her.

He stopped his pacing. Was that someone outside? No, just a passer-by who had something of the look of Christine in the set of her head, in the short little steps she was taking down the street. How odd, he thought, to know someone's body so well, for it to be so familiar, and yet so . . . He did not like to formulate the thought even to himself. Then something made him go on, some honesty which had been touched by his move away from Parkhouse Langabeer. Distant. So familiar and so distant. So separate. When did that happen?

He tried to think back, to put his finger on the disintegration of their love, of their friendship. He tried hard to be honest with himself, but the effort of imagination was too much. Before we stopped making love. Long before. Before I realised her baby was never going to be. It has always been her baby, never mine.

I wonder if she realised that? That line of enquiry was also too hard to follow. Why are we still married? Why had that question never occurred to him before? What does either of us get out of this? Security, maybe. Christine liked the security. But does she still feel safe now I'm leaving Parkhouse? Maybe she thinks I could leave her as easily. Maybe she's right.

The thought of freedom, of coming home to a bare flat, with no chintz, no cut lemon, no plumped cushions – and no Christine – made him almost dizzy for a moment. She can have everything, he decided, I don't need anything. I'll buy, rent – whatever, it doesn't matter. She can have the house and everything in it. Suddenly mad, he ran up the steps two at a time, looked in each room, opening cupboards, checking pictures on the wall. And back downstairs, the same again, checking, looking, making a crazy mental inventory of all their belongings.

As he searched, looking intently at familiar objects as though he were meeting them for the first time, he realised that there was nothing here that he could not live without. He could walk out of the house with his clothes and never look back. He would not care. He was breathless, beside himself, totally immersed in this extraordinary emotion. Freedom was near now: he would have a new job, a new life, cut free from all that had dragged him down.

'Bugger it, I'll laugh again!' he exclaimed, and although a little sane bit of his mind asked, *Who with, Herbie? It's not that easy to laugh on your own*, he pushed that traitor back and took what, for a mad moment, he hoped would be his last look around his dainty sitting room.

But what next? Sober suddenly, he knew it could not be that easy. Even if he were prepared to hand everything over, no man can walk away without a backward glance. He would have to see Christine, to explain, to apologise, to put up with her weeping, to do the gentlemanly thing with lawyers.

But he did not immediately lose his new hope. He could still begin now, while she was out. He was not going to wait around any longer.

He picked up his keys and shrugged on his coat. Every major move begins with a small step. His small step would be to take himself out to dinner. On his own. With a good book. He would eat well, and then he would come home to the spare bedroom. And tomorrow would be the first day of his new, truthful life.

It was not to be that easy, of course. Nothing ever is. Herbie arrived home at eleven o'clock, not entirely sober, not entirely in love with his new life of lonely restaurant eating, but still determined to carry it through. He would become used to it, and before long he would find other, lonely friends, who would eat with him, who would laugh with him and understand about the importance of truthfulness even if it led to loneliness. If he saw the police car parked outside his house he did not register its importance. It was only as he fumbled with the key in the lock and the two policemen stepped out of the car and up the path towards him that he felt the first flicker of alarm. Had he been burgled? Had there been an accident?

'Mr Langabeer? Mr Herbert Langabeer?'

'Yes? Can I help you?' Pulling himself together, trying to sound sober — although what did it matter, he had walked to dinner and back, he had done nothing wrong — Herbie felt the alarm grow. *What has the silly woman done?* he asked himself, but managed to keep his mouth shut.

'Mr Langabeer, may we come in?'

Of course, Herbie had seen enough police movies to know that when they asked to come in, they would be offering you a cup of tea within five minutes and were not chasing you for out-of-date parking tickets.

'I – I suppose so, yes, of course.'

He unlocked the door – suddenly his fingers had found their agility again – and led the way along the narrow corridor to the kitchen (they might as well be near the kettle, was his only coherent thought), switching lights on as he went. Then he turned to face them, and waited.

'Yes?'

'Wouldn't you like to sit down?'

'I don't think so, no, thank you.' They were running through every cliché in the book. 'What is it?'

The two officers exchanged glances. *We've got a right one here, doesn't know what's good for him.* Well, damn it, it was his house and he didn't feel like sitting down. He put a hand on to the back of a chair to steady himself. He wondered if they realised that he was not sober.

'As you like, sir. I'm afraid it's bad news. Do you know where your wife is?'

Herbie cast wild glances around the kitchen as though the answer lay somewhere within its walls. 'No. She wasn't here when I came home from work.'

'Is that normal?'

'Normal? No, I suppose it isn't.' He had an image of Christine sitting holding her magazine as he had seen her so many evenings – until tonight – and a feeling of loss swept over him. Where had it all gone wrong? When had that gentle girl turned into that pale woman? Only forty, but she seemed so much older. He felt younger than her, gayer, more light-hearted.

'Where is she?' he asked, gulping in sudden panic.

'You didn't report her missing?'

'Of course not! You would have thought I was mad. Yes, it was unusual for Christine not to be here, not to have left a note – but if I had rung the police and said a grown woman was not at home would they have listened to me? They'd have had me down as a nutter!'

'Possibly, sir. Were you at all concerned?'

'Yes – no, I don't know. I waited a while, and then I went out to dinner on my own. Please, tell me what has happened.'

'Has your wife been distressed recently, under any strain? Been behaving out of character?'

Herbie had no idea what they were trying to pin on him. As far as he was concerned, he had behaved normally. Christine had taken herself off, maybe because she felt as he did about their marriage (but that would make everything too easy, he could not hope for that), and he, part worried, part angry, had gone out to dinner. Now at last he sat down, and put his head in his hands for a moment before looking up again at the policemen.

'Yes, she has been distressed. Do you need to know everything about my life before you tell me where my wife is? All right, I'm leaving the family firm. It will mean nothing to you, but it means everything to my wife. She is very unhappy about my decision. I thought she had reconciled herself to it but ... please, Officer, where is Christine?'

He sounded to his ears as though he minded. He tried to feel as though he minded. He hoped she was safe. But he also hoped that she had found herself some other life, that for some bizarre reason she had called upon the local police to break the news to him. Perhaps she had gone abroad, perhaps only to Kent. It did not matter. As long as she was safe and somewhere else. He looked from one policeman to the other.

He was going to say nothing more until they told him where Christine was.

They waited too, and then the older one gave a big sigh and said, 'Well, sir, I'm sorry to tell you that Mrs Langabeer was found trying to climb into Highgate cemetery. She was in a very disturbed state. She said she had to talk to her father, but when we tried to find out where her father was she became increasingly incoherent. We took her to the station where the police doctor saw her. She has been taken into hospital and sedated. We found her bag and identified her.'

'Sedated?'

'The doctor was extremely concerned. Her mental condition was very unstable. At first we thought she was inebriated, you see, sir. She became very abusive when we approached her.'

'Abusive?'

'And violent, sir. But the doctor established—'

'Yes, yes, I understand.' Herbie sat, hands flat on the table in front of him staring blankly ahead. 'Can you tell me—?' His voice broke and he had to repeat himself: 'Can you tell me what she was saying? What was bothering her?'

'She said,' and the younger policeman actually took a notepad from his pocket and read from it, 'that she wanted to talk to her father.'

'He's not even buried in Highgate,' Herbie said, staring at the policeman, who paused, nodded, then continued.

'She said she needed to tell him that she had changed her mind, that she did want to work for Parkhouse and Daughter.'

'It was never called that. She's gone quite mad.'

There was an awkward silence. Then the younger of the two policemen said, his face going quite red with the embarrassment and effort, 'I think you're putting it a little harshly, sir, but as we said, she is rather disturbed. You should know that she also made certain allegations about your treatment of her. It has to be said that the police doctor could not corroborate them.'

In the moments that followed Herbie saw all his new plans crash around his ears. For better, for worse, for richer, for poorer, in sickness and in health . . . If he had left earlier she could have gone mad on her own, but he could not desert her now. She would recover, a little rest, some wonder drugs. She would be better, back to normal. Back to the chintz sofa, the sliced lemon, the face raised for a kiss when he walked through the door every evening. There was no room to hope for anything more than that. That was all there was left of Christine, and that would be returned to him.

And later? In a year or two, when she was fully recovered, when he was that much nearer retiring, that much nearer dying . . . would he be able to go then? No, not now. The spectre of her insanity would always be there, always a threat she would be able to hold over him, even if it were never mentioned. His lonely dinner now took on the aura of supping with the gods in Elysium. That was it, the beginning and the end of his freedom.

He gave a deep sigh and stood up. 'Where is she? Which hospital?'

The policemen looked relieved. 'We'll take you, sir. It's probably better if you don't drive.'

With bowed head Herbie passed between them, picking up his coat and keys as he went. He locked the front door and slowly, legs like lead, followed the policemen to their car. They would take him to his poor mad wife. There was nothing else to be done, nothing left to say.

Chapter Fifteen

Every major Waterstone's in the land wanted Melzi to do a book-signing. Oxford, Cambridge, Durham and Edinburgh universities all wanted him to speak at their unions. The tabloids were fighting for the exclusive interview, the *Sunday Telegraph* magazine was already booked up for a major piece, the *Guardian* was happy with the second slot. Taking the longer view, Antonio Carluccio had even agreed to take Melzi with him for one of the programmes in his next television series. ('Melzi in a cooking series! Are you mad?' Bruce had asked. 'No, she's brilliant,' Herbie had replied. 'Yours is exactly the reaction she wants. The only way to sell the books is to make people curious.') Given that books were almost the hardest product to promote, Penny was happy with the way the project was going. How many extra books all this would sell was a moot point, but Penny's job was to deliver the column inches and she was confident that she could do just that.

She sat down with a map of England and plotted the tour. Two weeks from Edinburgh to Bristol. It would be exhausting but it might be fun. Giovanna, who spent every weekend she could exploring England, was adamant that time should be made for Melzi to visit the cities properly. 'There's no point him spending three hours in a place, he has to see it properly. Italians are very chauvinistic, he must see how much England has to offer.'

'Who do you think is going to pay for his Baedeker tour? And, anyway, not all Italians are as anglophile as you.'

'Only because they don't look. And don't let him eat in provincial Italian restaurants. Those will put him off England.'

'He can't stay in every town he visits. He'll have to do two a day sometimes.'

'All right, but make them the ugly ones.'

'Like?'

Giovanna's passion for England was an office joke. She even claimed to find a certain romance in Reading station.

'Oh, I don't know, there must be somewhere ugly. Newcastle? Manchester?'

'Don't say that, you're looking at the obvious. Manchester's wonderful, Newcastle has its moments. Anyway, Giovanna, we're not running a tourist trip, we're trying to promote this book.'

'I know, but even so . . .'

Penny sighed and returned to the map. She normally found planning the itinerary the easiest part of the job, but this time she could not concentrate, and Giovanna was not helping her. Each time Giovanna sang the praises of a town, Penny imagined herself there with Melzi. King Arthur's Seat in Edinburgh, Prebends Bridge in Durham, Bath Abbey, an Oxford quad, a Cambridge courtyard . . . a roll-call of the sights of England, and in each place there she was, and there was Melzi, and it did not look as though they were discussing books.

Since she had returned from Exmoor, Melzi had not given up on her. He had every reason to ring her, after all. The tour dates were moving nearer and he was perfectly entitled to want to know where he was going, where he was staying, who he was supposed to talk to and what he was meant to talk about.

Penny pushed the map across the table to Giovanna. 'I need some coffee. I'm going across the road to get myself an espresso.'

'Do you want me to go?'

'No, I need some air. I'll be about fifteen minutes. Look, there's the list of places and fixed dates. Can you match up the rest? It's only a fortnight away and we must get moving, now. He never stops ringing me and I'd like to be able to give him some final answers.'

'About the tour or about you?'

Penny stood still in the act of putting on her coat, and looked at the back of Giovanna's bent head. 'What do you mean by that?'

Giovanna did not look up at her, but was brave enough to continue. 'No client has ever been so consistently on the telephone as Melzi. He's not a nervous first-timer, he's done promotion for films, which is much higher profile. He doesn't need to ring as often as he does, not for business reasons, anyway.'

'Oh, Giovanna, honestly. He's a terrible flirt, you said so yourself.'

'I know. But it's not me who checks my reflection in the glass whenever he's on the telephone.'

Penny sat down slowly in the chair opposite Giovanna, coat half on, purse still in her hand. She waited until her secretary could not help but look at her.

'What do you think is happening?' she asked softly. If there was office gossip she had better hear it.

Giovanna gazed at her steadily. 'Nothing.'

'So?'

'Yet. Nothing yet. I just wonder, Penny, I'm sorry, but I thought I ought to say something. I know those men, those Italians ... Are you sure you know what you're doing?'

Penny shook her head, annoyed. 'Oh, come on, Giovanna. Italians aren't the only men who flirt. He's no more dangerous than – than Bruce!'

'Yes, he is, to you. Not because he's Italian – I'm not that silly. I just think he's got to you. And you should watch him.'

Penny stood up again. 'I'm going to get myself that coffee, Giovanna. And don't worry about me. I trust Mario implicitly. Could you get on with that itinerary, please?'

Alone in the lift, she leaned back against its mirrored walls and looked at herself. No grey hairs (Beth already had some, to her rage), no lines apart from a few around her eyes, which she secretly quite liked. She looked well, rested after Exmoor and Kensington Gardens. Perhaps there was a little tension around the mouth. She forced it to relax, saw the change in her expression, saw herself look a good two years younger. She must remember to watch her mouth: she did not want to turn into one of those thin-lipped disapointed women who lurked around Kensington in expensive clothes.

The lift arrived at the ground floor and Penny made her way across the shiny fake marble floor of the hall, nodding at the doorman as she passed him. 'Cheer up, love, it may never happen,' he sang out (she must have tightened her mouth again) and she walked out, blinking in the bright cold light. She sat at an outside table, alone on the edge of the pavement, crunching a sugar lump and stirring the thick dark coffee.

She did trust Melzi. She knew a flirt when she saw one, and knew that she was in no danger from him.

She was in danger from herself. She and Melzi found each other attractive. He was single, rich, living the disconnected, carefree life of his age and income. She made him laugh. She was also employed to talk to him about himself and she had enough experience to know the attraction of that to a man like Melzi. To any man, probably. And he made her laugh. He flattered her. He looked at her as though she was interesting, important, as though her views mattered. She looked at him and wondered what his mouth would be like to kiss. What his left shoulder looked like underneath his expensive shirt.

The time had come. She was lonely. Melzi was there. There would be no commitment in an affair with him, and that was attractive in itself. Their affair (was she so certain of it?) would be a celebration of the physical. They would meet, laugh, talk, go to bed with each other, and part.

And she would be left with her guilt, her infidelity – and, she smiled to herself, probably some warming memories.

If she went with him on the author tour – as she was supposed to do – she was almost certain they would begin an affair. And she was equally certain that it would be she who would initiate it. She had two weeks in which she must decide what she should do.

And not very much more than that before John came home.

The Beth to whom Penny opened the door was a different creature from the ebullient, skirt-swinging girl of a week before. Penny had the advantage of a step, and Beth raised worried eyes to her. Helen hovered behind, hair back-lit by a street-lamp, looking like a guardian angel.

'Sorry,' Beth said. 'I'm very very sorry. Do you want me to go now?'

Penny looked down at her, relishing the moment for one

second longer. She knew Beth well enough to be aware that, once forgiven, she would forget the whole incident and probably spend the rest of her life denying that she had ever done anything wrong. 'For a day or two I thought Judas Iscariot was a good friend to have, compared to you.'

'I——' Beth began, but Helen poked her in the back and she fell silent.

'I honestly think it was a completely shitty thing to have done. But do you know what?' Penny went on – she had been planning her speech all day. 'I remembered something that my job teaches you pretty early on. Anything published in a daily paper is worth diddly-squat within forty-eight hours. So you'd better come in and have a drink. On the other hand,' she added over her shoulder, as she walked down the hall into the sitting room, 'if you think I'm ever telling you anything again, forget it. Not unless you pay me the thirty pieces of silver or whatever it was Sheena the Creep Vickery gave you.'

Beth opened her mouth again, but Penny gave her no mercy. 'You've said sorry. I accept your apology,' she said grandly. 'The subject is now closed.'

Penny had been right. Within half an hour the old Beth was back, boasting, laughing, telling a story about how she had talked to a soap star she vaguely knew in the hope of selling an interview to the *Express*. 'And did the actress know you were writing an interview?' Penny asked, not very subtly.

'Of course,' Beth said, eyes wide. 'Well, she did half-way through,' she admitted, and exploded into giggles. 'But by then she'd told me an *awful* lot about the others in the cast. Anyway, actresses don't mind. All publicity is good publicity. I thought you knew that.' Penny looked her straight in the eye, Helen cast her face up to the heavens, but still Beth did not make any connections and went merrily on with her story.

'Anyway, the piece was a humdinger and the *good* news is that it looks as though Sheena is going to get me some more work. A three-month contract, to start with, and then—'

'Is a three-month contract really worth throwing in the magazine for?' Penny asked.

'Of course. It's Fleet Street, Penny, that's what counts.'

'To a girl who spent two years on the *Bridgwater Mercury*, maybe – but to the bank manager?'

'Oh, *Penny*, don't be such a stick-in-the-mud. You're as bad as my mother. Yes, to the bank manager. I get paid a lot more.'

'For three months.'

'For three months initially, then more. Anyway, by then I'll always be able to go freelance.'

'Are you sure? Who have you got left to sell? You've already done me and the soap actress,' Penny could not help saying.

'You said the subject was closed,' Helen reminded her gently.

Beth did not mind at all, though. 'Oh, don't be silly, there are plenty of other people. And by the time I've done them all, people will be coming to me to be interviewed, watch me. Anyway, you never know who could come in useful.'

'Except North London aromatherapists,' Helen said softly.

'Who? Oh, them too. Oh, God, look at the time. Helen, we're going to have to go. Do you want to come, Penny? We're going to see the Cher movie.'

'Cher?'

'Judi Dench, too,' Helen put in. 'Although Beth probably isn't as interested in her. Do you want to come?'

Penny hesitated, but Terence had said he would not be back until later and she had been looking forward to an evening alone.

'I won't, thank you. I'm feeling a bit tired. I could use an early night and a bit of thinking time.'

Helen looked at her closely. 'OK. Hey, why don't you come and have a massage tomorrow? I've only one client in the morning – at eleven. Come on your way to work.'

Penny was sure that this was an invitation not for a massage but to talk, and was grateful. 'I'll see how I feel. I'll ring you first thing. But thank you. And, Beth . . .'

'Yes?' For a moment Beth looked wary.

'You know, in a bizarre way I'm quite proud of you. You know what you want and you're going for it. Good luck with the *Express*.'

Beth had the grace to look surprised. 'Thanks.'

'But don't touch me again, will you?'

Beth smiled. 'Wouldn't dream of it. You're stale news now, aren't you? What did you say? Not worth diddly-squat. Pastures new, that's me. Endless pastures new. And I'm going to love them.'

Penny watched the two women walking up the street. Pastures new, or the comfort of the home paddock. That was what she must think about tonight.

There was less point in a massage at the beginning of the day than one after work. Penny never had trouble sleeping and it seemed a little silly to bath and dress, only to undress again an hour later and be covered with oils. She also felt that she would like to talk to Helen, but knew that she would not be able to first thing in the morning. So she did not take Helen up on her offer, but rang and said she had to get to work: with Herbie about to leave there was an endless rush on, MacLaing had called another meeting – he had spent a lot of money in the West Country and had expected immediate returns, which were clearly not forthcoming. She needed to be energetic and business-like, not post-massage soporofic.

Helen offered a massage after work, but John was due to telephone today so Penny turned her down. 'What's the news on John?' Helen asked.

'Much the same. Only a few days away now. Chris keeps me posted, of course.'

'You said something about him putting off his return.'

'Yes, that seems to be going ahead. Chris and John have cooked up the idea that John should write a book — or have one ghosted. John's doing some sort of promotional tour on the way home.'

'Before he's got the book to promote?'

'I know what you mean. But so much of this business is raising money — sometimes I think that takes more time and effort than the actual walking. I suppose they think it's time they had some American money. It might mean taking an American with him next time, but I don't suppose that matters. He's just done a solo, he should be with someone sometimes.'

'So there will be a next time?'

Penny fell silent. Helen had touched on the very subject that made her angry. Neither Chris nor John had mentioned a next time, but the very fact that John was so immediately ready to start a promotion suggested that he had something in mind. Penny had asked Chris, who had been uncharacteristically vague. 'Something new, possibly,' he had muttered.

'Something or somewhere?'

'Well, maybe both.' And he would not be drawn any further.

'There'll always be a next time,' she said.

'He'll be too old one day.'

'Is that meant to comfort me? Am I going to keep hanging on until he finally agrees to stay at home, and brings back his washed-up dregs to me?'

'I don't know – are you?'

'Oh, of course I am, don't pay any attention to me. I'm fine. It just gets on top of me sometimes.' Penny managed a laugh, but it was shaky and not very impressive. 'Anyway, look, I really must go. Thanks for the offer, and I will come again soon. We still haven't done that supper, have we? Maybe one day next week?'

She hung up feeling vaguely dissatisfied, but whether with herself, or John, or Helen, she was not quite sure.

When Penny arrived at the office Giovanna looked up and said, 'Both the MacLaings – father and son, separately – have rung and so has Philip Veysey. Herbie rang and said he had to visit Christine in hospital on the way in so he would be late, could you hold Don Slater for him if he arrives first? He's a potential new client – big account, if it comes off – and he doesn't trust him to Dawn.'

'What's the company?' Penny asked, taking off her coat.

'Um, Narcissus. The makeup company. It's in the last-chance saloon – they're looking for a company to move them out of the fifties. Bruce is after the account, but I expect you'll get it if it comes through. Anyway, Herbie is terrified that Dawn will give Slater some of her views.'

Penny looked at her watch. 'I'm sorry I'm late, although everyone seems to have been hitting the telephones pretty early. Anyone else?'

'Yes, Chris Bellew, said he must just have missed you at home, wants to talk to you, any chance of lunch, and, of course, Melzi.'

'Giovanna!'

'Sorry.'

Penny felt awkward – she did not know whether Giovanna's interference the day before made this easier or harder to say, but she knew what she must do. Today at least. One day at a time. 'Look, Giovanna, could you do me a favour? You've got Melzi's itinerary all planned now, haven't you? I'll dictate a covering letter, then if you could fax it through to him. And then if he calls back again today say I'm busy and I'll ring him tomorrow.'

Giovanna looked at Penny searchingly. 'And will you?'

'Of course. I've his campaign to run.'

'And any more nooky dinners?'

'Oh, come on, there have been hardly any of those.'

'And after the tour is over, and the party, and the book is thoroughly launched, then what?'

'I told you, he's become a friend. I'm sure I shall see him from time to time.'

'*Va bene.* It's nothing to do with me, anyway.' She walked around the desk and gave Penny a sudden hug and a kiss on the cheek. 'I'm sorry. I've just been worried about you.'

Penny sat at her desk with the feeling of unfinished business hanging over her. She must decide what she should do, but she did not want to be pushed one way or the other by anyone else – by Giovanna, by Helen, by Melzi. Even, in his absence, in his ignorance, by John.

She began with the easiest calls. First to Donald MacLaing, who asked her out to dinner, which she laughingly turned down, reminding him in mock-strict tones about the existence of Mr Brunel. 'I'm sorry,' he said, not sounding at all penitent. 'I thought you were separated. You know, on your own.'

'No, but we don't go on each other's business trips.'

'Of course not. It wasn't that. You just seemed separated. Anyway, please don't take offence. I just thought it would be nice to see you again. Worth a try.'

Penny laughed, agreed and hung up. She had thought Donald MacLaing an idiotic, if agreeable, product of too much ready cash and a half-formed public-school education. She was flattered he had asked her out – after all, a compliment never hurt anybody – but would never have wanted to spend much time with him. She returned to her post, but found she could not quite put him out of her mind. Not him, so much as something he had said. *You just seemed separated. You know, on your own.* What had he meant by that? He was a man she would write off as having no imagination, no finesse, no perception. And yet he had quite coolly looked at her and felt – what? Was she giving off some vibe without even realising it? Donald MacLaing probably did not have many skills, but as a rich bachelor he probably had a fair idea about women. Men were very good at avoiding the women with the mad glint of matrimonial desperation in their eyes, approaching those with whom they sensed a good time was available. Wasn't that, after all, precisely what Melzi was doing? And he was not the first. Her months of grass widowhood had taught her a few lessons about men who claimed to be friends, whose wives were her friends, but who could not quite put away the hope that her aloneness made her in some way available. She despised these men, for trying it on, for complicating or ruining what had been a friendship, for their laziness in not looking further afield for their kicks. Melzi was not in this category: he had at least come to her new, fresh, with appraisal as much as friendship in his eye from the start. Nor, for all his faults, was Donald MacLaing. He had looked at her, liked what he saw, and read not lonely-married-ready-for-a-good-time, but on-her-own-self-sufficient, and presumably ready for a good time.

She must learn not to write people off so quickly. It would never have occurred to her that a man like Donald MacLaing could unnerve her. But he had.

Giovanna brought Don Slater into her office, a distraction Penny welcomed. But she who had always been so good at role-playing was finding it more and more difficult to slip in and out of character. It took her a good five minutes to push MacLaing's comment out of her head, a five minutes in which the energetic Mr Slater looked at her with increasing puzzlement. Only when she had finally rid herself of MacLaing and his comment did she return to her role as go-getting public-relations woman and did she, and Mr Slater, relax.

Lunch with Chris Bellew. Why was he in such a hurry? He had been reticent with her recently, so why should he suddenly ring up and ask to have lunch with her on the same day? Normally he would ring her at least every other day to keep her up to date with developments. Now it was more like once a week. Maybe he thought that Terence was keeping her informed, but if so he knew a different Terence from her silent stepson. Maybe there was something he did not want her to know – an illness, unexpected danger, another long-term project. He always hated to give her bad news, would ring regularly when there was nothing to say and go silent when times were bad. She understood that well enough, was inclined in that direction herself.

Which still did not answer the question of why he had suddenly changed tack. *Lunch?* She never lunched with Chris.

After Slater left her she rang Chris back and said she did not have much time, but if he needed to see her they could meet for a quick lunch in a pasta bar round the corner from her office. 'Unless you want to meet after work? John is ringing at seven thirty, but I could probably squeeze in a quick one if you could make it over here soon after six. Or tomorrow, I've more time.'

'No, lunch would be better. Today. If you don't mind.' He sounded nervous, jumpy.

'Chris? What is it?'

'It'll wait till lunchtime.'

'Should I be worried?'

He gave a camp little giggle, sounding more like himself. 'I don't think so. I hope not.'

'John?'

'John? Oh, no, it's not about John. I'll see you later, then. Half one, you said. I'll see you at Mario's.'

For a moment she panicked. What did he know? Or think he knew? And then she remembered that the Italian restaurant was called Mario's, and this time it was her laugh that sounded foolish.

'Yes, Mario's at one thirty. See you then.'

Although she arrived five minutes early Chris was already waiting for her. He was drinking a spritzer and picking at a bowl of olives. The menu was in front of him but it was clear that he was miles away. He jumped when Penny touched his shoulder.

'Chris.'

'Penny, pet, good to see you.'

Penny sat down and waved for a waiter. 'I was beginning to think you were avoiding me. A half-bottle of your house white, please, and I'll have the *tagliatelle ai carciofi* and a side salad – green. Chris?'

He was flustered, looked again without seeing at the menu,

played for time, muttered something about mushrooms, let Penny, who was trying unsuccessfully not to be impatient, order for him, then suddenly took an interest in the breadsticks.

She was willing to wait – for a moment or two. She could see that whatever he had to say would sweat itself out of him pretty quickly, and until she had had some wine she did not have the energy to make too much effort. She hoped Chris was not about to announce that he wanted to give up working for John – now of all times she was not strong enough to take back control of her husband's career.

Finally, after she had drunk half a glass of wine and Chris had expended a lot of nervous energy on the breadsticks, she could bear it no longer.

'Well? You look a nervous wreck, Chris. You go silent on me, then ring up in a panic and now can't talk. What's going on?'

He tried to look her in the eye, but failed. 'It's quite complicated, like,' he said, sounding distinctly Geordie, a sure sign that he was rattled.

'Try me.' She took another sip of wine. 'Come on, Chris, I did warn you I didn't have much time and at this rate you won't even be out of the starting gate by the time I have to leave. Please, Chris, is John all right?'

For the first time he looked straight at her. 'Of course. Oh, God, I'm sorry, did you think ...? Of course you did. No, John's fine.'

'Only he's due to ring me tonight and I thought maybe you were in such a rush to see me because he wouldn't be able to for some reason.'

'No, no, oh, pet, I'm sorry. No, John's fine.' Another pause. 'But you're right, I did want to talk to you before John did. It's about Tel.'

'Terence? He seems a new person since he started with you. More relaxed about life, we're getting on better. Mind you, I see much less of him. Is it not working out? You mustn't keep him on out of charity.'

Chris shifted in his seat, and Penny noticed his ears turning slightly pink. 'Chris? What is going on, please?'

'He's working out very well. Works hard, has picked up the ropes, seems to know what's needed. He's very focused.' It had taken him a long time to begin, so Penny let him have his say but she found it hard to believe that he was talking about the same Terence she knew. 'You know,' Chris went on, amazing her still further, 'he reminded me very much of John when I first saw him, physically, but he also puts me in mind of John himself, the way he is, know what I mean?' Again, the Geordie accent was coming through thick and strong, and Penny wondered what on earth was going to come next.

'So, I've been thinking. John should arrive at the Pole in the next few days. Then we've had quite a few bites in America, from a couple of TV shows and one or two universities. There's a small town on the Canadian border that wants to give him the freedom of the city – it has some annual festival and this would tie in nicely. He'd go to the ceremony, make a speech, and would aim for some sponsorship from the local fibreglass factory. It all adds up. It means putting off John's return to you, but not by much.' He paused, finished his spritzer, passed her his glass for some white wine. He had lost his nervousness now, seemed more animated. 'Then I had this idea, thought I'd run it by you. I want to send Terence to meet him.'

'Terence? Where from? What do you mean?'

'Well, I don't mean Heathrow. No, I want to send him out to Canada to meet John at the ops base there. Then they'd do the American tour together. I might even send Tel all the way.'

'All the way? To the Pole?'

'Possibly. Look at it like this, it would make a fantastic story. I know I could get the papers interested. Combine human interest with adventure and we'll have the world eating out of our hands.'

'Terence already told me that there was not much copy in an almost thirty-year-old drop-out turning up to fling his arms around his father's neck. What's changed?' Penny knew she sounded aggressive, but the idea had taken her by surprise. She wished she had had some warning, some chance to consider her position, but that was why Chris had asked her to lunch: so that he could stun her into agreeing.

'The angle.'

'How?'

'Well, you know we play the mystery son bit, play up all about how his mother disappeared with him, John searched for him, couldn't find him, and now here's Terence, good-looking young man, coming to find his father. John gets to the Pole, and then the support team turns up on the ice with Terence. Wonderful!'

'Sounds a bit American to me. Too Jerry Springer for words.'

'Exactly. And that's where we're going, isn't it?'

'We?'

For a moment Chris lost pace, faltered, then he picked himself up and ploughed gallantly on. 'Yes, I'm going on this one. Not on to the ice, obviously, but to the States.'

'So you thought you'd take Terence along,' Penny said slowly, the first glimmer of light breaking on her mind.

'Well, don't you see?' Chris sidestepped the implication. 'The son goes out to meet the returning warrior, hero, call it what you will. It's a sort of handing over to the next generation thing, a sort of "The king is dead, long live the king."'

'Except that John is not dead, and is unlikely to hand over any sort of crown to Terence. Nor, I think you'll find, would Terence want to go adventuring. He finds it tiring enough getting from Drogheda to North Kensington. A helicopter flight in a padded suit for a photo-opportunity on the ice might suit him, but I doubt it would go any further than that.' Penny's mind was turning, trying to catch the tail of the elusive idea that had begun to break upon her. Chris was muddling her, probably deliberately.

'I don't know. It's possible, for our next project, that we might get Terence to join in ...' Chris began, but tailed off. 'Anyway, that's not important now. But I like this idea. It's heroic in its proportions, don't you see? We have you, waiting loyally at home – don't worry, there'll be no Sheena Vickery mistakes – then we have the son going out to bring his father safely home. You know, like that bloke, you know what I mean ...'

'Odysseus,' Penny said slowly. 'Telemachus went to bring Odysseus home. That's what this whole thing is all about.'

'Who? No, I'm thinking of some bloke I saw on the telly, it doesn't matter. But I think it's a great concept, don't you? Then he can accompany John on the tour, maybe do a TV appearance or two with him.'

'So he gets to be famous, after all.'

'John?'

'No, Terence. His mother will be pleased. I don't suppose you want to take her along for the ride, too?'

'The mother?' Chris looked nervous again. 'I'd very much doubt it, wouldn't you? No, I don't think that would be the thing at all.'

The waiter arrived with the food, and while he was fooling

around with the pepper-pot Penny took a moment to think. Her instinct was totally against the whole idea, but she wanted to be honest with herself as to why. Of course, it was supremely tacky but, then, so was ninety per cent of public relations. Part of the reason she had handed John over to Chris on their marriage was that she knew her personal distaste for self-exposure would stand in the way of her doing a good job for her husband. This emotional reunion did seem too much, though, she was sure of it. But there was more to it than worrying about good taste.

'I can see you don't like it, Penny, but think hard of the coverage,' Chris pleaded. He tasted his pasta, grinned, added more cheese, took a sip of wine, but all the time he was watching her. 'Do you want to go, too?' he asked.

'I'm too busy right now, there's so much going on at work.'

'That's not what I asked. I said, do you want to?'

'No.' There was too much going on out of work, too, although that was not an answer she could give him.

'So why don't you want Terence to?'

'It's tacky.'

'And?'

'And – inappropriate. And if you think John will be prepared to talk about Tel and Rowena and all that business on television, you can't know him as well as I thought you did. And if you think he'd like to hear Terence spilling his orphaned soul out on the television you're wrong too.' *And I don't trust Terence and I don't know what he will say to John and he will get it all wrong anyway. And it's all coming too fast, too close to home.* 'What does John say?'

It was Chris's turn to choose his words carefully. 'We haven't really discussed it with him yet. I was thinking—'

'You were thinking that I would suggest it tonight? And that I could persuade him to say yes? Oh, no, Chris, that's going too far. You're in charge of the PR and sponsorship, and John's in charge of his own actions. The whole reason I gave the job to you in the first place was so that I didn't have to be involved in either these kinds of discussions or the decisions. I don't like the idea at all, but it's not up to me. So I'm not going to get involved. This one's for you, Chris, and you know it.' She poured some wine into his glass hoping that he would not take her antagonism to the idea personally. 'Apart from anything else, I don't see why both you and Terence need to go out. Either he's up to the job or he isn't. If he isn't it must be a waste of money for him to go out. Unless you're admitting that he's no good at his job but is a good PR tool. I don't get it.'

'You don't want to get it, pet. I don't understand why you feel threatened by Terence. He's not trying to be his da, you know.'

'Isn't he? Well, I wonder what he is trying to be? I'm glad you get on with him so well, glad all that's working out, if it is, but isn't it time he moved on? He's twenty-seven years old. He shouldn't be living with his stepmother, working for his father's support group, for no rent, no salary. He should find something else to do with his life.'

Chris looked at her steadily. 'He's stayed with you too long.'

'Yes, I suppose so. Oh, don't say anything to him, I don't want to throw him out, but I don't know if he should be here when John comes back. And on the other hand, if I ask him to leave just as John returns, we'll get back into all that jealousy thing again and I just don't feel strong enough for it.' To her own and Chris's amazement, she heard her voice wobble. For a moment she had been close to tears, she who never cried in public. She felt overwhelmed, exhausted. She just wanted to be alone, and to sleep, and to wake up and discover which way her life had gone while she had been sleeping.

'Well, that's something else I wanted to talk to you about.'

Chris spoke calmly, but he was gripping his fork so tightly that the white bone shone through the soft skin and Penny was sure that whatever he was about to say next carried his heart with it.

'Given that John agrees to Terence coming out to America, doing the meeting, the tour and all – and even if he only agrees to the meeting, it will be worth it. Terence can just use the rest of the tour to learn how these things are organised. I can understand that you might not want Terence there when John is home, especially if it's not for long.' Penny cast Chris a sharp glance, but did not interrupt. One hurdle at a time was enough. 'I thought maybe it would be a good idea if Terence moved in with me. For a while.' He stopped, sipped, looked at her, down again at his plate, wound some pasta round his fork but did not lift it to his mouth, looked at her again.

'I thought it was John you loved,' Penny said, and blushed for shame. 'Oh, my God, I'm sorry, Chris, I don't know why I said it, oh, God . . .'

To her amazement Chris held her gaze for the first time, and seemed almost proud, as he answered, 'Don't worry. We've never talked about it, but you've known, and I've known you've known. And somehow it hasn't mattered. Yes, I've loved John. But I knew he was straight, I always knew it. So I'd go off looking for him in other places. It was daft, I know, but a bit of me always hoped. Not for – you know – just that . . .'

'It's all right.' Penny felt deeply sorry for him. His passion had been such a joke between her and John, but now, hearing him express it for the first time, she saw the wretchedness and the bravery that had kept him going for so long and none of it seemed funny any more. It had never occurred to her how lonely he must have felt, working for the man he loved, and seeing him come home again and again, with a smile and a handshake and a pat on the back for Chris, and then with an arm around his wife turn and walk away and close the door between them. 'And now you think you've found him. In Tel.'

'I don't know. Tel is different, of course he is. He's more vulnerable, more mixed up. But there's a lot in him I recognise. I've known John for a long time. I do see him in Tel.'

'And isn't that a mistake? Aren't you just projecting John on to Tel?'

'I don't think so. I was frightened about that at first, of course I was. I'm not daft. But Tel ... You know, I thought John needed me, that's what kept me going.'

'He does.'

'Aye, but anyone else who could do the job would do. You know that. John doesn't need anybody. Not even you, Penny, if you're honest. And I need to be needed. Tel is needy.'

'I know that,' said Penny, who had found her stepson's neediness increasingly tiresome. 'But all I'm saying, Chris, is that you should be careful that his neediness doesn't take you over. He needs to be free of us all, that's what should really happen to him. All of us, and his mother. You may be the first step to freedom, but I doubt you'd be more than that. He's not a giver, you know. I don't mean of things, I mean of himself.'

'Oh, but he is.' The cry was so impassioned Penny could only look at Chris with amazement. 'He is. Penny, he's given me hope.'

'It's not just hope you want, though, is it? It's love. That's what you both want.'

'He's given me the hope of love, that's a beginning.'

'But Terence isn't—'

'Gay? Didn't you know? Of course he is. Of course Terence is gay.'

They sat in silence, staring at each other as the waiter cleared away their plates and hovered, waiting in vain for a pudding order. 'Zabaglione? Tiramisu?' he offered, trying to catch Penny's eye.

'No, no, just coffee. Two large espressi, please.' And as the waiter backed off, grinning at the opening of a love affair, which he thought he was witnessing, Penny said, 'Say that again, please.'

Chris said. 'Terence is gay. Always has been. Always will be. And I love him. And I think that before long he may find that he loves me.'

And Penny, thinking of Beth's determination to hook Terence, began to laugh with relief and joy and at her own folly. 'I'm not laughing at you, Chris,' she managed, 'but, oh, if you knew how everything is falling into place.'

Chapter Sixteen

There were three notes on her desk when Penny returned from lunch: one from Bruce, probably just to point out that he had been in the office while she was carousing elsewhere, one from Charlie Ackroyd, which sounded furtive and personal (she suspected he wanted the gossip on Christine), and a reminder of the unreturned call to Philip Veysey.

Penny wondered why Giovanna was so worried about Melzi and so unconcerned about Veysey. Veysey called her almost as often as Melzi did, she had actually eaten out with him more often (although Giovanna was not to know that) and, in Penny's eyes, he was every bit as attractive as the Italian. Less obvious, more intense, but very attractive. Penny sat at her desk, staring blankly at the paper on which his name was written. His launch was not far away either, the publicity machine in full motion, air time booked with every arts programme, a few London signings: nothing on as big a scale as Melzi but, then, he was 'only' a novelist, with no connection to the big-money world of films.

Penny's daydreams about Veysey were much purer than her musings about Melzi. There were no clinches on famous bridges, no four-poster beds in provincial hotel rooms. When she thought of him she imagined sitting with him, books to hand, one on each side of a log fire. They were Gabriel Oak and Bathsheba Everdene, 'Whenever you look up, there I shall be – and whenever I look up, there will be you'. They were in Hardy country, walking the top of wind-blown cliffs, or in Coleridge's world, sitting under a lime tree and talking, always talking. She imagined being with him, always trying to live up to the challenge in those fiercely questioning eyes. Time spent with Melzi would be intense, almost to violence, time spent in cities, in expensive restaurants and hotels all over Europe. Time with Veysey would be physically more gentle, more tender – more true. She felt that she understood Veysey without having reached his depths, that in many ways they were as one. She understood Melzi totally: he, after all, was another side of herself, the flippant, flirtatious, amused and amusing side that was all most people saw. But Veysey . . .

With an effort she pulled herself together. She should not be thinking about either of these men in any context other than promoting their very different books. She should be able to go with Melzi on his tour, and answer Veysey's telephone call, without a qualm. She was John's wife. Soon he would be home, and she would be there to welcome him as always. Within a week of his being home she would have forgotten all such foolish thoughts, holding them only as faintly embarrassing memories . . . wouldn't she? It depended, of course, on whether she did or did not set off with Melzi next Monday morning. Would it hurt so much if she did? John would never know, never suspect. She had undertaken enough PR tours in her career; to John this would be just another one.

But she did not like the image of herself as an unfaithful wife. Where would they be on their return, after all? She would have to slide off to his flat on the way back from work, arriving home with some ready-made Marks and Spencer meals in a plastic bag, claiming pressure of work, a sweet false smile on her face for her husband, her hair either too rumpled or suspiciously brushed. Where would the intensity of romance, of sexual fulfilment, be then? She imagined her attachment for Melzi as some fairy-tale goblin, fair and sweet at the beginning, gradually transforming itself into a crooked little troll, hiding in the dark, not daring to show its face. She would nurse it, needing to continue to love it for her own rather than its sake, until one day, surprised, it would pop out into the light and she would see it for the ugly little liar it really was. Would the few weeks or even months of sweetness be worth the long, slow nurturing of the monster that would follow? Almost certainly not. But, oh, how she longed for the sweetness. She could almost taste it, her desire was so intense.

She looked up and saw Giovanna watching her through the glass. How much did Giovanna really understand? Very little, she was sure. She was acting on gossip, on her own muddled perception of Penny, her distrust of her own countrymen, her Catholic clinging to Right. Penny sighed, stood up, opened her office door. She could not bear to be watched, but did not like to flick down the blinds that would shut out all stares.

'Giovanna, can you be an angel and go over the road for a cappuccino for me? I forgot to pick one up on my way back in and I've a lot to get through before the end of the day. And on your way out could you tell Bruce that I've a couple of calls to make, but if he wants to see me I'll be free in about twenty minutes? Is Herbie in?'

'He's been in and out again. He said to say that Slater was very impressed with you, and he thinks we've got the account. They've planned one more meeting, in ten days' time, when we must make our presentation. He wants to talk to you about it. Bruce is desperate for it, and Herbie can't decide whether or not you should work together on this one. Anyway, he looks dreadful. He's gone back to see Christine.'

'Did he say how she was?'

'Reading between the lines, still drugged up to the eyeballs and not making much sense. The doctors claim she's making progress, though. He'll be back later in the afternoon, and I've pencilled him in for four thirty with you. Hope that's OK. He's only got another ten days here himself and I think the whole thing's getting to him.'

'Poor man. Yes, four thirty's fine. Here's the money for the coffee.'

She went back into her office and sat back at her desk. She must keep her mind clear: too much was happening all at once.

Bruce, Charlie, Veysey. She looked at the three notes. There was no contest, really. She picked up the telephone and dialled Veysey.

Sometimes she felt that her whole life revolved around telephones. She thought with envy of Patrick and Marie, who did not even own a mobile, who spent their days in the clear air of the moor. And the wind and rain, she reminded herself. And the stink of slurry and the backache of shearing and the long winter nights of lambing. Tiny veins were breaking on Marie's cheeks and she had long forgotten – if she had ever known – what a kitten heel was. Perhaps North Kensington had its points.

Penny was over the worst of her nicotine withdrawal, but it was at moments like these – as she waited for John's voice – that she longed for the comfort of cigarettes. This time it was more difficult than usual. Was she supposed to tell him about Terence and Chris or not? Would he mind? Would he feel threatened by Terence's homosexuality? Maybe he had known all along, but somehow she doubted it. Neither of them had given all that much thought to Terence, neither of them had heard his cries for attention as more than the irritating whine of a mosquito on a summer evening. They welcomed him when he arrived, fed and watered him, talked to him – but did not listen. It occurred to her that maybe John would even be jealous. He did not want Chris, but then he had become so used to his attention, to his devotion, he might not like it to be withdrawn. That was a funny thought. 'And serve him right,' Penny said out loud. 'He's had too many of us at his feet for too long.'

The telephone rang, but it was not the tinny sound of the long-distance link that Penny heard. 'Penny? It's Mario Melzi. I'm sorry, I tried to reach you today in your office but I kept missing you.'

'Mario, hello.' Penny flushed with guilt. She felt ridiculously pleased to hear his voice.

'It was just that I am going to a drinks party in your elbow of the woods this evening and I wondered if you would like to come with me. My friends live in Ladbroke Gardens – that's not far from you, is it? He's a cameraman, has worked with me a couple of times and she's a lovely girl, a nursery-school teacher, very pretty.'

'I can't, I'm waiting for something.' She was reluctant to tell him that she was waiting for a different telephone call, knew she should put him off, clear the line, but wanted to keep on talking.

'Oh.' He sounded genuinely disappointed. 'How long will you be?'

'Not very. Half an hour.'

'Well, that's all right, I could come and get you then. Please.'

'Mario, I – I'm waiting for John.'

There was a silence. Then, 'John? The husband?'

Penny could not help but smile. 'Not *the* husband. My husband. And it's neck.'

'Neck?' Now he sounded truly bewildered. 'You're waiting for your husband's neck?'

'No.' Penny suddenly had a vision of John's neck. It was not his finest feature. Too thick-set for his finely boned face, it looked like the neck in a child's game of consequences, a rugby player's neck put absurdly between a starlet's body and a little girl's face. 'No, I'm waiting for John to ring. It's my neck of the woods, not elbow of the woods, that you're finding yourself in.'

'I wish – no, I don't.' He stopped himself, but Penny had heard the flirtatious banter in his voice and knew the sort of thing he had been about to say. 'Well, I do, but if your husband's there, technically speaking, or about to be there, this is not the moment for that sort of talk.'

'No,' said Penny, somehow wishing that it was. 'Oh, Lord, Mario, you'd better get off the line.'

'Yes, of course. But you will come? I can come and get you? And then dinner afterwards?'

Penny, her mind back on John, and Terence and Chris, hesitated. But not for long. 'Of course you can. Thank you. That would be lovely.'

She would only cry otherwise. She usually did after talking to John.

She called Helen at midnight. She was a little drunk, very confused, not sure if she were a wife of great or no virtue. Her heart had not leaped at John's voice as it had for Melzi's, nor had it sung as it did for Veysey's. He had seemed remarkably relaxed over the idea of meeting Terence on the ice, and she had felt a little chill pass over her as she realised he was almost enthusiastic about the idea. 'I know it's not the sort of thing I normally do and, no, I don't really like it. But Chris is right, it will be tremendous copy. And we really do need it.'

'The copy?'

'Well, the money it will bring, I hope.'

'John, we don't need any more money. We have stacks of the stuff. What do you want more money for? We've got our house, we can go where we like when we like, I have everything I need, everything material, I don't have the time to spend all the money we have. I suppose you mean sponsorship, but you've money signed up for years ahead, practically to the end of your career, I shouldn't wonder. What is it?'

'We could always do with more. Money is important.'

'Only if you haven't got it, and we have.' What was happening to John? This was so unlike him. He had always been an adventurer because adventure called him, had always said that no challenge ever completely satisfied him because there was always the next one beckoning. 'In a way, when you build up, little by little, each challenge is in the end only slightly more difficult than the one before, and in the end that is not enough, you have to push yourself further,' he had once said on a television programme. 'I started with the Duke of Edinburgh award schemes. I couldn't have gone straight to gold, it would have been impossible. But gold was only a little more difficult than silver, which was only a little more difficult than bronze. It's the same with these treks. I could not have begun by walking solo to the Pole. But walking solo is only a little bit harder than walking in a pair, which is only slightly harder than working with a team. So next there is solo and unsupported.'

'And are you ever afraid?' the interviewer had asked, a breathy blonde, leaning close to him on the red leatherette sofa, her upper lip faintly damp under the lights, or perhaps under the gaze of John's blue eyes.

He had narrowed them, looking straight back at her, his brown face giving the lie to her fake tan. 'Afraid? Occasionally. I feel almost let down if I reach the end of a journey and have never felt fear.' And the audience had drawn in its breath and clapped and the interviewer had leaned back on the sofa, nodding and smiling, never taking her eyes from his.

Had that been the same man as the one who was now talking about money, about parading himself and his son on American television to talk about their past, about finding some half-witted writer to turn his heroism into a series of clichés designed for serialisation in the *Daily Mail*?

He had also greeted the idea of Terence moving in with Chris as a good one, without seeming at all to grasp its implications, and Penny, exhausted and despairing at this new John – or maybe not a new John, maybe the John who had always been there – had not had the energy to deal with that subject any further.

'Listen to the news, then,' John had closed. 'I'm almost there now. Chris is organising the meet.' And he did not ask her if she wanted to come too, perhaps because he knew how distasteful she found the whole plan.

'Or perhaps,' she said to herself, as she put down the receiver, 'because he does not particularly want to see me. Either,' she added, just for the devilry of it, and to see how it sounded. As she went up the stairs to change for Melzi's friends' party she thought that actually it sounded rather good, and prepared to wait for Melzi without any guilt.

The party was perfectly enjoyable, his friends were very

welcoming. Penny did wonder under what guise she had been introduced – friend, lover, potential lover, potential new friend for her neighbours – but she decided not to worry about it. Sandra, the girlfriend, had just left the City to become a nursery teacher, and was forthright and engaging. Penny sensed that she could become friends with her. The cameraman was hairy and monosyllabic, but there was a humorous glint in his eye that Penny thought boded well.

Sometimes she hated going to parties where she knew no one: the social effort was so enormous, the temptation to cry in the lavatory or go home sometimes overwhelming. But tonight, after all the emotional upheavals of the day, she found it a relief to be talking to strangers who knew nothing of her and cared less. Seeing herself from the outside, she knew how well she was performing, saw the laughs, felt the eyes following her. She was not even showing off, she did not need to tonight, she was just flying.

Afterwards a group of them walked to Lancaster Road and ate at Alistair Little's. The people she was with were also friends of Melzi, but they already felt like her friends. She did not need to make an effort, but just enjoyed herself and felt that she was earning Melzi's approval. She realised, too, that with such easy, funny, clever and, above all, nice friends as these Melzi must be a nice man, not just an enjoyable flirt. 'The more I see of you the more surprised I am by you,' she said afterwards, as they walked the short distance back to her flat. 'You give no clues to the nasty side when we meet – but it must be there.'

'Why?'

'Because of the films.'

'Nonsense. It's *not* there because of the films. All my – nastiness, as you call it, comes out in the films, leaving behind the sweet, charming person you see before you.' And they laughed.

Penny knew that in a minute they would be at her door and she would have to make some sort of a decision.

They hesitated at her door. Melzi followed her up the three steps and waited while she fumbled for her key. She opened the door, but he made no move to follow her, just looked at her. The house was in darkness, Terence was either in bed, or out, but she was not thinking of Terence. She looked at Melzi and he looked at her, and then she gave the tiniest shake of the head. 'Goodnight,' she said. 'It really was fun. Thank you for taking me. I think I would have been sitting here in a gloom, watching rubbish on television and trying to summon up the energy to go to bed, if you hadn't rung. Thank you.'

'Thank you for coming,' he said, and suddenly all flirtation was gone and he was serious, almost gentle. 'I know it's not entirely easy,' he said. And he leaned forward and kissed her. And she kissed him back. And almost asked him in, almost changed her mind, but pulled away and shook her head again, more firmly this time, and said, 'Goodnight,' and gently shut the door between them, leaving him on the doorstep.

She stood in the dark hall, tears running down her cheeks. If kissing him made her feel this bad, how could she even consider anything else? She made her way, stumbling slightly, to the telephone and dialled Helen's number by touch. 'Helen,' she said, 'do you mind very much coming over? I know it's late, but . . .'

'Of course not,' said Helen's faintly muffled voice. 'Don't worry, I'll be right there.'

When Penny opened the door to Helen and saw that she had brought her little bag of aromatherapy oils with her she managed a laugh. She had been sitting by the light of one side lamp, drinking whisky and waiting. It had taken Helen only ten minutes to arrive, but already in that time Penny had regretted the impulse that had made her call her friend.

'I wasn't expecting you to come and massage me,' she said, with a watery smile. 'I'm not so spoiled that if I can't sleep I ring you up expecting a treatment.'

Helen looked at her gravely. 'I know,' she said. 'But I know you. For the first time in our friendship, probably in your life, you ring someone up for help. I guessed you'd think better of it before I got here. So I thought if I brought the oils it might help. Might get you to sleep afterwards, too.'

'You do know me, don't you?'

'Of course I do. So do you want a massage?'

Penny shook her head. 'No, thank you. Really not. Do you want a drink?'

'Each to their own.'

'Their own?'

'Crutch, or support, or whatever. You do find drink helps, don't you?'

Penny went on to the defensive, clutching her glass to her as though Helen would snatch it away. 'I suppose so. Are you saying I drink too much?'

'Almost certainly by all that units-per-week talk, but no, not really. I've rarely seen you drunk. But that's all to do with your not wanting to lose control, isn't it?'

'Hey, I didn't ask you round here in the middle of the night to give me a hard time.'

'Didn't you? Penny, I don't know what's been going on recently, but you've changed. Tell me what the problem is.'

Penny poured Helen a glass of red wine and, looking at her whisky, decided it was a mistake and poured herself some wine as well. She rummaged in her cupboard in the hope of finding some Pringles or crackers, but knew she was playing for time and knew from Helen's stillness, her calm look, her refusal to lead the conversation, that she, too, was aware of what Penny was doing.

So she turned another light on, and lit the gas fire, more for company than warmth, and took a deep breath. 'I think I've got myself into a terrible mess,' she said. And extraordinarily, perhaps it was the drink, perhaps it was the kiss, perhaps it was just because she was ready to, she poured out the whole story. The flirtation with Melzi that was developing dangerously fast, but which she just could not resist, the slower-growing but almost certainly deeper friendship with Veysey, the way Terence had been watching her, silently accusing her almost since he had moved into her house. 'Do you know, I wonder whether all this stuff started *because* Tel assumed that it was already happening. I mean, he suspected everyone, Herbie, every man at that blessed party I gave. And meanwhile his ridiculous mother was assuming that I was after her son, who turns out anyway to be gay.'

'Didn't you know?'

Penny looked at Helen in amazement. 'You mean you did? Did he tell you?'

'Of course not. In fact, he almost came on to me once.' She shuddered at the memory. 'He slightly gives me the creeps, if I'm honest. I think he was testing me, it was a power thing, not a sex thing But maybe he'll be better once he's out. It's often the way.'

'But how did you know? I mean, he flirts away, he's not remotely camp, or soft, or anything—'

'Anything obvious, you mean. Don't be silly, Penny. You know as well as I do that half the gay men in London appear completely straight. It's not all *La Cage aux Folles*.'

'But Terence—'

'It's funny how the families are always the last to see it, however relaxed they think they are about it all. So he's come out? What did John say? Did he already know?'

'I don't know. I talked to him tonight, but I didn't mention it. There's too much else going on.'

'Of course. So that's why he was so watchful.'

'Terence?'

'Yes.'

'Because he was gay?'

'No. But because of his mother, and father and you ... It's obvious, really. He doesn't know how mothers are meant to behave. His clearly doesn't play the part properly, she's all wrong, he knows that. So he looked to you. And, of course, you're not his mother. Or anyone's. So you didn't fit. And if you're not a mother, what are you? A whore, clearly. That is the only alternative. But you didn't fit that either. He's the one who's confused. But don't think him suspecting you of some kind of immorality pushed you into feeling attracted to other men. That's just silly.'

'Well, I don't know what to do. I really don't. I don't know why it happened.'

Helen looked down into her wine-glass, then straight up at her friend. 'Are you asking me if you should have an affair with Melzi? Because I don't really think that should be my decision.'

'No. Of course not.' But a part of her had hoped that Helen, so wise despite her New Age philosophies (or maybe, dreadful thought, because of them), might be able to wave a magic wand and tell her what to do. 'I've just lost my way. I don't know where the truth lies.'

'In a fling with Melzi, in love ever after with Veysey, or with your husband?'

'It sounds a bit silly put like that.'

'But it doesn't *feel* silly at all, I know that. You know Terence didn't push you into this state of mind any more than you or his mother or John pushed him into being gay. But I suppose he might just have pointed a few things out to you.'

'Like what?'

'Oh, Penny, you've always been so self-sufficient. You never talk to anyone, turn to anyone. We've all come to you weeping about something, or just asking for advice, and you've helped us all. Sometimes without even noticing it. I would never have set up on my own without you, honestly I wouldn't have.'

'That was nothing. It was easy for me to do, and you paid me back ages ago.'

'I'm not talking about the loan, although of course that was brilliant of you and made it all possible. I mean, I would never have had the nerve to do it if you hadn't sat me down and almost bullied me into being brave enough. You gave me such confidence, and all the time I knew that you didn't even believe in aromatherapy, thought it was a load of nonsense. Yet you knew it could work as a business and, more importantly, you knew *I* could make it work. And you made me see that. And what have any of us ever done for you?'

'You've been good friends.'

'How?'

'Well, you know, we've had a laugh.'

'Exactly. That's all you'll ever let your friends do for you. Have a good time with you. You've never asked us for anything.'

'Anyway, you've convinced me about aromatherapy. Either you're particularly brilliant at it or it's everything you've always said it was.'

'Thank you. But don't change the conversation. I'm on

about you, your self-sufficiency. I've known you've not been particularly happy for ages, but you've never let me get close and I haven't wanted to push.'

'What do you mean I haven't been happy?' Penny was stunned, and once again remembered Sarah's words, *you married for love and you're not really very happy, are you?* What do they all know that I don't? she wondered.

'Penny, this didn't come out of nowhere. You can't blame Terence for making you emotionally vulnerable. Blame his father, if you like, but not him. The only thing Terence might have done is make you realise you were vulnerable. I don't know, it's not to do with me, it's all between you and John, but you know you've changed. Your face used to light up when you said his name, but now if someone mentions him your face closes.'

'But I love him,' Penny said, and the words hung in the space between them and she could not look at Helen.

'Penny, all this stuff with Veysey and Melzi, none of it would have happened if you had been happy, if you really love John the way you tell yourself you do. It's not just a case of loneliness and a pretty face wandering by. You could go off and have a good time with Melzi, go on this trip next week, spend two weeks in bed forgetting to go to book signings or talks or whatever he's supposed to be doing. You could come back, go to his launch party and never see him again and you'd barely regret it – either the affair or the farewell. You could welcome John home and, with a little difficulty, pretend it never happened. Remember Isabel Letts? She had a rip-roaring affair, that's all it was, no illusions about true love or a future with the man, went on with her husband without a care in the world, thought when it was all over that that would be that. And in a sense it was. She said it was amazing how little guilt she felt after the first few weeks, how easy it was to pretend. But it was only later that she realised that although she was right in that the affair did not matter, what did matter was that she had had one. There was a reason. It's the same with you. In a sense Veysey sounds more of a threat to John than Melzi, but why is that threat there?'

Helen stood up and poured them both some more wine, while Penny, feeling as though Helen were driving over her with a steamroller, sat numbly.

'You know why you fell in love with John,' Helen said as Penny took the wine.

'Of course, I . . .' Penny paused, trying to remember anything, even what John looked like. 'I loved his stillness. I loved how he looked at me, straight at me, as though he could see through all the rubbishy outside I put on for people.' Veysey looked at her in the same way, she realised, with a shock. 'I loved that he didn't seem to care what people thought, that he was who he was without having to pretend. I suppose I wanted to be like that, instead of being a flibbertigibbet who could make people laugh. He never tried to make people laugh.'

'He doesn't laugh much himself, though, does he?' Helen pointed out.

'Doesn't he?' Penny remembered Veysey asking her more or less the same question, remembered how she had refuted the suggestion that she and John did not laugh together – and what had she come up with? A centuries-old shared joke about penguins. Did John really not laugh?

'Not any more,' Helen answered. 'And he never really did much. I don't know, that's not the be-all and end-all, is it?'

'I laugh less when he's around,' Penny said.

'I know. You've taken to looking almost nervous when he's home.'

'Nervous?'

'As though you don't want to . . . I don't know, offend him, or irritate him, or something.'

'Well, of course I don't.'

'But you shouldn't be worrying about it all the time.'

'I don't.'

'Don't you? Penny, you're the straightest person I know. You say what you think, you're unafraid of everything and everybody. I love that about you. But you know, recently — and I don't mean very recently, not in the last few months, not since Terence tipping up which is where you seem to date everything from, but in the last year or even two — I've been wondering if you're really truthful after all.'

'Of course I am.'

'With everyone else I know you are. But not with yourself. I don't think you've been telling yourself the truth for ages. That's what all this is about, all this Veysey-Melzi business. It's about telling the truth. It's about not pretending.'

The front door slammed, and the two women jumped. They heard a low whistle as Terence double-locked the front door behind him. They heard him walk down the corridor and pause outside the sitting-room door, then he stopped whistling and walked slowly up the stairs. Penny stood up. It seemed important that Terence knew she was sitting in the half-dark with Helen, not Veysey or Melzi or Herbie or anybody else. Then, catching Helen's eye, she sat down again. What did it matter, after all? She had never been frightened of what people thought before, there was no reason to start now. But she had had enough of talking about herself. She was not used to it. She did not like the things that Helen was saying, although she admired her bravery in speaking out. Penny was aware that she was not an easy person to approach — she had spent long enough building up those defences, after all.

'You'll stay the night, won't you?' she said, formal now, unable for the moment even to thank her friend. 'Terence is in the best guest room, but there's the little one at the top of the house.'

Helen knew Penny had reached her limit, was amazed at how much her friend had stood. She nodded. 'If you don't mind. It's late, and now I've drunk this wine . . .'

The two of them made their way upstairs, kissed each other goodnight and went to bed. It was as though nothing had been said, as though they had spent a relaxed evening eating pasta and watching a video. 'And yet,' Penny said, as she undressed, looking at her face to see if all this showed on it, 'I think my whole world has just shifted its orbit. I wouldn't be surprised if John got to the Pole and found it was not there, after all, that it had somehow moved.'

She lay in bed, thinking that her mind was spinning too much for her to be able to fall asleep, yet suddenly, magically, it was eight o'clock in the morning and she had slept the sweet and peaceful sleep of the untroubled.

Chapter Seventeen

The deep sleep left her refreshed and strong. She could meet Helen and Terence over breakfast, and deal with them both with equilibrium. Terence eyed her a little strangely, told her that plans were going ahead to send him north. He would probably leave within a day or two. He even thanked her for her hospitality. He did not mention Chris.

Helen drank some of the herb tea she always carried in her bag, ate a piece of toast, smiled sweetly on Terence and congratulated him on his new life – congratulations she made deliberately vague and he took with baffled pleasure. Helen knew her work was done, and just hoped that Penny would be brave enough to act upon their conversation. One way or the other. 'Just look at the world clearly,' she said, as she left. 'You'd be amazed what a beautiful place it is,' and she kissed Penny and wandered off into a day that held just the smallest hint of spring.

Penny set off for work feeling she could deal with everything and anything – from Bruce to Veysey, taking in Melzi along the way.

Her composure was destroyed only an hour later when her

telephone rang. 'I can't quite understand what this woman wants, or who she is,' Giovanna said. 'She says she's John's wife or something. She's crying. I don't know what's going on. I've hung up on her twice, but she keeps calling back. She says she will until she talks to you. I'm sorry, but I just don't know what to do. She sounds a complete nutter.'

'John's *wife*?'

'I know. But she says she'll be on a plane from Dublin this afternoon unless you talk to her.'

'Dublin? Oh, God, it's Rowena. It's Terence's mother. You'd better put her through.'

'What the *fuck* is going on?'

Penny took a deep breath. What a way to begin a conversation. 'Rowena, I presume. Good morning.'

'Don't you good morning me. Would you like to tell me what's happening?'

Penny's impulse was to send her up, to feign ignorance of the likely cause of Rowena's distress. Instead she decided to preserve her energies, thank heaven that she had arrived at work feeling so relaxed, and finish the conversation as soon as she reasonably could. 'I suppose Terence has just been talking to you?'

'Yes, he has, with the most ridiculous story I've ever heard. You put him up to this, and I won't have it.'

Penny was genuinely unsure whether Rowena was in a rage about Terence's trip to meet his father, or about his plan to move in with Chris. She could ask Rowena straight out, of course, but she did not want to cause any more trouble. 'It's no good talking to me about it, Rowena, it's nothing to do with me. I think, though, that Tel thought you would be pleased.'

'And that's another thing, it's not Tel. It's Terence. Or Terry, if you're his mother. This Tel rubbish, cooked up by you and John, it's not a name. I chose Terence.'

Penny could not help but be sidetracked. 'I think that was it, really. That John had no say in the naming of his son. He didn't particularly like the name Terence, he told me, and he wanted something more friendly-sounding to call him.'

'It's a good Irish name.'

'For a good Irish boy?'

'What are you implying? Terence is his father's son.'

'Of course.' Penny suddenly felt tired. 'Rowena, I'm sure you didn't ring me three times to bicker about your son's name. I've certainly got other things to do. Now, how can I help?'

'My God, you're nothing but a jumped-up little secretary,' Rowena hissed. 'I don't suppose you can help at all. I think I might have credited you with too much intelligence when I supposed that you'd encouraged Terry away from me towards his father. You're not evil, you're too stupid to be evil. I want my boy back. I forbid him to go.'

'Rowena, neither one of us can forbid him to do anything. He's twenty-seven years old.'

'He's always come home before. I can't believe he's not coming home.'

Rowena's voice had changed to a pathetic wail, but that did not arouse Penny's sympathy. She tried to speak calmly. 'Rowena, look, I'm really sorry if you don't like the idea. If I'm totally honest neither do I. But I would like to say that this had nothing to do with me, nothing at all. I think the whole plan is ghastly. Chris says—'

'I've heard enough about what that Geordie faggot says.' She had forgotten the abandoned-mother wail and was vicious again. 'That's all Terence could talk about. Chris this, Chris that. I thought it was a girl on whom he had a crush. Then on the line he comes, "I think you'll find, Miss Smith Stourton," Penny could not help smiling into the receiver, Rowena had

Chris's educated-Geordie accent, the one he always came out with when he was trying to impress, down pat, "that this'll be the making of Terence. It's a real adventure and he'll be doing something to help his da." As if I want Chris bloody Bellew's cheap psychological insights into my son. Something to help his da! As though his so-called da has ever done anything to help him.'

Penny sighed. This was old ground. 'Well, they see it as some grand gesture in the Greek heroic mould. I think Terence has always wanted to be a hero.'

'He is a hero, the way he's looked after me . . .' Pathetic mother again.

'Well, you know, something rather, well, *larger*. And you know there's no danger. He'll be flown out with a photographer and a reporter and he'll hop out on to the ice, be photographed, and be flown back to camp. Easy.'

'It's time he came home.' Rowena sounded like a stubborn child.

'Tell him that. Honestly, Rowena, it's nothing to do with me.'

'It is. You introduced him to this Chris, got him the job. If you'd thrown him out he'd have come home.'

Penny thought of all that Helen had said to her the night before, realised how true it was not just in her case but in life. 'Yes, Rowena, but it's what went before that counts.'

'What do you mean?'

'I mean that the past is not the past. Nothing springs fully formed from nothing, except Aphrodite from the shell or Minerva from Zeus's head.'

'Don't you get all clever with me. I've got a writer here.'

That surprised Penny, who had assumed that Rowena's hysteria stemmed from the disappearance of her lover. 'Well, good, talk to him about it. I must go, I have work to do.'

She did not want to hang up without a formal goodbye, so she waited a moment to allow Rowena the chance to behave in a civilised way. The calm voice she heard next, more Roedean than Drogheda, no malice, no self-pity, took her by surprise.

'What do you mean by the past not being the past?' And Penny suddenly felt sorry for this lonely, lost woman whose past included so many mistakes.

'I mean that the past informs the present, and the future. All the things that happen to us make us what we are. I don't mean the old Larkin thing, that we can blame our parents for everything, but in the old nature-and-nurture argument you must see that the two work together.'

'I don't understand.' Rowena sounded very sad.

'I mean that, say, three-quarters of what Terence is comes from inside him, from before he was born. But that all the stuff that's happened to him – John not being around, and you being, well, you – all that kit brings out different parts of him, but parts that were always there, that might have stayed hidden.'

'They will stay hidden, even from him.' Rowena sounded firm.

So she did know, had known all along. She knew her son was homosexual, thought he did not know himself. She clearly did not know, or would not let herself know, about Chris. And yet she had skirted so close – said she thought Chris was a girl Terence had a crush on. It almost took Penny's breath away. After a moment, she went on. 'All I'm trying to say, Rowena, and please believe me, is that nothing that happens to Terence now can be dated from his arriving on my doorstep. It was all waiting there, for something, some catalyst. Any more than I can blame him for—' She stopped. She may have made great advances in self-revelation but she doubted she would ever be able to talk frankly about herself to Rowena. There was too much past there, even though they barely knew each other. Whatever happened between Penny and John, Rowena would always be the enemy.

'Blame him for what?' Rowena was sharp again.

'Nothing. You know, we just sort of bumped into each other, me and Terence. We're just coincidences in each other's lives.' And yet Rowena was right. Maybe, without Terence, Penny would have drifted on in her half-life for ever, and maybe, without Penny, Terence would have continued his good son/bad son routine for the next thirty years, never admitting that he was not up to being a hero, would achieve nothing great himself, but might be worthy of being someone else's hero, someone else's muse.

'There's nothing wrong with being a muse,' Penny said, forgetting Rowena for a moment.

'What? Penny, I used to have you down as a wicked stepmother, but you're not, are you? You're probably not interested enough. In him, or John, or anyone but yourself. I've told you what I think and, yes, you're probably right, it's his mother the boy needs. They tell me he's leaving the day after tomorrow. I'll be there tomorrow morning. I assume I'm welcome in the house my son is living in? Don't worry, I won't be bringing Pip with me. Goodbye.'

Penny hung up and sat staring at the receiver. 'Mad. She's quite, quite mad,' she said, and felt time pressing ever closer to her. She did not have much longer. She had to decide.

She leaned forward and buzzed Giovanna. 'Could you get me Mario Melzi, please? See if he can come into the office this afternoon, or make an appointment for this evening. It doesn't matter. I must see him. And, Giovanna, how would you feel about running an author tour for me?'

Of course, Melzi was far too busy to be able to come into the office that afternoon. In fact, the only time he would be able to see Penny before the author tour was due to begin was that evening, over dinner. This time Penny took control. She chose the restaurant, the time, told him she would meet him either at the office or at the restaurant but, no, he need not pick her up from home nor would she go to his flat. Helen, Terence, Rowena, John . . . it was all too much. She had to clear the decks, and hope her mind would become clear at the same time.

She had sadistically chosen an Indian restaurant, the Red Fort in Frith Street, in the hope that an Italian, even one who went to the cinema often, would not feel most at his ease faced with a Prawn Vindaloo. She badly wanted the upper hand and knew that Mario being charming about artichokes in Italian would immediately put her at a disadvantage. She also felt that there was something so deeply unromantic, not to mention unsexy, about eating a plateful of curry and too many side dishes that she would not be tempted to change her mind.

She ordered spicy poppadums and cold beer, and he looked disappointed and asked for plain poppadums and pink wine. 'I'm sorry to ask to see you in such a peremptory way,' she said, dipping a poppadum into strong lime pickle, 'but time is running out.'

'I'm delighted. I was beginning to think you were avoid-ing me. Your charming Giovanna has become slightly cold towards me, I fear, and I was worried that she was acting under orders.'

'Giovanna? I hope she hasn't been rude.'

'Not quite. She's begun to tell me that you're out of the office in Italian, in case I haven't quite understood the message in English.' They both smiled. 'Were you avoiding me?' he asked. He was good at the switch from relaxed and humorous to concerned and gentle. It was unnerving. She wondered how much of it was meant, how much was part of his reflexive instinct to charm.

'No. I've been very busy. Mario, the tour is completely in hand. I hope Giovanna sent you the full itinerary?' She laid a copy of it on the table between them.

'Yes. It looks very interesting. I've been barely anywhere in England. I look forward to discovering it.'

'Yes, well, there won't be much time for all of that. Although Giovanna would love there to be.'

'Giovanna?' He looked surprised. 'What does she have to do with it?'

Penny took a deep breath. This was not going to be easy, not least because she was in many ways going against her own desires.

'I'm very sorry to have to do this at the last moment, but I'm deputing Giovanna to accompany you on the tour. It's no longer possible for me to come with you as planned.'

He looked absolutely stricken. 'But we're friends!' he said, and sounded just like a little boy after being told he could not have the lolly he had been expecting.

'Yes, I know we are. More to the point, as far as this goes, I feel as though I'm letting you down professionally.'

'So what's happened?' He was slightly belligerent now, and Penny realised that he was used to having his own way. That was the problem with charm.

'You know about John, my husband, that he's near the end

of his trip. He's going to reach the Pole in the next few days, all going well. There were a couple of hold-ups early on in the expedition, otherwise he would have arrived already and I would have been in the clear to come with you.'

'I don't see how it makes any difference. He's still on the other side of the world. Are you going out to join him?'

Penny could not help but notice the tiny edge of malice in the question. She drank some beer to give herself time. 'Of course not.' She nearly told him about Terence, but felt that she should keep away from any sort of intimate conversation. She was trying to handle this as a professional, not as a friend. 'But I need to be contactable.'

'And there aren't telephones in hotels in the north of England?' He flicked a hand at the itinerary lying between them. 'It all seems organised enough to me.'

'It's not that—'

'I know it's not. What are you afraid of? Me? I thought we were friends.'

She looked at him steadily, weighing her words carefully. She could not tell him that she was afraid that she would make a move, that they would end up in bed together. That although she wanted that, she did not want that to be the way her marriage ended. If her marriage was over, it must end in recognition of its failure, not for any other reason. But he was right, they were friends, she should not be lying to him. He deserved more than lies.

'We are friends, Mario. And you're right. I'm using John as an excuse. I don't want you to be an excuse.'

'What do you mean?'

She faltered. What did she mean? That she did not want to use him as an excuse to end her marriage. But could she really tell him that? Of course not. That in itself would be an invitation. 'I feel that I've been unprofessional,' she began.

'Not at all. Look at all this ground-work you've done. All I have to do now is go out and talk, and you know how good I am at that.' He was trying to bring the conversation back to a lighter level, to stop her saying what he must know she would say. By now, though, Penny would not be diverted. She almost quailed at all the truths she was going to have to face in the next few days or weeks – this was just the first, but she must keep going.

'It's because we're friends. We shouldn't be such friends. Not until all this is over, anyway.' Well, that was the truth, if deliberately vague. He nodded. Veysey would not have let her get away with that, she knew, and her heart sank at the thought of facing him. Perhaps she would not have to: he was a problem she had to deal with on her own.

'So you will send *la bella* Giovanna with me to hold my hand?'

'She will love it. She doesn't know that she's going yet, but she's been determined all along that I should – that you should be converted to the beauties of England. You'll have your own tourist guide to show you every gargoyle on every cathedral the length and breadth of the land.'

He sighed. 'That wasn't quite what I had been imagining.' She met his eyes, and remembered her own imaginings, and knew that she must be honest.

'Me neither. But you know . . .'

'Respectable married lady?'

'Something like that.'

The curries arrived, sizzling. 'Don't think that I've never had curry before,' Melzi said, 'but I must admit I have never understood the English passion for them.'

'Oh, it's all to do with our imperial past. They comfort us,' she said, and laughed.

He looked at her thoughtfully. 'I'm never quite sure how seriously to take you,' he said.

'Good, that's how it should be. Do you want some of my beef Madras? It's quite hot.'

'But I'll tell you one thing. I don't take your refusal to come with me to Edinburgh and points south as anything but encouragement,' he said. 'It shows you take me more seriously than you're letting on.'

'Or my marriage.'

'Possibly. I don't think that's completely it, though, do you?'

'Madras?' she repeated, spoon poised over the dish. And this time he allowed himself to be diverted.

Penny arrived back in Cambridge Gardens quite early to find Terence and Chris drinking beer and eating a takeaway. Terence was livid when he heard that Rowena was arriving the next morning. Penny lost her temper with him for the first time, pointing out that none of it was her fault, that he had run away from Rowena and she had welcomed him with no questions asked, and that he had to face up to his mother himself. Chris pulled a lot of faces at Penny behind Terence's back, terrified that she would say more than she should and wreck his delicate courtship.

The plans were in place and the two men were to leave London the following lunchtime, flying north to meet John. Terence was on a high, excited and pleased and talking non-stop. He even apologised to Penny, agreeing that she could not be held responsible for his mother and that it might even be a good thing to be able to talk to Rowena, 'not that she'll listen', before he left. Penny managed tactfully to suggest that it might not be a good idea for Chris to be part of the meeting, and said she thought she should be somewhere else herself. 'Work, in all probability,' she said gloomily. Now that she had done the right thing about Melzi she was left feeling irritable and unhappy. She could not bear how cheerful Giovanna was going to be when she heard that she would definitely be accompanying Melzi – it was the first time she had been given such responsibility so it was a significant advance in her career as well as a two-week freebie around the England she loved.

'There's something else, too,' Terence said, clearing away the remnants of the takeaway, which Penny watched with some amazement. 'After we get back, Chris, I don't think I'll go on working with you. Not for long, anyway.'

Penny could not bear to see the disappointment on Chris's face, and turned away so that she should not be witness to his pain. 'Why not?' he asked, as soon as he could trust his voice.

'Well, this trip is one thing. It'll be good fun, an experience. And it'll be nice to spend some time with John. But you know, PR, it's not really my thing. And PR for John – I don't know enough about him, or what he does, and in some ways I know too much. I shouldn't be doing it, I see that now.'

'But you're making a fine fist of it.'

Terence looked at Chris with gratitude. 'Thanks. And thanks for giving me the chance. But, you know, I've messed around for too long. I'm not going to write that book my mother's waiting for, and I'm not going to be prime minister. But I wouldn't mind doing something, after all. Offices aren't such bad places, it turns out. All that chatting round the coffee machine and free telephone calls.' He smiled. 'I don't know what I will do, and I know it won't be easy. I haven't got the greatest track record. But there must be something, even if it's just setting myself up properly as a house painter. One thing that working with you has reminded me of is how boring it is doing nothing.'

Chris nodded. 'It's up to you, of course.'

'And, you know, if I'm living with you,' Terence went on, 'I don't want to be under your feet all the time.'

Chris's face was transformed. 'You mean you still want to come to mine?'

'Yes. If that's all right.'

'Of course it is. I was counting on it.'

'You know I won't be able to pay you much rent?'

'I wasn't counting on it for the rent, Tel,' Chris said, looking at Terence with an open affection that went straight to Penny's heart.

She said goodnight to them and made her way up to bed. 'Tomorrow,' she said, as she turned out her light, 'I get my house back. And very soon after that I think I may find I get my life back too.' Without wondering any further what she meant, she fell asleep.

When Penny came downstairs the next morning Terence was up and dressed. He had even made her some coffee. 'I wanted to talk to you before I left, and I couldn't last night because Chris was here,' he said, cutting bread for toast. 'Sit down, there,' and he passed her her coffee. 'First of all I want to say thank you. You've been very generous. And I know my mother abused you and I've sometimes been – not very friendly. But I'm aware of how long I've been here and you've never asked for anything, not even thanks.'

'That's all right,' Penny said. She did not like other people's gratitude, it embarrassed her, so she hoped that he had reached the end of his speech. 'You're John's son. It's normal. And we get on.'

'We used to. If we still do, it's no thanks to me. I know I was—'

'It doesn't matter what you were. It's over.' As she said the words she wondered how much over it was. She felt a certainty that she would never see Terence again. Except maybe on some satellite television station, standing in the shadow of his father. Her husband.

'Not quite. I don't know if you realised it, but when I came I thought maybe you were – you know – playing around.'

She smiled. 'You weren't very subtle about it.'

'No. I don't suppose I was. And my mother didn't help. But I mustn't blame her, not entirely anyway. I was worried about John, and I suppose I was, I don't know ...'

'Jealous?'

He looked at her hard, and she realised that he was finding this conversation much more difficult than he was showing. 'Maybe. Of John. Of you. Of you and him, or at any rate of how I thought you and he were.'

'How you thought?'

'You know, all that happy-ever-after stuff. I thought you had it and I never would.'

'And now?'

He could not meet her eyes, but he did try to answer. 'I don't know ... I'm not sure you do have it, after all. And I think ... I think I might.'

'Why are you saying all of this now?'

He brought her her toast, fetched the butter, Marmite, a knife. She never ate Marmite but did not want to break his flow, so obediently spread the black paste on to her slightly burnt toast.

He turned his back on her and looked out of the small kitchen window on to the bedraggled gardens outside. 'Chris. He told me I should mend my fences with you. He's right, of course. He so often is. I want to tell you what I thought I was going to say to John when he came home. No, let me. I thought I was going to find out who you were having an affair with and warn him. I was going to tell him about all those men mooning around after you, waiting for – I don't know what, for him to die or just not come home. Circling like vultures, waiting for the last trace of your – purity to die.' There was the same nasty edge to his voice that had disturbed her intermittently throughout his stay.

'Hey, you're coming on a bit strong.'

He ignored her. 'That's what I *was* going to say. I was going to warn him about his faithless, distracted wife. I wanted to see him come back and see them all off, sort you out, maybe even leave you. I didn't like how he was being treated.' He stopped, made an effort, corrected himself. 'How I thought he was being treated. And then, when this idea of Chris's – that I should go out to meet John – was first suggested, it seemed even better. I imagined going out to him, telling him all this, then coming back with him, having the upper hand, I suppose.' He turned and paced the small kitchen, still not looking at Penny.

'That was what you *were* going to say,' she reminded him, after a while.

'Yes. But I think,' another effort, another correction, 'I know that I've done you wrong. I'm sorry. Even up till the other night when I realised you were in the sitting room with someone, I was still thinking men, and the next morning there was Helen

299

and I realised I had probably been wrong about everything. So I want to say, well, I think—'

'Sorry?' she suggested, but with a smile.

'Yes, sorry.'

'That's all right. Apology accepted.' She began to stand up, but he turned and almost pushed her back into her chair.

'Please, I haven't finished yet. I want to tell you what I'm going to say to John now.'

'Oh, Terence, do you need to say anything?' she said wearily.

'Yes. I think I need to tell him to watch himself. There's a Janis Joplin song – "A Woman Left Lonely".'

'It's not to do with being "left" lonely,' Penny said, moved more than she could have realised possible by Terence's belated attempt at honesty.

'But it is something to do with being lonely, isn't it?' He could look at her now, but she found it hard to look at him. What had happened to him in the last few days? It was as though he had suddenly done all the growing-up that he had missed out on over the years. She hoped that his mother's arrival would not undo all the good that Chris – and maybe she, or maybe just time and distance – had done.

'Yes, maybe. Just a little bit.'

There was another pause, but one in which Penny felt nothing but relief. Facing the truth was not so very hard after all.

'So what I'm going to tell him is that he should look after you a bit better. It would be very sad if – if you were to become what I thought you. I do want to see off all those men that hang around you, but just not in the way I thought I did.'

Penny felt tears rise to her eyes. So now he was on her side. He came over to her, helped her to her feet and put his arms around her. After a second he let her go and kissed her cheek. 'Thanks, stepmother,' he said. Penny realised that although he had suffered her embraces in the past, this was the first time he had ever volunteered any form of physical contact. She looked at him and could not hold back a couple of tears. He smiled and wiped them away. 'Thank you,' he said. 'Sorry, and thank you. I'd better go and pack.' She watched him walk out of the kitchen, heard his step – so much lighter now than it had been – as he made his way up the stairs. She thought how young he really was, in experience, not years. His emotions were as raw and unformed as an adolescent's. He had distrusted her with an adolescent fierceness, and now he set off to mend her marriage with an adolescent's optimism.

'But I think it's too late,' she whispered to herself, as his footsteps faded away. 'It's all too late.'

Chapter Eighteen

He had arrived. Penny sat alone in her sitting room with her gin and tonic, her television and her now recovered cat. She sat through the Balkan news, the political news, photographs of Tony Blair smiling at an uninterested crowd somewhere in the Midlands, the arrest of a man suspected of murdering five women, one of them a minor radio presenter. And then there they were. A man who could have been anyone but was apparently John, muffled up to the eyebrows, standing with his sled in a landscape that could be anywhere but was apparently the geographic North Pole. The film was taken from the plane, jumpy and indistinct at first, then closer and closer. The cameraman obviously left the plane first, zoomed in on the lonely figure of the explorer, then turned back to the plane. Another, slighter figure was hesitantly climbing down from it, walking with unsteady feet towards the larger figure. And then John put out his arms and Terence walked into them.

'A likely state of affairs!' said Penny. 'That's probably the first time they've hugged in their entire lives.' And she despised them both for playing the public-relations game, the game by which she lived. 'Yes, but it's different,' she muttered into the cat's fur. 'I get paid for it, it's my job.' And then she remembered her last conversation with John on the subject and knew how the money aspect was taking over from the adventure for him and was saddened.

Long into the night, until she was almost asleep on the sofa, she sat in front of the satellite news channel, waiting for more pictures, more coverage. Again and again she saw Terence walk into his father's arms, heard the saccharine reporter's voiceover: 'And so, in the strangest of reunions, in the strangest place in the world, the son has come to find the father. Twenty-odd years ago John Brunel searched England for his son. He found his son, but they remained estranged. John Brunel later married, but cannot be said to have settled down. Maybe his constant travelling has been in a sense a search for the son he lost so young. Maybe now at last John Brunel will find peace.'

Chris had done his job well, there was no denying it. The photograph of John and Terence would be on the front page of every paper in England the next day. Whether the English media would follow the steps of his American tour would be another matter, but there would almost certainly be a snapper or two waiting when he arrived at Heathrow. John's solo walk was an achievement, an event, but the Terence slant made it into a story.

Penny went to bed but, having been so tired on the sofa downstairs, found herself unable to sleep. She wondered what Terence was saying to John, what they were finding to talk about – more than just her, she hoped. Half an ear was cocked for a telephone call, but none came. No one. Not her family, not John's, not a friend. And not John himself.

She woke feeling hung-over from the gin and red wine and drained from lack of food and sleep. It was Sunday, so she did not have work to distract her. Tomorrow she should have been setting off with Mario for Edinburgh. She wondered if she could still change her mind, but knew she must not and would not.

She spent most of the day in front of the television again, and finally saw John back on real land, in a television studio in northern Canada. It was always a shock to see John at the end of an expedition. He would spend months at home making himself fit, and set off, strong and hopeful, a gleam in his eye and flesh covering his bones. He would disappear and the next time she saw him he would be a different man, listless after the first adrenaline high of success, thin and weak. He never looked less like a hero than when he was most of one.

Hero. 'So what is a hero?' she wondered, as she wandered around her empty, silent house. (Who would have thought that she would miss Terence's mess, the tinny sound of his radio coming down the stairs?) On impulse, she went to the dictionary. She had used the word so often, not always in jest, when she referred to her husband. What had she meant? 'A man of superhuman strength, courage or ability', she read, and looked up at the television screen where a brown-faced, weak-looking and, yes, almost *old* man smiled with practised charm at a television interviewer half his age. She supposed he was strong, but were heroes meant to weaken? He had courage, but would he be brave in a burning house? Was his courage not something entirely selfish? Were these expeditions really heroic or were they just some peculiar form of self-gratification? She thought of her mother-in-law, who had driven three of her four sons so far away from her. Was running away, from your mother, your responsibilities, from *life*, really the act of a hero? He was not fighting a war, was not smuggling Jews out of Nazi Germany or aristocrats from the threat of the guillotine. Percy Blakeney, now there was a hero.

Penny smiled to herself and returned to the dictionary. 'A

demi-god, an immortal.' Well, she had once thought that he was something of a demi-god. She had been almost embarrassed at her near-worship of him. But perhaps Melzi had been right: perhaps she had worshipped him because she needed a shrine, and he had been there.

She skip-read through the list of definitions, half hoping, half fearing to find something that still fitted her elusive husband. 'One who does brave or noble deeds, an illustrious warrior'. No, no warrior, and not that noble. 'A man who exhibits extraordinary bravery or greatness of soul ...' There, that was it. The greatness of soul. That, perhaps more than anything, was what she had believed in, hoped to find. She put down the dictionary and leaned her head against the cool glass of the window. Greatness of soul. Unlike many men, John could be alone with himself for long stretches of time, indeed he sought them out. She had believed that to mean that he was at peace with himself, that he had a soul he could bear to contemplate. Now she wondered whether he thought at all. She had assumed that a man who spent so much time surrounded by nature at its most inhospitable, at its cruellest, must be a man with the soul of a poet. To see the beauty in the cruelty, to live with it and learn to love it – did not that mean that he had an extraordinary soul?

Now, as she watched him on television, half heard him playing the self-deprecation card, she thought maybe it meant that his soul was underdeveloped, not overdeveloped. That he did not think about the beauty, but looked past it and only into himself. And what did he find?

The last definition finally struck home. 'The chief male personage in a poem, play or story'. That was it. That was what John was. The chief male personage in his own life, the chief male personage in hers, but it was a story, not real life. Their lives did not touch any more – had they ever? She had invented John Brunel, and had fallen in love with her own invention. Their relationship had been based on nothing more than once-upon-a-time with the old happy-ever-after lie tacked on at the end. She had loved John Brunel honestly and truly and deeply. But she had not loved *him*, she had loved the man she had created for film and television and newspapers. She wondered if she could have turned anyone into a hero – Bruce or Chris. And then fallen in love with him and married him and realised she had been only pretending all along.

So what should she do? Realise that her husband was no hero and try to love him all over again for what he really was? A man running away from life, loving his own power over his body, loving his own self-discipline more than he loved his wife? She had thought that he hated his fame, played along with it as a way of funding his expeditions. Now she was not so sure. There had been no need for him to stage the Terence stunt. No need at all, unless it was the need for more glory, more column inches. And he still had not rung her.

The telephone finally rang at six o'clock. It was not John, but Philip Veysey.

'Hello, Penny.'

She knew his voice at once, although it was not the one she had been expecting. 'Philip. Hello.'

He sounded oddly hesitant. 'I didn't know if I should ring. Are you all right?'

'Me? Yes, I am.'

'I saw your husband has arrived. Congratulations.'

'None due to me. But thank you.'

'So will he be home soon?'

'No. Not for ten days or so. He's doing some promotional lecture tour in America.'

'I see.' Did he? She was not sure she did herself.

There was another pause while she waited and he thought. Then he said, 'Penny, I don't know if you'd like to but I'd love to have dinner with you again. I was going to ask you to join me and some friends after the launch next week.'

'Thank you. I should like that very much.'

'But — I don't know if it's what they call "inappropriate" in caring circles, but—'

She smiled, then laughed. An hour ago she had felt as though she would never laugh again, but there was hope after all. 'But?' she prompted.

'But, well, would you like to have dinner before then, with just me, I mean? Maybe tonight if you're on your own. You might be feeling a bit odd just now, I do understand that.'

And, yes, she knew he did understand it. She knew that here was a man with emotional imagination, who did look beyond himself. He laughed at his own tag of writer with the bleak vision, but it was the fact that he had vision outside himself that drew her to him. John did not, she knew that now. And neither, really, did Melzi. Not in the same way.

Suddenly she knew what she should do. 'Philip, I should love nothing more. But I don't think I will. I have some things I must do first.' She took a deep breath. 'Of course I'll be at your launch, and come to dinner afterwards. But aside that, do you mind if we put — anything else — off for a little while?'

'For ten days or so?' he suggested.

'Yes. Until after. After.'

A silence. Then a gentle, 'All right.'

She hung up. She was going to do everything in the right order. She was going to tell the truth and stop pretending. She sat in the darkening room and waited for the telephone to ring again. Waited for John.

And as she did so she sat and thought of the four years of her marriage.

All those years of wasted loving.

A selection of bestsellers from
Hodder and Stoughton

Her Husband's Children	Sophia Watson	0 340 64041 3	£5.99	☐
Strange and Well Bred	Sophia Watson	0 340 64043 X	£6.99	☐
The Perfect Treasure	Sophia Watson	0 340 68888 2	£6.99	☐

All Hodder & Stoughton books are available at your local bookshop or newsagent, or can be ordered direct from the publisher. Just tick the titles you want and fill in the form below. Prices and availability subject to change without notice.

Hodder & Stoughton Books, Cash Sales Department, Bookpoint, 39 Milton Park, Abingdon, OXON, OX14 4TD, UK. E-mail address: order@bookpoint.co.uk. If you have a credit card you may order by telephone – (01235) 400414.

Please enclose a cheque or postal order made payable to Bookpoint Ltd to the value of the cover price and allow the following for postage and packing:
UK & BFPO – £1.00 for the first book, 50p for the second book, and 30p for each additional book ordered up to a maximum charge of £3.00.
OVERSEAS & EIRE – £2.00 for the first book, £1.00 for the second book, and 50p for each additional book.

Name _____

Address _____

_____

_____

If you would prefer to pay by credit card, please complete:
Please debit my Visa/Access/Diner's Card/American Express (delete as applicable) card no:

Signature _____

Expiry Date _____

If you would NOT like to receive further information on our products please tick the box. ☐